EXPOSED
The Consequences of Truth

RHONDA SWAN

Author of

BUSTED:
Never Underestimate a Sista's Revenge

SASS Publishing Co.

This book is a work of fiction. Names, characters, places, and incidents are either the product of the author's imagination or are used fictitiously, and any resemblance to actual persons, living or dead, business establishments, events, or locales, is entirely coincidental.

Exposed: The Consequences of Truth
Copyright 2013 © Rhonda Swan

Printed in the United States of America
Library of Congress Control Number: 2006908071
ISBN 13: 978-0-9742645-1-6
ISBN 10: 0974264512

ACKNOWLEDGEMENTS

A special thanks to Percy Allen for your time and interest in my literary pursuits. Your constructive criticism, insight and suggestions have been invaluable and helped make this a much better book. Thanks also for your great sense of humor and making me laugh even when you were telling me how bad a particular chapter or character was. I hope to get the opportunity to return the favor when you write your book!

To "Mama" Freda Malone who's been my distributor, publicist, literary critic and most of all, my sister and friend. I love you.

To my Temptation Island Cruise shipmates, Kaprice Brewer, Tiffany Nobles and Karina Little for your support and suggestions. You guys are absolutely wonderful!

And of course to the readers who have supported my work, especially Toni McDaniel (Ms. Toni), Crystal Nolden and the other wonderful ladies of Only One Keystroke Away (OOSA) online book club. Please keep up the good work you do supporting black authors.

And finally, to Elysia Richardson for your keen copy editing skills.

EXPOSED

THE CONSEQUENCES OF TRUTH

One
Arianna

Karma is a bitch.

So I shouldn't have been surprised when someone tried to kill me.

After all, I had taken a life.

It was an accident, but somehow I don't believe the universe cares about those little details. The media and the small-minded people of Philadelphia sure as hell didn't.

And they wasted no time kicking a sista while she was down *and* out, literally.

"You reap what you sow," one ignorant man told a TV reporter doing a man-on-the-street interview about my shooting. Journalism lingo for ask any asshole his opinion about something they know nothing about.

"Fuck you," I wanted to shout at the TV. But the words remained stuck in my brain because I couldn't speak.

I was lying unconscious in a hospital bed, listening to the news.

That's right listening. You see what most people don't know, or refuse to believe, is that a lot of people in comas can still hear.

I was one of them.

My husband still finds it hard to believe that's how I verified he was having an affair. I had suspected for months since it had been that long since he touched me.

In fact, the day I got shot, I'd left my house in the middle of the night frustrated because I couldn't get laid.

An hour later, I was laid out on the floor of my office in a pool of blood, struggling for each breath.

I hadn't been to the office in days because I was routinely accosted by angry men carrying picket signs scrawled with hateful and stupid words such as, "SCORNED BITCHES GET A LIFE," "PLAYAS NEED LOVE, TOO!"

"DON'T HATE THE PLAYA, HATE THE GAME!"

Since the players invented the game, I never quite understood that one.

All this fuss was over ExposeHim.com, a Web site I created where scorned women put the men who'd done them wrong on Front Street.

They posted pictures and told their stories in hopes of saving another woman the heartache they'd been through.

Men, of course, hated the site.

Most women loved it.

It had saved more than a few sistas from wasting their time, affection and in some cases their money, on womanizing losers.

The office for ExposeHim.com was a former Laundromat on Ridge Avenue in East Falls, an urban neighborhood known for being the place where Grace Kelly grew up and where the Pennsylvania governor lived.

It was a little after midnight when I pulled up in front of the building. I went to enter the code for the alarm, but it had already been disabled.

I assumed that Keisha, my assistant, must've forgotten to set it and went in.

I flipped on the hallway light switch. The place suddenly felt eerie. I walked slowly to my desk. Goosebumps emerged on my arms, pulling my hairs into a standing position as I wondered whether I was there alone.

I ignored my instincts, attributing my anxiety to my frustration at home and the late hour. Turned on my computer and waited for it to power up, tapping my boot-clad foot on the floor beneath the desk -- a nervous habit I'd had since childhood.

I logged onto the Internet and went straight to the company inbox. There were at least two-dozen new postings of cheating men for me to process. One in particular caught my attention as I scrolled down the list.

It read:

LORENZO TATE IS A LIAR AND THE TRUTH AIN'T IN HIM.

"Please let this be a joke," I whispered as I clicked open the e-mail. Lorenzo was my best friend Nicole's husband.

My request was denied.

Lorenzo Tate is not who he pretends to be. This cheating man of God is the devil incarnate. He is lying to his wife, lying to God and lying to himself. He lives in two worlds...

Just as my eyes were about to land on the real information, the light went off. I gasped at the realization that I wasn't alone after all.

"Who's there?" I shouted across the room.

My hands frantically searched the desk for something I could use as a weapon. I came across a clay paperweight my daughter made for me when she was in elementary school, grabbed it and held on tight.

"We don't keep money here," I yelled, my voice cracking to the rhythm of my shaking hands. "What do you want? Who are you?"

"I don't want yo money and don't worry 'bout who I am," said a deep voice coming from the doorway. "Move away from the computer," he said.

I slowly got up from my chair, paperweight in hand, and eased to the right of my desk toward an empty area near a window with a view of the street that fronted the building.

"Come toward me," said the voice. "Closer."

"No," I shouted, the fear inside me growing. "What do you want? Why are you here?"

"You need to shut down," he said. "Shut down the fucking Web site, you hear? Or you'll be sorry."

"Why? Are you on it?" I stammered.

"No!" he shouted. "Who cares why? Just do it 'cause I said so. And 'cause if you don't, I'll come back and hurt you."

Anger and fear were racing each other to my throat in a battle over which would control the next words from my mouth.

Fear won.

"I'll shut it down, OK? You can go now," I said, my hands shaking like an alcoholic going through withdrawal.

"You think I'm stupid, bitch? You're not gonna shut down just like that."

Adrenaline flooded every cell, igniting my internal furnace. Beads of sweat began to form on my forehead, under my arms and beneath my breasts.

"Yes, I will," I squeaked, my voice cracking. "I got the message loud and clear."

"Yeah, I'm gonna make sure. Move outta my way."

He raced toward me and pushed me to the side. I tripped, but caught myself before falling. The moonlight seeping through the blinds on the window cast a shadow. I saw him pull something silver and shiny from his jacket pocket.

Pop! Pop! Pop!

He killed the monitor and computer.

"Please stop!!!" I screamed.

"Shut the fuck up!" he turned toward me and yelled, spraying me with his saliva.

Though I couldn't see his face, I could tell he was only a few inches taller than my five-foot five inches and not very big. In the light of day, he'd hardly be scary.

His breath carried the stench of cheap liquor. The smell nauseated me and I felt faint.

Despite this man's puny size, panic gripped me like a pair of shoes one size too small. I was afraid he'd try to rape me, or worse, kill me. I reached up and smacked him across the head with the paperweight, then turned and ran.

I must not have hurt him too badly because he came right after me.

"You fucking bitch!" *Pop! Pop!*

My flesh sizzled as I dropped to the floor, pain searing my body.

Semi-conscious, life slowly ebbing from my body, I pretended to be dead. Rank breath didn't even bother checking for a pulse, just stepped over my prone body and raced toward the door.

He was met by someone I assumed was his partner, because he or she sure as hell didn't come to see about me. And I was sure that person heard the gunshots.

Their hushed, arguing voices were the last thing I heard before my world went black and I entered the Twilight Zone.

‡‡‡

After 12 hours of surgery, the doctor said I was touch and go. I lay in intensive care with a myriad of questions swirling through my mind, including whether I even wanted to live through this nightmare.

If death was like this – serene with no pressures or responsibilities - I could do it. Dying was a hell of lot easier than living, which meant waking up to an uncertain medical future, having to make a decision about my marriage. Stay with my boring-ass husband or walk away?

He was a good man, but I needed more. Still, could I take my daughter away from the only father she'd ever known?

And what was Nicole's husband up to and would I have to be the one to tell her?

Damn. If I let the Grim Reaper have me, I'd miss out on my daughter's teen years, my son's college graduation.

I wouldn't be there for my friend when she'd probably need me most.

And I'd never get back at the slack bastard who'd plugged me with these projectiles of hot metal.

I could hear my friends telling me that should be the least of my worries. That revenge isn't sweet. And I, of all people, should know that because if it were, I'd had enough to get diabetes.

But they weren't lying in a hospital with other people's blood running through their veins, hooked to machines to breathe, eat, shit and pee.

I made my decision.

I was going to fight to live!

I was going to find out who the hell shot me. And I was going to make him pay.

Two
Nicole

I was hanging a custom-framed print of a gorgeous little black girl eating a spoonful of biblical knowledge on the living room wall of my new home when I heard the news.

"Arianna Singleton, best-selling author and CEO of the popular and controversial Web site ExposeHim.com, has been shot by an unknown assailant, according to Philadelphia police. Officials at Temple University Hospital say it is unclear whether Miss Singleton will live..." the anchorman said.

I dropped the hammer and nearly fell from the chair I'd been standing on.

"Oh my God! Lorenzo! Lorenzo!" I was screaming hysterically trying to get my husband's attention.

"What is it, Nicole?" Lorenzo dashed into the room wearing anxiety on his face like a tight sweater. "What are you doing standing on that chair? Are you all right? Is the baby OK?"

"I'm fine," I squealed, already in tears. "It's Arianna. She's been shot!"

"What? *Your* friend, Arianna? Are you sure?" he asked in disbelief.

"Yes. Can you please take me to Philadelphia? I have to get to the hospital."

Lorenzo helped me from the chair. I was just more than two months along, yet I'd already gained 10 pounds and felt like a whale.

"I don't think that's a good idea," he said, worry still clinging to his face. "We'll just call and find out how she is. You're too upset. Going there might be even more upsetting. Remember the doctor told you to limit your stress."

"They tell all pregnant women that, Lorenzo. My best friend has been shot. I'm going to be upset no matter where I am. Please take me to the hospital. Me *and* the baby will be fine."

"How bad is she? What happened?"

"I don't know. They just said on TV that she was shot and they didn't know whether or not she would live," I screamed through tears. "She's at Temple University Hospital. Can you please just drive me there?"

Jamal Jr. emerged from the hallway where he'd obviously been listening. My screaming no doubt pulled him away from whatever video game he was playing.

"What happened, Ma? Is Miss Arianna gonna be OK?"

"I don't know, baby," I said shaking. "I need to go to Philadelphia to make sure. Come on. You need to ride up there with us."

"Can I stay here, pleeeze?" he whined. "I'll be all right. I'm old enough. You guys can just call me when you get there."

I looked at Lorenzo. He shrugged his shoulders and made a question mark with his face. We'd been together well over a year and married for several months, yet he still didn't feel comfortable advising me when it came to my 12-year-old son.

I guess he figured Jamal had a father and that since I'd been raising him alone for so long before we met that I didn't need his advice. I did. And since the man is supposed to be the head of the house, it was time for him to take his rightful place in that department.

Besides, he needed the practice with us about to have our own bundle of joy.

That conversation would have to wait, though. I had to get to Arianna.

"All right, Jamal," I said, hurriedly putting on my coat with Lorenzo's help. "Don't answer the door for anyone. Don't answer the phone unless you see Lorenzo's number or mine on the caller ID. And..."

"Ma, I got it. I'm old enough to stay home by myself for a few hours. My friends do it all the time. Just go and see about Miss Arianna. I promise. I won't burn the house down."

Lorenzo smiled and reached in his pocket and handed Jamal a 20-dollar bill.

"Here you go, son. Order yourself a pizza or something."

"Cool, thanks."

"You're welcome," he said to Jamal, and then turned to me. "Come on honey. I'm doing this against my better judgment..."

"I know. I know. I know. Let's just go."

I rushed from the house, racing down the stairs.

Lorenzo came up on the side of me and grabbed my hand.

"Take it easy down these steps, Nicole. Arianna will still be there when we get to Philly. And I don't want my wife or my child getting hurt rushing to get there."

I exhaled. "OK, sweetie. You're right," I said, slowing down.

God, how I loved my husband.

Not just because he was fine with a face the color of powdered ginger and hair with waves deep enough to swim in. It helped, of course, but I was long past being that superficial.

Lorenzo was a praying, God-fearing man with character and values -- qualities most of the men I'd dated in the past definitely fell short on.

Arianna had urged me to take more time dating him before getting married, but I knew Lorenzo was the one.

I'd prayed on it and God confirmed what my gut already had told me.

I'd learned to depend on Him and not make any decisions without His guidance after my relationship with Chauncey, a man I'd met online, turned out to be a disaster.

I loved Arianna dearly and I knew she meant well, but she was no expert herself when it came to picking men.

Not that she should've had any problems. She certainly was attractive; a fitness nut with flawless cinnamon skin who'd gone from a size eight when we first met to a six in the past few months.

Too small in my opinion. Maybe because I'd spent most of the past 12 years at a size 16 until my wedding when I worked my butt off to get down to a 10.

Arianna had grown out her hair and wore locs. She faithfully dyed it chili powder red every eight weeks and the color and style framed her face perfectly.

When it came to fashion, she thought she wrote the book.

I prefer a conservative, business casual look. She's diva glam, even during the day. The only pairs of flat shoes she owns were workout sneakers in every color to go with her matching tight Lycra sweat suits. She has a walk-in closet devoted to shoes and boots, all of which have three-inch heels minimum.

Whenever we went anywhere together, she was the one who turned heads. Not that I didn't get my share of attention, but it's no secret most brothas prefer the smaller sistas.

Despite her outside beauty, Arianna hadn't had much luck in love.

Her first husband, the man she says was her soul mate, died from cancer.

And she was already having problems with her second.

Kenny seemed like a genuinely nice guy and treated her kids like gold. I just never got the feeling Arianna loved him the way he loved her. Or the way I loved Lorenzo.

I always felt like she wasn't as happy as she should be.

And fact is she had picked Chauncey, too.

That's how she and I met. When I found out he was cheating on me with her, along with many others, I warned Arianna about him. We bonded over our mutual betrayal and eventually became best friends.

Chauncey may not have broken her heart like he did mine, but he definitely made fools out of both of us.

Arianna was so angry, she wound up killing him.

It was an accident, of course, but I warned her not to go after revenge. I told her to let the Lord handle it. If she'd listened to me, Chauncey would still be alive.

Now I just had to pray that whatever she'd gotten herself into this time, God would keep *her* alive.

Three
Nicole

Seeing Arianna in the hospital was almost as depressing as visiting my mother in the nursing home.

Except my mother could actually talk to me.

Even though she had Alzheimer's and barely recognized me from one week to the next, she could still communicate.

Arianna just lay there, surrounded by machines and looking like a ghost.

The fierce woman who never left the house without her mouth covered in shimmering gloss had been replaced by a frightened-looking, sallow-skinned girl with dry, cracked lips.

Lorenzo had the good sense to call the hospital from his cell before we pulled out of our driveway the night she'd been shot. He found out she was in intensive care and couldn't have visitors.

I called Kenny and he arranged for us to see her a few days later. Each day, I devoted an hour on my knees in prayer for her.

Three nights in that place had added years to Arianna's appearance. Her hair looked as though she'd been struck by lightning and the nurses had yet to bathe her. I could tell because dried white stuff lingered around the corners of her mouth and eyes.

As my eyes traveled the lines of her face, I noticed for the first time a sadness I'd never seen before and the pain I'd always assumed was arrogance.

The woman lying in that hospital bed was not the formidable figure I'd grown to love, but who often exasperated me. For the first time, I pitied her.

It was a feeling foreign to me where Arianna was concerned. She had been the one I leaned on. Tears flooded my face.

"Baby, I told you we shouldn't have come here. Look how upset you're getting," Lorenzo said as he gently caressed my shoulders.

"I can't stand seeing her like this, but I'd be more upset if I had to stay home wondering what was happening to her. Can you pray for her, please?"

I wiped the tears with the sleeve of my shirt before standing up and joining hands with my husband. We closed our eyes.

Lorenzo's booming voice filled that small hospital room like it did the sanctuary of Truth and Light Missionary Center when he delivered the rousing sermons that first attracted me to him.

"Father God in the name of Jesus, touch your daughter lying here in this bed. Awaken her mind, Lord, and bring her back to us, to my wife and the other people who love her. Father, you can do anything and you said that if we believed it, we could receive it. We believe right now and we claim her healing in the name of the Father, the Son, and the Holy Spirit."

In unison, we said, "Amen."

Lorenzo followed his prayer with a kiss on my cheek and an announcement that he was going to the cafeteria to give me and Arianna privacy.

He must have sensed that I needed to be alone with her.

I grabbed her hands and held them tightly in mine.

I leaned in and whispered in her ear.

"You are going to come out of this, Arianna. Your kids need you. I need you. Believe in your healing and claim the victory. Don't let the devil win."

I closed my eyes and prayed again in silence. Arianna had never been much on faith so I needed to believe for both of us.

Four
Arianna

Nicole was a holy roller who went to one of those nondenominational Pentecostal churches and prayed about everything from what she should eat for breakfast to what color pantyhose to buy.

Calling on God was her specialty, something I was used to. Hearing her talk about the devil, though, made me want to crack up.

The little man with the horns and red suit that Christians liked to blame for everything bad that happens in life didn't exist in my reality. But, he was almost as powerful as God in Nicole's brand of religion.

I knew that brand all too well and had long ago decided it wasn't for me.

I was raised on a weekly diet of fire and brimstone and for years lived by a set of stupid rules that made simple things such as wearing pants and going to the movies a sin and one-way ticket to everlasting hell.

Then I grew up and started thinking and reading for myself and realized it was all bullshit. So I shunned the church once I left Connecticut and no longer had my mother, Missionary Blanche Pearson, guilt-tripping me into the pew every Sunday.

I still believed in a higher power, though, and if Nicole wanted to pray for me, who was I to stop her?

Besides, the sound of her voice gave me comfort and a sense of peace I hadn't had since my descent into the world of unconsciousness.

I wanted so badly to ask her if they'd found the man who shot me. She had to know I'd want this information. Yet, she insisted on reading scriptures, praying and talking about everything but that subject.

"The kids are fine," she said. "I talked to Kenny and he said they're going to let Akilah and Amir come and see you once you're out of intensive care.

"The bad news is I shut down the Web site. Most of our subscribers are upset and demanding their money back but they'll have to find another way to investigate their men. ExposeHim.com is out of business for now. I didn't know what else to do. The media's been camping outside our offices since you got shot. About a dozen more frivolous lawsuits have been filed. I need you to wake up so you can help me figure out this mess.

"Kenny told me not to tell you this stuff, but I know you. You'd want to know. You're a fighter. And I need you to help me fight so wake up, girl.

"Do you hear me, Arianna? All hell is breaking loose out here and you know how much you love being in the thick of things and running the show. Plus, you don't want Kenny to spoil that daughter of yours any more than he already has," she laughed. "I can't wait to drop this load I'm carrying and have those same arguments with Lorenzo. I know he's going to spoil this child rotten."

An uneasy feeling crept over me. Lorenzo was up to no good. I didn't know exactly what, but I assumed it was another woman based on that e-mail I never got the chance to finish reading.

What should I tell Nicole? Would she even listen?

ӨӨӨ

Nicole thought she had finally snagged Mr. Right with the Reverend Lorenzo Zechariah Tate.

Many sistas think snagging a brotha of the cloth is like winning the black man lottery. As far as I was concerned that cloth just meant they were prepared to wipe away the tears or dry the wet spot.

Nicole was moving too fast. Lorenzo had proposed only six months after they started dating. But she said he was the man God had ordained for her to marry.

I went along with that, but asked her to keep in mind that most preachers are men with superiority complexes, not supernatural powers. I swore when she looked at Lorenzo, she saw the second cumming.

She wasn't that far off. His milky complexion, wavy dark brown hair and slender mustache could've put him in the running for a Jesus look-a-like contest. If you believe Jesus was a hippy looking white guy, which I don't.

Nicole called him her six-foot tall glass of champagne whenever friends teased her for going from jet black to light and bright.

But Lorenzo's fair skin was one of the things that had attracted her.

Had he looked anything like Chauncey, the man who broke her heart, wallet and spirit, she would've never given him a second look.

She hadn't wished him dead, but I knew she hoped he was turning in his grave at the happiness she'd found with the man of her dreams.

After him, she'd kept her legs closed -- scared she wouldn't recognize another snake unless he bit her -- and she put her heart on ice.

It began to thaw a year later, the day Lorenzo sauntered into the pulpit of Truth and Light Missionary Center.

And he was everything the men who'd preceded him weren't.

Honest. Faithful. And most importantly, he loved the Lord as much as she.

Or so she thought.

Lorenzo was the man Nicole had prayed for. Once she made that discovery, a month after their first date at a tent revival, she wanted to part her legs like Moses did the Red Sea. The good reverend, however, insisted they wait for their wedding night, giving Nicole even more reason to be in awe of him.

She'd been celibate for so damn long, it was a sacrifice she was more than willing to make. That and not wearing the pearl-colored sheath she always dreamed would cover her lithe body the day she walked down the aisle.

Thanks to six months of diet and exercise she'd manage to turn herself into a dime for her special day. And even though some sistas wore white for their second and third trips to the altar, she wasn't about to perpetrate that pure-as-the-driven-snow fraud before the Heavenly Father.

Said she wasn't a virgin, had a son out of wedlock and shacking up with Chauncey made her a tainted woman.

"Tainted? Girl you can't be serious," I said, giving her one of my "chile puhleeeze" looks.

But she was dead serious and decided to wed in silver. A strapless, iridescent organza gown that drew attention to her full breasts and away from the generous hips no diet could erase. The silver dress glowed against her golden skin. On top of the gown, she wore a sheer, long-sleeved, organza coat. The beaded embroidery on the coat sparkled, radiating the joy that beamed behind her nervousness.

Inside the bridal chambers of the mega Washington, D.C. church Nicole chose for the wedding, her soror Candace, cousin, Sherie, sister Pam and the flower girl took direction from me. Her brother Mark, who was giving her away, waited in the hall.

Lorenzo had insisted they get married in D.C. since that's where most of his family lived and his family outnumbered Nicole's.

Pam, a slightly overweight caramel sista with a short brown bob, was on the pastor's aide committee and got her the use of the church where she worshipped. Pam and her family, a philandering husband and 14-year-old son, had recently moved to Silver Spring, Maryland.

Since I'd had two weddings under my belt, I convinced her that a wedding planner was a waste of money. I'd also been a bridesmaid more times than I care to remember so I chose dresses that the wedding party – read myself – could wear more than once. My satin platinum bustier with matching floor length skirt would be turning heads long after Nicole said, "I do."

I was surprised our friendship had lasted long enough for her to include me in the wedding.

Nicole and I couldn't be more different.

I'm confident, though some call it arrogant, with zero tolerance for bullshit.

Nicole is undemanding and pious. Her ego naps in the basement or dances on the roof depending on the day of the week.

Unlike sistas who tear each other's hair out over triflin' brothas, we became friends when we learned we'd been sharing the same man.

I nearly destroyed that relationship when I manipulated him to his final resting place, and then used his exploits in cyberspace as the subject for a book. The two years Chauncey shared a mailbox with Nicole were featured prominently.

But I did such a sorry-ass job hiding Nicole's identity; even the janitors who worked in her building knew the most intimate details of her love life.

Reporters had mentioned her name in the bottom of stories about Chauncey's death as one of his many online victims, but I got the brunt of the media attention.

It wasn't until the book was published that she got her 15 minutes of fame and then some. She switched churches to avoid the stares of the large women in big hats. And put her son, Jamal Jr., in a new school.

Candace, an attractive mahogany sista with a bad attitude, couldn't stand me and tried to convince Nicole that I intentionally set out to hurt her. And for a while Nicole was very aloof. But a sermon Pastor Gill gave on the power of forgiveness one Sunday at Truth and Light motivated her to pardon me and give our friendship a second chance.

Nicole says she's one of the few people who can see the vulnerability hidden deep beneath my emotional armor of steel. I'm not so sure it exists, but I'm glad she thinks so, 'cause not too many people are willing to put up with my bitchy ass.

She and I not only became best friends, but business partners.

Readers of my book seemed to particularly enjoy the part where the main character – me – put a profile of Chauncey, complete with a picture and details about his ways of seduction and manipulation, on virtually every online dating site that catered to African Americans. The goal, of course, was to warn women away from this player.

Hundreds of women practically begged me to start a real-life site where they could do the same to warn sistas about the scandalous men in their lives. And get a little revenge to boot.

That's how ExposeHim.com was born. In addition to posting photos and information about the men who did them wrong, subscribers also could investigate potential mates for a fee. They got access to public records on marriages, divorces, and paternity and bankruptcy cases, as well as other must-have information.

It took some convincing, but I hired Nicole, who had worked in public relations for the city of D.C., as the marketing and public relations director for the site. I reminded her that when she learned about Chauncey's deception, the first thing she did was send out e-mails to all the women she suspected he was involved with to warn them. If it hadn't been for that, she and I would never have met.

"I'm just trying to do what you did for me and those other women on a larger scale," I told her. She smiled and agreed.

Later, when the Web site was up and running, I had to persuade her to use our resources to check out Lorenzo.

But our snooping turned up nothing.

Unfortunately, not everything you need to know about a man can be found in public records.

"This is it, Nicole. The day you've been praying for," I said as I adjusted a glittering tiara on the swirl of chestnut-colored micro braids crisscrossing the crown of her head. "Your hair is so pretty like this."

I had to stand on my toes since at 5 feet, 10 inches, she towered over me, especially when she wore heels.

Nicole fidgeted with her bouquet, a mix of white roses, pink and red carnations and baby's breath. "Thanks, girl. I can't believe I'm so blessed."

"Why not? You deserve to be. Besides, Lorenzo is the one who is blessed."

"Do you really think so?"

"Nicole, why do you always do that?" I snapped.

"Do what?" Nicole asked, as if she didn't know where the conversation was heading.

I took her by the hand and yanked her in front of the full-length mirror in the middle of the room.

I stood behind her, grabbing Nicole's shoulders. "Look at the woman in the mirror, Nicole. What do you see?"

"I see myself and a mean looking woman standing behind me," she laughed.

"Funnnnnyyyy. I see a beautiful woman, inside and out. One who constantly questions her value and shouldn't. Scripture says a man who findeth a wife findeth a good thing. Not a woman who findeth a husband. Lorenzo is lucky to have *you*."

"I heard that," shouted Sherie, a petite ghetto diva with smooth skin the color of rust. She waved her French-manicured four-inch nails in the air for emphasis. "The man who finds me is gonna be one lucky brotha."

Laughter filled the room. Nicole giggled then turned her attention back to me. "I know you didn't just quote the Bible."

I let a smile creep across my face. "I wasn't always a heathen who went to Bedside Baptist, you know. I did my time in Sunday School."

"I can't tell," Nicole said, rolling her slanted brown eyes.

I rolled mine back. "I'm a down-low Christian, OK? Can we just get you to the altar, please?"

"Wait a minute," Candace said. "We didn't finish the something old, something new, something borrowed, something blue."

I rolled my eyes again. "I don't know why you guys are insisting on that European good luck tradition when this is supposed to be an Afrocentric wedding."

Attitude gripped Candace's tongue as she grabbed her petite waist with her small hands. "And I told you we were doing it Miss Wedding Planner."

Sherie jumped in. "Right. Pam did it at her wedding and it was Afrocentric."

Pam nodded her head. "Yeah, who cares where it comes from? Black folks got married in cotton fields back then, too, but you don't see us having this ceremony outside in the woods."

"Come on, Arianna," Nicole pleaded. "My dress is new. Candace bought me a blue garter and I'm wearing the pearl necklace my mother wore at her wedding for something old. You said you'd let me borrow your tennis bracelet. Did you bring it?"

I sucked my teeth and gave in. "Yeah, but I would've let you borrow it even if it wasn't for this silly tradition."

"Do you have a good marriage?" Candace asked.

I looked at her like she was stupid. "What does that have to do with anything?"

"You're not the only person in this room with wedding knowledge," she hissed as I searched my purse for the bracelet. "I did some research. The something borrowed is supposed to come from a happily married friend whose good luck is supposed to give the bride good luck in *her* marriage."

Hell no my marriage wasn't happy. But I wasn't about to admit that to Miss Attitude.

"Oh," was all I could manage. "Shit. I can't find the bracelet. Pam do you have something your sister can borrow?"

"No," Pam said. "That was your job."

"Are you sure you can't find it?" Candace said with an accusatory tone. "Maybe you're just being contrary because you don't want to do it."

The heifer was starting to get on my nerves.

"Contrary? I haven't heard that word since my grandmother was alive. Get over yourself, Candace. Maybe I left it in the car."

I looked at Nicole. "I'll be right back."

۞۞۞

As I rushed toward the church parking lot, I saw Lorenzo and another light-skinned man talking about six cars away from my silver Volvo. The closer I got to my car; I realized they were arguing. Their voices were low, so I couldn't hear them. But the younger man was so heated, the cool October evening was beginning to feel like a hot summer night.

I pretended not to see them as I opened the trunk and searched my overnight bag filled with things I didn't need but bought anyway at the Arundel Mills mall on the drive down.

The man Lorenzo had been trying his best not to yell at stormed off slinging, "The truth shall make you free, Rev," over his shoulder. He headed toward me and I couldn't help but notice his youth. He wasn't much older than my son, Amir, a sophomore at the University of Maryland. He was a few inches shorter than Lorenzo and handsome, magazine cover handsome with jet-black curly hair.

"Damon, wait!" Lorenzo shouted, grabbing him.

When Lorenzo noticed me staring, he let go of the man and forced a smile in my direction.

Damon pulled away and anxiety replaced the anger that held Lorenzo's face. He put his hands together as if he were praying and spoke to the man in a pleading manner. Damon just shook his head, pointed an accusing finger in Lorenzo's face, mumbled something and stomped away.

I finally found the bracelet in my cosmetic bag, grabbed it and went back inside the church. As I ascended the stairs toward the bridal chamber, Lorenzo called out my name.

I turned around to face him. "Yeah, Lorenzo. What's up?"

"I'm sorry you had to see that," he said. "I mentor some young men and they are used to having me at their beck and call. I was trying to explain to him that this was my wedding day and his problem had to wait, but he kept insisting he needed to talk now. Some of these young brothas don't know how to take 'no' for an answer."

In the year he'd been dating Nicole, 'hello' and 'how are you' were the most words Lorenzo had ever spoken to me. Even during the wedding rehearsal the night before, he simply followed my instructions with an occasional nod and limited conversation. I didn't understand his sudden need to explain something that clearly was not my business.

My internal alarms were beeping loud as hell, telling me my girl was making a big mistake. But no way was she going to become a runaway bride because my instincts were working on overtime.

Without facts, there was nothing I could do but smile and wish her the best.

"I hope he works out whatever his problem is," I said dryly to Lorenzo. "Nicole will be ready in a few minutes."

I decided not to mention Lorenzo's argument with Damon to Nicole. The tension between Candace and me was still hanging in the air and she didn't need any more drama on her special day.

"Here you go," I said, handing her the two-carat yellow gold tennis bracelet Kenny had bought me for our first anniversary.

"You found it. Great!" Nicole said. "I hope it brings me and Lorenzo luck."

"Nicole, you're a woman of faith. Believe in that, not this bullshit, OK."

She must have sensed there was more behind my acerbic comment than mere annoyance with the old, new, borrowed and blue.

"Is everything OK with you?" she asked, concern washing over her face.

I walked behind Nicole and started fluffing her train. "Today is not about me, Nicole. It's about you. You've got all your accessories and you look beautiful. Let's get you downstairs so you can become Mrs. Tate."

The sanctuary of the church was cavernous and dark. Brightly colored stained glass windows filtered whatever light tried to shine through during the day.

The candle lit ceremony was scheduled to begin at six. It was twenty minutes after.

Silver holders with white battery-operated candles were fastened with navy blue ribbons to the outside edges of every pew. Those were Nicole's colors, silver and navy blue. She wanted real candles, but the church wouldn't allow it for safety reasons.

Just before the procession of the wedding party, I instructed the ushers to turn on the bulbs of each candle, giving the room a warm glow.

Kenny's band was set up to the right of the pulpit where the church musicians usually banged out shouting tunes by Kirk Franklin and Fred Hammond.

Though Kenny was an accountant by day, his passion was music and for years he played drums as part of a jazz band.

He'd dropped out of the group after holding an all-night pity party several months earlier, but I begged him to play one last gig for Nicole and he consented.

A trio of African drummers sat in the choir loft. When I nodded, they began to play. While they slapped their Djembe drums, the ushers and a nurse escort whom the rest home provided rolled Nicole's mother to a spot at the front of the church where her wheelchair wouldn't get in the way.

Then they seated Lorenzo's parents and maternal grandparents.

Lorenzo made his entrance to the beat of the drums. When he was in place, the drummers stopped playing, stood up and summoned the divine spirits.

Rev. Gill had let me know during the rehearsal he was none too pleased about this part of the service, calling it devil worshipping.

I explained it was just another way of worshipping God and he reluctantly gave in.

When the spirits were safely in the room, I signaled Kenny and the boys who played Carmen McRae's *When I Fall in Love.*

The song was the cue for Nicole's niece Kiara, Mark's daughter, to start marching down the aisle.

The cute almond-complected preteen with Shirley Temple curls was given the title junior bride so Nicole's son Jamal could have someone to escort. At 12, he was too old to be a ring bearer, so she made him a junior groomsman.

Each bridesmaid carried a candle similar to those attached to the pews. Only theirs were wrapped in velvet, navy blue drawstring pouches. The pouches and a pair of pearl earrings were Nicole's gifts to her wedding party.

Jamal, a lanky preteen with a mouth full of metal, nervously twisted the bulb of Kiara's candle, turning it on, and then took her arm in his. They walked to imaginary beats in their heads instead of the one Kenny and the band played, amusing the guests.

Pam, Sherie and I followed with our escorts, handsome acquaintances of Lorenzo's, who also turned on our candles before taking our arms and leading us to the altar.

Next, Candace made her way down with Wesley, Lorenzo's best friend and the finest brotha in the room with milk chocolate skin, dreadlocks to the middle of his back and a smile that could light a path through the darkest night.

The flower girl, a 6-year-old with empty spaces where her two front teeth used to be and silver ribbons tied throughout her hair, followed them, throwing red rose petals on the white carpet runner.

When she was halfway down the aisle, I nodded again to the band. They stopped playing McRae and smoothly transitioned to Etta James' *At Last*, Nicole's substitute for the played-out *Here Comes the Bride*.

A sista from the praise team crooned the lyrics and Nicole stepped gingerly down the aisle, arm in arm with Mark.

Between the flashes of blinding light from digital and video cameras, I caught glimpses of her as she approached the altar. I never took that stuff about brides being radiant too seriously because all the ones I'd seen, including myself, were happy but too damned nervous and stressed to glow. But Nicole was beaming like a tacky neon sign.

Her gaze, wet with tears, bounced between Jamal and Lorenzo. The rest of us were mere window dressing.

By the time she arrived at the altar, awash in light from the candles held by each bridesmaid and the Christmas-like bulbs strung through the white arch that welcomed her, Nicole was in tears.

Lorenzo smiled as he took her arm from Mark and joined her under the arch.

Candace took a handkerchief and dabbed at the saltwater streaming down Nicole's face, trying not to smear her makeup.

Then Rev. Gill prayed for what seemed like an hour before raising his bowed head and instructed the new family to share their special promises to each other.

Lorenzo looked at Nicole and took her free hand. "I honor you for your love and devotion to your son Jamal. I will assist you in your care and nurture of him in whatever way I can. I will seek to grow in love toward him as I grow in love toward you."

He then turned to Jamal. "I promise to love and care for you as I would my own son."

Tears stung at Jamal's eyes, but he fought them back. "I promise to respect and care for you," Jamal said.

Candace gave Nicole the handkerchief and she dabbed her eyes as she turned to face Lorenzo.

"I am grateful for your willingness to join with me and accept the challenge of child-rearing above the covenant which we make to each other for our marriage," she said, her voice shaking. "I promise to support you in your care and nurture of my child, even as I have promised to support you in all other ways."

By then, half the females in the church needed tissue, and there was more to come.

"Now, Lorenzo and Nicole will say the vows that will unite them as one before God," Rev. Gill said.

Nicole handed Candace her bouquet and placed both her hands in Lorenzo's.

He cleared his throat. "I, Lorenzo Tate, take you, Nicole Harris, to be my wedded wife. With deepest joy I receive you into my life that together we may be one. As is Christ to His body, the church, so I will be to you a loving and faithful husband. Always will I perform my headship over you even as Christ does over me, knowing that His Lordship is one of the holiest desires for my life. I promise you my deepest love, my fullest devotion, my tenderest care."

He lost me with that headship stuff, but apparently I was the only one who wasn't feeling it because by now all the women in the sanctuary were wiping their eyes.

Nicole needed a minute to compose herself before responding.

"Take your time, my sister, the reverend said. "You got him this far, he ain't goin' nowhere now."

The church burst into laughter, giving Nicole a little more time to get it together.

"I, Nicole Harris, take you, Lorenzo Tate, to be my wedded husband. With deepest joy I come into my new life with you. As you have pledged to me your life and love, so I, too, happily give you my life, and in confidence submit myself to your headship as to the Lord. God has prepared me for you and so I will ever strengthen, help, comfort, and encourage you. Therefore, throughout life, no matter what may be ahead of us, I pledge to you my life as an obedient and faithful wife."

No wonder she refused to actually say the vows at the rehearsal. She knew I would have given her shit for promising to obey and submit. All I could do standing at that altar, though, was bite my tongue and smile.

After saying their vows, they lit a unity candle, and then Pastor Gill said another prayer.

It felt like yet another hour had passed, as we stood frozen in place.

When the good reverend said, "Amen," the ushers appeared with a straw broom spray-painted silver with blue ribbons and white flowers wrapped around the handle. They gave it to the bride and groom then took their places on either side of the aisle.

Nicole and Lorenzo turned toward the congregation gripping the handle with their hands wrapped over each other. As I explained the symbolism behind the broom as it relates to the joining of the couple, the combining of two families, and the need for the community to support them, they swept the red carpet in a circle until I finished.

Then the ushers took back the broom and laid it on the carpet. Nicole and Lorenzo waited while they gathered her train to prevent her from tripping.

When they gave her the signal that all was clear, I instructed the audience to count.

"One! Two! Three!" Nicole and Lorenzo jumped the broom into their new lives as husband and wife .

Five
Nicole

Arianna's chest heaved up and down as a respirator pumped air into her lungs.

Liquid nourishment dripped into her veins. A catheter collected her pee.

I couldn't wrap my mind around the fact that she was helpless.

Why would someone want to turn such a vibrant woman into a vegetable I wondered? Would I ever get my friend back?

Her dreadful appearance was all the more shocking to me because the last time I saw her was on my wedding day.

She was my coordinator and not only did she look almost as radiant as me, she was in total control, as usual.

Because of that, she and my maid of honor, Candace, got into it. I think Arianna was jealous that I hadn't chosen her as my matron of honor. She and I had grown closer, but I'd known Candace longer.

And I knew Arianna could handle not being chosen better than Candace.

Except for their little cat fight, things couldn't have run smoother.

My wedding was everything I'd hoped for and the guests couldn't stop talking about the reception.

Lorenzo spared no expense.

Arianna had helped me find the venue through her brother who lived in D.C.

Though I used to work in Chocolate City, I rarely socialized there and knew little about its catering halls.

I couldn't have picked a better place than Evermay, a private, historic Federal-period mansion that overlooks Rock Creek Park in Georgetown.

When Arianna told me how much it cost to rent, my heart stopped. I was even more shocked when Lorenzo agreed to sign a contract.

Though he was an engineer who made six figures, I didn't think he'd want to spring for it. God knows I couldn't afford it. Arianna paid me well, but not that well. Tuition at Jamal's private Christian school kept me one step ahead of the bill collectors.

Lorenzo said I deserved it and handed me a check for the deposit without blinking.

I felt like a princess bride.

Valets parked our cars as we pulled around the circular courtyard. As the wedding party took pictures near a pool with angel sculpture fountains and in the rose garden, the guests dallied in the drawing room and on the grounds, dining on lobster-stuffed mushrooms, scallops in bacon, coconut shrimp, vegetable spring rolls and skewered chicken served by the wait staff.

I was one of the many people who particularly enjoyed the fact that all the servers were white, while the guests were predominantly black.

There were constant lines at all three open bars on the rose garden terrace, the rear terrace and in the Orangery, a tented area off the kitchen.

African dancers joined the drummers from the wedding and set up near another fountain on the huge property.

When we were done with pictures, we went inside the house, just to come out again to be introduced.

After Lorenzo and I made our grand entrance as Mr. and Mrs. Lorenzo Zechariah Tate, the dancers pulled us onto the grass, grabbing our waists in an effort to get us to rock to the beat of the Djembe drums and shekeres, hand-held percussion instruments that sound like loud rattles.

We moved like bricks in the wind. Lorenzo and I had never gone out dancing. He thought it was inappropriate for a minister to be seen in the club, so I had no idea how bad a dancer he was.

I was no video vixen but I could hold my own. African dancing, however, was not my forte.

Candace and Pam and their reluctant escorts joined in to show us how to move.

The sight was comical to say the least.

My mother, who was having one of her more lucid days, put an end to the fun by pointing out it wasn't yet time for Lorenzo and I to have our first dance.

On that cue, Arianna asked the guests to gather for a libation ceremony before heading to the tent and taking their assigned seats.

She explained that the ceremony, like communion, is an act of remembrance to keep families linked to their familial legacy and to prevent them from becoming isolated and adrift in society.

"And for anyone who has lost a parent or other family member, it can be a moment of emotional reconciliation and celebration," she said.

The wait staff brought glasses filled with just enough white wine to pour a few drops for the libation ceremony. She instructed the guests in her commanding voice to call out the name of a deceased loved one as they poured.

"May the spirits on high, as well as the spirits below, fill you with grace," she said, then turned to me and asked me to go first. Lorenzo cleared his throat and twisted his face. I took it he was letting me know that as the man, he should go first.

I deferred.

He called out the name of his paternal grandmother.

I called my father's name. As wine flowed from my glass, tears streamed down my face. My father was my first love and I so wished he had lived to see me get married.

Arianna called out the name of Michael Singleton, her first husband. I could see the tears pooling in her eyes, but she kept them from falling.

She always had to be strong. Any show of emotion was a show of weakness.

I cried for Arianna as I recalled that day. Her worst fear had been realized.

She couldn't have been any weaker. And the whole world knew it.

Six

Arianna

The man who tried to take me out of this world was caught and arrested three weeks after putting me in the hospital.

They let him out the next day when someone put up $15,000 dollars, 10 percent of his $150,000 dollar bail.

Somebody cared a lot about that two-bit punk, I thought.

I learned his identity on the six o'clock news where I was still lying in a coma, the TV still keeping me company.

I'd had a parade of visitors during those weeks, including my children, my brother Greg and his wife, Gina. Nicole. And Agnes, a woman I'd met at a book club meeting who quickly was becoming my surrogate mother.

Blanche also came. My mother and I had never been close, but I knew she loved me in her own way. She'd even said a tearful prayer, asking God to open my eyes.

I also had a visit from a man whose voice, though vaguely familiar, I couldn't recall.

"Who's sorry now, bitch?" he hissed, venom dripping from his tongue. Fear filled the room, turning up the humidity tenfold.

A nurse came in and shortly after, I heard hard footsteps making a quick exit. The panic he stirred in me, however, remained. Perhaps because he wasn't the man who shot me, which meant there was someone else who might want to do me harm.

I knew he wasn't the shooter because the voice wasn't the same. The voice of the man who shot me was permanently seared on my eardrums.

A voice, according to the news, belonged to a man named Darryl Crump.

"In our top story this evening, police have arrested the man they believe is responsible for shooting Arianna Singleton, author and owner of the controversial web site, ExposeHim.com."

The TV announcer's voice echoed through my body, stirring the fear inside. My heart raced and my breaths struggled to keep up. By then, they'd taken me off the respirator and I was breathing on my own.

"Police have identified the alleged shooter as Darryl Crump, a convicted felon, whose last known address was in Virginia," said the woman whose throaty voice sounded like it belonged to a sista. "Ms. Singleton has been in a coma since she was gunned down inside the East Falls headquarters of ExposeHim.com nearly three weeks ago.

"Police believe Mr. Crump was not acting alone, but declined to release the names of other suspects or provide a possible motive for the shooting."

Then a male voice chimed in.

"Mr. Crump has been arrested and charged with attempted murder based on physical evidence found at the crime scene. We have not yet determined a motive, but this case is still under investigation."

The female anchor identified the speaker as detective Lester Howard of the Philadelphia Police Department.

She then continued.

"While police have declined to speculate on a motive for the shooting, many believe it may be related to Ms. Singleton's Web site, ExposeHim.com, which allows scorned women to post pictures and identifying information about the men who they say have cheated on them or otherwise done them wrong," she said. "The Web site has been making headlines for months. Ms. Singleton and other company officials have said the site, which also lets subscribers investigate the marital and credit histories of potential dates and mates for a fee, provides a much-needed public service. Detractors, however, say the site is an invasion of privacy, allows users to post inaccurate information and has torn apart families.

"In the weeks before the shooting, male demonstrators picketed outside the Web site offices daily demanding that Ms. Singleton shut it down. Several libel suits have been filed against ExposeHim.com since the shooting. Company spokeswoman Nicole Tate said she is confident the courts will find in favor of the Web site as they have in the past. Two of the three libel suits filed against the company before Ms. Singleton's shooting were dismissed.

"Mr. Crump was extradited from Virginia to face charges here. No further details about him are available. It is unknown whether he was ever featured on ExposeHim.com. In other news..."

I'd never heard of Darryl Crump. Now his name sent chills down my spine. And if he wasn't working alone, who the hell was he working with? Or for?

Could it be that hateful man who'd just left?

Seven

Nicole

Another suicide bomber killed dozens of people in Iraq. President Bush was still defending the war there even though there were no weapons of mass destruction.

Osama bin Laden was still on the loose. Gas prices had never been higher at more than three dollars a gallon.

And New Orleans Mayor Ray Nagin, despite the lousy job he did protecting his people from Hurricane Katrina, the worst natural disaster to hit the country, was claiming to be the best man to run the city in an upcoming election that Bill Cosby, Jesse Jackson and Al Sharpton were trying to stop.

And in case America forgot, the news anchor was sure to remind us that only a couple of weeks before, Nagin had said New Orleans should remain a Chocolate City because God wanted it to stay black.

I laughed. People sure did blame God for a lot of stuff.

Just when I thought the six o'clock news couldn't get any worse and I grabbed the remote to change the channel, the newscaster said they'd made an arrest in Arianna's shooting.

"More after the break," he said.

I put down the remote and waited impatiently for what seemed like a hundred commercials to be over. When the news finally came back on, the white man with perfect hair and teeth announced the man who'd shot Arianna had been arrested. My relief disappeared when the announcer said the man had been released on bail.

First, I was scared for Arianna. Then I was scared for him. Well, not him exactly, but the trouble Arianna could get herself into because of him.

His name, Darryl Crump, was familiar to me, but for the life of me I couldn't recall where I'd heard it. I wondered whether he was one of the hundreds of cheaters we'd featured on the Web site and made a mental note to check later.

Mr. Crump would probably be safer if he stayed locked up.

All Chauncey had done was lie to her and she was hell bent on making him pay. And she did.

In the worst way.

Darryl Crump had tried to kill her. No way was he going to escape her wrath.

I prayed he would be back in jail by the time God saw fit to wake Arianna up.

"Hey honey, what'cha watching?" Lorenzo asked as he dropped his briefcase on the floor and joined me on the couch. I'd been so engrossed by the news, I hadn't heard him come in from work. I kissed him on the cheek and brought him up to speed.

"Well, that's good. That'll be one less thing she has to worry about when she comes out of the coma," Lorenzo said. "He can't be stupid enough to go after her again while he's out on bail. He'd be the first person they'd suspect."

"At this point, I'm more worried about what she'll try to do him," I said.

Lorenzo laughed. "Yeah, from everything you've told me she's not a lady to be messed with."

"It's not funny, Lorenzo," I said. "I've got this bad feeling that this guy being arrested is not the end of this."

"What do you mean?"

"I don't know," I said, standing up and making my way toward the kitchen. "I just suddenly have this feeling something bad is going to happen."

Lorenzo followed me. "Since when do you have ESP, Nicole? Besides, something bad has already happened. Maybe what you're feeling is indigestion."

I couldn't help but laugh. "Why are you always cracking jokes? I told you I was serious."

He wrapped his arms around my expanding waist. "That's the problem, honey. You're always serious. Loosen up. Stop taking the weight of the world on your shoulders. Arianna's burdens are not yours to bear."

"She's my friend," I insisted.

"Exactly. She's your friend, not your responsibility. She's got a husband and kids and a mother to worry about her. And right now she can't hurt anybody anyway. So why don't you worry about me?"

He kissed me on the forehead.

"What do I need to worry about besides making you dinner?" I asked, feeling his nature rise against my thigh.

Lorenzo smiled mischievously. "The fact that we are still newlyweds. Did Jamal's dad pick him up for the weekend, yet?"

"They left about an hour ago. We have the house to ourselves."

"Great," Lorenzo said with lust in his eyes. "Dinner can wait a little while."

He thrust his tongue between my lips and into my mouth. I cocked my head to the side and grabbed the back of his neck as our tongues glided across each other at a frenetic pace.

Lorenzo brought out a passion in me I'd never known with any man before him. I'd been content with the missionary position and occasionally getting on top. And the only place I'd made love besides a bed or the couch was the shower.

That all changed after I took my vows.

The Bible says the marriage bed is undefiled so I let my husband have me in any way and anywhere he wanted. I was shy at first, having sex in the bathroom, holding on to the wall behind the toilet as he entered me from behind. In the garage on top of the brand new Lexus he bought me shortly after our honeymoon that he wanted to christen.

Seemed he wanted to christen every room and piece of furniture in our new home. And my being pregnant did nothing to lessen his appetite for me. So with each new experience, I gained more confidence, wearing off a little more shyness.

Lorenzo lifted me and gently placed me on the kitchen table, still passionately kissing me. He lifted the red maternity dress I was wearing with one hand and slid my panties to the side, inserting a finger inside my already moist vagina.

He slid his finger in and out, in and out. With his other hand, he reached inside the dress and pulled a breast from my black lace bra. He pulled his mouth away from mine and wrapped it around the nipple, sending tremors between my legs.

I ran my fingers through the waves in his hair, trying not to scratch his scalp as ecstasy overwhelmed me. I was never one for loud noises during sex, but Lorenzo loved it when I voiced my pleasure so I was learning to let go.

"Ahhh. Ahhh. Oooo Lorenzo," I moaned.

"You like that baby?" he asked, taking a break from my nipple, which was hard as a missile.

"Ohhh yeah, baby. I love it."

"Tell me how much you love it."

"I really love it, baby."

"How much?" he insisted.

"More than anything."

I knew he wanted me to say dirty things to him, but I wasn't quite there yet. I even felt funny calling out God's name when I was making love. Lorenzo had used naughty words with me. I told him it made me uncomfortable, particularly since he was a preacher.

He said even preachers enjoyed sex and had a naughty side. God understood and wouldn't hold it against him.

Lorenzo removed my panties, slid my butt to the edge of the table and planted his head between my legs. He caressed my clitoris with his tongue and slid his finger back inside my warm place, igniting a fire there. With his other hand, he massaged my nipple, picking up where his tongue had left off.

The intensity was more than I could handle. I writhed underneath his head, my pelvis moving up and down as his licks and the thrusts of his fingers became quicker and quicker. My body shuddered and to my surprise, cum gushed all over Lorenzo's face.

I'd heard that women ejaculated just like men when they reached orgasm. I never had and never thought I could. I wanted that feeling to last forever.

Before I had time to fully revel in the moment, though, Lorenzo was inside me, basking in his accomplishment.

"You like the way I made that pussy come?" he said, panting and thrusting his way to making me come again.

"Yes!" I shouted. "Yes!"

"Whose pussy is this, baby? Huh? Whose pussy is it?"

"Yours, baby. Yours. You own this pussy, Lorenzo. It's nobody's but yours."

I couldn't believe the words coming out of my mouth. I'd never referred to my womanhood by that vulgar term. Hated it when men did.

But my insides were on fire and desire had taken over my tongue. My husband's penis had become like a drug and I was a-dick-ted.

It was as if some other woman had taken over my body.

"Fuck me, Lorenzo. Fuck me," I shouted, embarrassed as soon as the words fell from my mouth.

Lorenzo was as shocked as me. But he was turned on even more.

"Say it again, baby. Say it again."

"Fuck me."

"Again."

"Fuck me."

Each time I said it, his thrusts came faster and his penis seemed to get bigger.

Seconds later, his hot fluid was splashing against my vaginal walls and we both were screaming our joy.

"We didn't hurt the baby, did we?" Lorenzo said, after dismounting me and rolling off to the side, his breaths short and quick.

I lay on the table breathing just as fast, sticky white fluid streaming down my thighs.

"No, sweetie. I told you the doctor said sex was OK."

"I know, but I was in there deeper than usual today."

"I noticed."

"You OK? I didn't hurt you did I?" he said, suddenly concerned.

"No. I'm fine."

"You sure?"

"Yeah."

"It's your fault, you know. What came over you any way?"

"You did. I've never come like that before."

"Never?"

"No."

"Well, I'll have to try and remember what I did so I can get that kind of reaction out of you all the time."

He kissed me on the lips. "Now I'm hungry. What's for dinner?"

I laughed. "Now I'm tired. Take-out. Besides, I don't think I can eat off this table anymore."

Eight
Arianna

Detective Howard wanted answers, like me.

He came by the hospital several times the first few weeks I was in La-La Land, hoping each time there'd been some improvement and that I'd be able to offer him assistance in figuring out why I'd been shot.

He came by one day while Kenny was visiting.

"Any leads on Crump's accomplice?" Kenny asked.

"Not yet, Mr. Washington. Has there been any change in your wife's condition?"

"No, but the doctors still think she has a good chance of waking up. Why do you think Crump was working with somebody?"

"Well, he didn't know your wife for starters. He wasn't one of the men posted on her Web site. So as far as we can tell, he had no motive that we can ascertain," the detective said. "It wasn't the kind of business where money was kept on the premises, so we doubt it could've been a robbery."

"But, Arianna wasn't even supposed to be there," Kenny said. "She didn't work nights, so he couldn't have gone there expecting to do anything to her. Maybe he didn't know there was no money. Or maybe he wanted the computers. Junkies sell those on the street to support their habit all the time."

"We thought about that, but your wife's office was trashed and the computers were vandalized. And according to her secretary, nothing was missing," the detective said. "This appears to be personal. Plus, Mr. Crump had several thousand dollars when we arrested him so I doubt he needed money bad enough to rob the place. In fact, we think the money we found on him may have been a payoff from the person or persons who paid him to trash your wife's office. Crump was working as a janitor. No way did he come by that kind of cash legally.

"Mr. Washington, I know we asked you this before, but can you think of anyone who would want to hurt your wife personally or professionally?"

"Just the names of the people Nicole gave you," Kenny said. "It has to be one of them. I can't think of anybody else. Crump won't tell you who he was working with?"

"We've tried. But there's a certain honor among thieves. And snitches don't fair very well in prison. At any rate, we're checking out the information you gave us and, of course, we're checking out the other men posted on your wife's Web site and relatives of Mr. Cockfield, the man she accidentally killed a couple of years ago. We'll find out who was behind this, Mr. Washington. If you think of anything else that might help, please give us a call. I hope your wife gets better soon."

"Thanks. By the way, detective," Kenny said. "You never told me how you caught Darryl Crump?"

"That was the easy part," the detective said. "DNA. There apparently was some kind of struggle because we found blood by your wife's desk that wasn't hers. We used the FBI's national database of DNA for people with criminal histories. It took us a while, but we finally found a match. In law enforcement, DNA is priceless. I don't know what we'd do without it these days."

Shortly after the cop left, Kenny's cell rang.

"Hello. OK, I guess, just stressed by this whole investigation and everything. How about you? No not tonight....I'm taking my daughter out. She needs me more now that her mother's in the hospital...what?"

He lowered his voice and spoke angrily.

"You're not seriously asking me to choose between you? I'm spending the evening with my daughter. If you can't deal with that, too bad. Maybe we should end this now....I'm really starting to think this was a mistake in the first place ....OK, all right. I'll see you tomorrow."

He walked out shortly after ending the call.

Anger bubbled inside me. Why? It wasn't as if I hadn't long suspected he was seeing someone else.

Kenny and I began to drift apart after my novel, *Busted: Never Underestimate a Sista's Revenge,* hit the stores.

Kenny's anonymity disappeared with each page and he couldn't take the constant scrutiny of his life – or more precisely his manhood.

Our marital discord started with my first major book tour.

Kenny accompanied me to a signing in New York where the audience threw as many questions at him as they did me.

Why didn't he kick me to the curb after our first date when I told him I wasn't attracted to big men? Or when I started dating another man? Definitely after I killed that man?

His answer was always the same: Because he loved me.

That didn't play well in New York or New Jersey, and by the time we arrived back home in Philadelphia, Kenny was tired of being the objection of disaffection.

While I continued with signings in Maryland, D.C., and Virginia, he decided to stay home and finally read the book that had put him in the spotlight.

The night I dragged Akilah home and myself from the last event on the tour, I found him sitting in the dark, alone in the living room listening to the blues.

"You care more about those groupies addicted to the Internet than you do your own husband," he slurred.

I sent Akilah to bed and turned on the light. An empty glass and half-full bottle of cognac sat by his feet. "Musicians like you have groupies, Kenny. And they're book lovers, not people addicted to the 'net."

He tried to stand, but slipped back into the gold recliner I'd bought him for Father's Day, collapsing under the weight of the liquor and the bricks he'd been carrying on his shoulders.

"Fans, groupies, whatever. You spend more time with them than you do me and the kids."

"What the hell is your problem? I'm only gone on weekends when you usually have gigs anyway. Amir is away at college and most of the time I take Akilah with me. I'm here all damn week, but when you get home from work, all you want to do is eat, watch TV and sleep. *That's* our chance to spend quality time together."

"What do you tell those book lovers when they ask you about me, your fat ass husband, now that I'm not there to hear your answer?"

I couldn't believe he was going there. Was it my fault he put back on the 25 pounds he'd lost before we got married and another 20 after? I wasn't responsible for his self-esteem issues.

I just gave him a cold look. "Kenny, please. You're drunk."

"Please what, Arianna? You had to tell the world about my weight problem? That you didn't really want me? That I was second best?"

The seeing people of the world didn't need me to tell them Kenny had a weight problem, but I didn't say that to him.

"When did I say all those things?"

"In your damn book."

'That's not what I say about you, Kenny. And if you believed you were second best then why did you ask me to marry you?"

"I didn't believe it, then."

"But you do now?"

"Yeah, seeing it in black and white. Reading about you and that bastard having sex. How much you enjoyed it."

I turned down the music, stomped across the room and stood in front of Kenny, waving my finger in his face. "I asked you to read my book the whole time I was writing it. You couldn't find the time. I told you I was writing about Chauncey and me. I told you I was writing about us. Now that it's in stores, you want to complain about what I wrote?"

He managed to sober up enough to stand and return the finger pointing.

"It was supposed to be fiction, damnit! You wrote the truth and just changed the names. I figured at least you would make me your knight in shining armor the way I stood by you. He was an asshole, but he still came out looking like..."

"Like what?" I interrupted. "Like the lying cheat he was. You did come off as my knight, Kenny. Everyone who reads the book tells me they're glad we ended up together."

"He still looked like a stud! All my friends just call me a sucker. Say I came off soft."

I threw my keys and purse on the cocktail table and backed away, unable to stand the stench of his breath.

Patience has never been my long suit and by then, I was running on empty.

"Fuck your damn friends. You're a nice guy, so that makes you soft? You know how ridiculous that sounds? Besides, I didn't make you out to be something you're not. So if they think you're soft, it's not because of *my* book and you need to pick some new damn friends."

"Maybe I need to pick a new wife. One who doesn't embarrass her husband in front of the whole world."

Kenny's words were laced with contempt and hit me like darts. If he was aiming to hurt me, he'd struck a bull's eye.

For once, I was speechless.

I grabbed my purse from the table, ran up the stairs to our bedroom and slammed the door.

I didn't realize it but that night was the beginning of our ending.

Nine
Nicole

I got a call from the detective in charge of Arianna's case the day after they made the arrest.

He wanted to know whether I was acquainted with Mr. Crump. I told him I was sure I'd heard the name before but couldn't place it. I knew I'd never seen him before from the mug shot they showed on TV.

"Is there anything more you can tell us, Mrs. Tate?" he asked.

"No detective, but if I remember anything, I'll definitely give you a call."

I'd already told him everything I could.

Three men had tried to sue ExposeHim.com, claiming we'd libeled them. Two of the cases were dismissed before they ever made it to court.

That's because it isn't libel if it's true.

And the women making claims against these men had proof of their scandalous behavior.

No doubt these men were carrying a grudge.

The first was Scott Heath, a white man whose poor wife sent us this e-mail:

DIRTY DANCIN'

My husband, Scott, had an affair with a stripper he met at the gentlemen's club he and his co-workers frequent nearly every Friday after work. I guess it would be more accurate to say he had the affair with me since he was with her before, during and after our marriage. I had the marriage certificate, but she had the husband and kids, two to be exact. Scott lives in Dallas and is an architect for a big firm that has a lot of contracts with the city. I'm sure all his co-workers knew about the relationship and had great laughs behind my back. When I found out about it, he denied it for weeks. So I confronted her. She was more than a little upset to find out the father of her two children had gone out and gotten married on her! So she went with me to his job and we both confronted him! Later, he told me he married me because being a respectable teacher I was "marriage material" and he needed the right image to advance at the firm. He actually told me that he loved the stripper! Can you beat that!

So respectable ladies beware. If a six-foot two-inch tall architect approaches you and says he is looking to settle down, run in the other direction!

Lisa Heath, scorned in Dallas.

P.S. Thanks for creating ExposeHim.com. I wish this site was around before I married the jerk. You are providing a wonderful service to women around the world.

Scott lost his job and both women. He thought winning a libel suit against us could help him clean up his reputation. But everything his wife said was true and the mistress ended up suing him for child support. The DNA test proved he was the father of her children.

There were days when I questioned whether I made the right decision going to work for Arianna and ExposeHim.com. Then we'd get e-mails from women like Lisa and I couldn't help but feel her pain.

The second case was just plain ridiculous.

The man was mad because not only did the woman he piss off expose his infidelity, she told the world he had a little penis. I didn't even want to post her e-mail. It was in poor taste. Arianna, however, took great pleasure in humiliating this man.

"Like TLC says, girls talk about the booty, too. Especially when they're mad and the shit ain't good," she laughed. "We are definitely posting this one."

LITTLE MAN

My cheater's name is Darnell Watson. This pencil dick muthafucka has the nerve to try to be a playa when he can't even satisfy a woman! Most of the playas I know at least can put it down in the bedroom. Not him! So you know I'm pissed.

Darnell is good-looking and spends hours in the gym every week pumping iron, so the brotha is buff. From the waist up, that is.

We dated for several months before I finally gave in and slept with him. He wined me and dined me, made me believe I was special. Had me convinced I was the only woman he wanted to be with.

When we finally have sex, I am disappointed to say the least. His dick is the muscle he needs to be working on in the gym. He's about as big as my pinky toe!

Anyway, despite the terrible sex, I decided to keep kickin' it with the brotha because he's a nice guy and I just didn't have the heart to kick him to the curb just 'cause he wasn't swinging. Like they say, no good deed goes unpunished. A few weeks later I'm at the club with some co-workers for a girls' night out and who do I see all hugged up with another woman slobbin' him down? You guessed it!

She was grinning from ear to ear so I'm sure she hadn't had the displeasure of sleeping with this fool yet. Mind you, I'd called him earlier that day and he told me to make sure I didn't have too much fun without him or give any guys my number!

I want all my sistas in the state of Washington to know that Darnell Watson is NO GOOD, in bed or out!

Sexless in Seattle

Sexless even sent naked pictures of Darnell taken in the shower to prove her point. I insisted that we edit her e-mail, and removed the expletives. Arianna at least had the good taste not to post the images. But when "Darnell the dickless," as she called him, tried to sue us, she let his lawyer know that not only would she use the pictures as evidence, she'd tell her friends at the *Press-Herald* who would have a field day with the story and the rest of the world would find out about Darnell's "little" problem.

That case was dropped, too, and Darnell had plenty of reason to be mad at Arianna.

The third case, which was still pending, had us scared. That's because Arianna was in danger of losing everything. I'd just lose my job, which Lorenzo was pushing me to quit anyway. Still, I was worried about her.

It turned out the man who'd done the cheating was the police chief in a small town in Virginia. The person who'd posted his information had used a false name and e-mail account so when we went looking for the woman to verify the story, we couldn't find her.

Arianna hired an investigator to try and prove the claims posted on the site that the man was going through his third divorce because he was having an affair, but no one would talk. They were scared of him.

He had a list of character witnesses a mile long and was more arrogant than Muhammad Ali before Parkinson's disease.

The soon-to-be ex-wife was chief of police in a neighboring community and wasn't talking. She didn't want the bad press.

So the only thing we could prove was that he was indeed going through a third divorce. And the wife had cited irreconcilable differences, not adultery.

Unless a miracle happened, he had a great chance of beating us when our day in court arrived.

Ten
Arianna

Mommy, please wake up."

Akilah's voice pulled me from a lustful dream and brought me back to the present.

As much of the present I could be aware of while trapped in my own mind in a hospital bed.

It felt good to hear that word.

My daughter had stopped calling me "mommy" when she started middle school, preferring the label, "Ma."

That's about the same time our relationship entered the rocky stage.

Adolescence had stolen Akilah's innocence and turned her unconditional love for me very conditional.

As long as I supplied her with spending money, a cell phone, the latest designer fashions and the freedom to socialize with other wannabe-divas, we were cool.

The minute I made any demands on her, or took away any of those privileges she perceived as her civil rights, it was on. Eleven brought breasts, twelve ushered in a menstrual cycle and by the time thirteen came, her budding attitude was likely to be the size of Kobe Bryant's ego.

The little girl who owned my heart had become a young woman with a tongue sharp enough to pierce it.

This wasn't one of those days when she used it as weapon, though.

Akilah talked to me as though we were at home in our living room, telling me about events at her school. She told me about the teacher who always got on her last nerves, as if her 12-year-old butt actually had nerves.

Then there was the verbal altercation she'd gotten into on the bus that resulted in her getting kicked off for two days. This, of course, was not her fault.

I lay there trying to remember the last time she shared her day with me in such detail. Her conversations usually were limited to one and two word sentences. Three at the most with "uh-huh' and "yeah" being her favorites.

When she ran out of tales to fill the silence, she joined it.

I wanted desperately to see her face, hold her hand, and wrap my arms around her. Yet, only her fear was palpable.

It washed over me like a tidal wave, threatening to take me under. I struggled to keep from drowning, to get my head above water where I could breathe freely and actually see and feel my child.

Then Akilah asked again.

"Mommy, please wake up."

And that time, I heard her for real.

At first, I thought my senses were playing tricks on me.

Then my eyelids fluttered, letting in flashes of light until finally, they were able to remain open. My head felt like Kenny's reclining chair with him in it. I summoned all the strength my newly awakened body could muster to turn in Akilah's direction.

My vision was fuzzy, yet I could see her face, covered with worry, staring into space.

Except for her amber complexion, Akilah was the spitting image of the biological father she never knew with large, deep-set eyes and a nose that peaked like a mountain at the tip. Her long brown hair cascaded in curls that danced around her shoulders. She had traded in her ponytails for a more grown-up look on her twelfth birthday.

I tried to speak, but my words were still asleep. Then, she noticed me straining to bring her face into complete focus.

A smile as big as my hospital room spread across her face. "Mommy!" she yelled. "Are you really woke? You can see me?"

Since I couldn't speak, I let a smile do my talking.

Tears pooled in her eyes. Akilah flung herself across my prone body, moistening my hospital-issue gown with her delight.

As she lay on top of me, holding on as if I would suddenly disappear, Kenny ran into the room with a nurse.

"Akilah, what's the matter? Why were you yelling? Is your mother OK?"

She jerked off me.

"She's woke, Kenny! Mommy's woke!"

Akilah stepped to the side, allowing Kenny and the nurse to approach the bed, but didn't take her eyes off me.

Kenny looked down at me with his brown eyes. "Arianna? Do you know who I am?"

Yes, Kenny. I do, I said with my eyes, wondering if he could read them.

He looked as if he'd lost another 10 pounds since the last time I'd seen him. Kenny was handsome, his fair skin the color of roasted peanuts. But my husband's weight had bounced up and down since we met when he topped the scales at 260. That was too much weight for a man five foot, eleven.

I'd put him on an exercise program, worked out with him and with the exception of soul food on special occasions, made sure he ate nutritious foods. When he was religious with his workouts and about his eating habits, he could drop 20 pounds easy.

Kenny would often backslide, though, sending me to the gym alone and pigging out on desserts. Then he'd put on more weight than he took off.

As he hovered over me, I couldn't help but wonder if this latest weight change had anything to do with the woman he was seeing.

"Excuse me, Mr. Washington," said the nurse, a petite redhead in need of a tan. "I need to examine your wife."

Kenny backed away from my bed and moved closer to Akilah.

"Is she really conscious?" he asked. "I heard some coma patients open their eyes in a reflex action, but they're not conscious."

The nurse ignored him, concentrating her attention on me.

"Ms. Singleton, if you can hear me please blink your eyes twice," she said.

I did.

She touched my hand. "Can you feel that?"

I blinked twice again.

She took my blood pressure.

"I'm going to call her doctor, but I think it's safe to say your wife is out of the coma," she said.

"How come she's not talking?" Akilah asked.

"Sometimes, it takes a while before people who've been in a coma get all of their physical abilities back, honey," she said in a gentle, reassuring tone.

"But she will be able to talk again, right?" Kenny asked.

"I'd rather you ask the doctor those questions," the nurse said. "Let me go call him now."

With that, she turned and left the room.

"Are you gonna call Amir?" Akilah asked Kenny, her eyes suddenly bright and big as silver dollars.

"Yeah, I'm gonna go outside to do it, though. Stay here with your mother and I'll be right back. I've got to call your uncle and grandmother and a few more people, too."

What was so secret about telling my family and friends that I'd risen from the dead? I wondered.

Then I realized he probably needed to break the news that I was awake to the mistress.

Kenny walked toward the head of the bed, smiling. He looked down and met my eyes with his, then began stroking my hair.

"It's good to have you back, Arianna." He bent over and kissed my cheek, then hugged Akilah. "See baby, I told you everything was going to be OK."

Akilah and I smiled at each other and she resumed her position across my breasts.

"I knew you were gonna wake up, Mommy. I just knew it."

Eleven
Arianna

D r. Balaji paid me a visit a few hours after my return to consciousness. He told me I'd been in the coma for four weeks, the result of swelling in my brain from the trauma to my head when I hit the doorjamb after being shot.

My inability to talk or move my limbs was normal and my functions most likely would return with therapy, though there were no guarantees. He poked my legs with a needle to see if I had feeling. One of the bullets had come dangerously close to my spinal cord and he was worried about the possibility of paralysis.

I didn't feel a damn thing.

He told me to give it a few days; they'd do some tests to see if there was permanent damage that would keep me from walking.

In the meantime, don't worry, he said.

Yeah, right.

The other cheery details of my condition he felt the need to share were I'd probably have memory lapses - some memories could be lost to me forever – I might become depressed and there could be changes in my personality.

I woke up for this bullshit?

I didn't bother telling Dr. Balaji or anyone else that I could hear just about everything they said while I was unconscious.

When the nurses finished their usual poking and prodding, I turned to find my six-foot tall son standing in the doorway of my room with a smile as bright as his complexion.

"What's up, Ma?" Amir said, clearly happy to see me awake.

He kissed me on the cheek and wrapped his arms around my shoulders.

I smiled and tried to utter a greeting. The words wouldn't come.

"It's OK," Amir said, pulling up a chair next to my bed. "Kenny told me you couldn't talk yet. Save your strength. You're gonna need it for when you get outta here.

"I'm so glad you're out of the coma, Ma. You really had us worried. I tried to spend a lot of time with Akilah. She was barely eating and kept trying to get Kenny to let her stay home from school. I know she's probably floating on Cloud Nine now."

A tear trickled down my cheek.

"Don't cry, Ma. Everything's gonna be OK now that you're awake," Amir said, wiping away the tear.

I slowly reached up my arms and he lay on my chest. I wrapped my arms around his neck.

Holding Amir felt good. It was the first time I'd seen him since Christmas Day when he'd dropped a bomb that left me crying like a baby on my living room floor.

ĦĦĦ

It was the first Christmas I'd spent in Philadelphia since moving there. Normally, I'd drive the kids to Connecticut and spend the holiday with Blanche, Greg and his family.

But I was in no mood to deal with Blanche's bullshit on top of the tension between Kenny and me. He wanted to eat at his mother's since we weren't visiting with mine, but I insisted on cooking and dining at our house.

On the menu were turkey, macaroni and cheese, collard greens, yams and peach cobbler. Blanche wasn't much of a mother when it came to love and affection, but she did teach me how to throw down in the kitchen.

We'd decorated the tree the night before with red and silver garland, silver balls and ornaments and a huge silver star on top. It stood in a corner of the living room clashing with my gold and plum love seat and sofa.

Kenny had hung icicle lights on the outside of the house where Akilah had insisted we plant a fake snowman. I'd never been much into holiday decorations but I relented for her sake.

On Christmas Day, soulful carols blared from the CD player in the living room entertainment center, the aroma of soul food filled the house and the mood was festive.

Kenny and Amir were in front of the TV watching football; Kenny in his recliner, Amir on the sofa. I insisted they turn off the volume since Akilah and I wanted to hear the music and they didn't need an announcer to tell them what their eyes could clearly see. I let Amir have a beer even though he was only 19. If he could die for his country, he could have a drink.

Akilah was helping me in the kitchen.

It was going to be a nice, quiet day with my nuclear family. So I thought.

After dinner, Akilah planned to go to the movies with some friends and Amir had a date with a new friend he'd met at college. Kenny was going to stop by his mother's house and come back for a quiet evening at home with me. We'd been getting along all day and I hoped that meant I'd get some loving that night.

I was happy Amir was finally dating. My son was handsome, high yellow with soft hazel eyes and curly dark brown hair. He was taller than his trifling father, a man I'd met in college who left me shortly after Amir was born. And unlike his father, he was well built with a six-pack and bulging muscles all over his body.

When he was old enough, I started taking him to the gym with me. I wanted to instill good exercise habits in him early. Frank, his father, was overweight and couldn't fuck to save his life. I figured Amir's girlfriends would teach him how to please them and I would teach him how to stay attractive.

Especially since he had a hearty appetite.

Amir had three helpings of macaroni and cheese to Kenny's two. "What? It's good," he said when I raised my eyebrows as he plunged the serving spoon into the pan a third time. "Almost as good as Grandma Blanche's."

"Almost?" I said, pretending to be offended.

"Nah. Just kidding. It's just as good."

"Everything was good, honey," Kenny said. "You put your foot in those greens."

"Thanks, baby," I said, grateful for his kind words.

"Ugh!" Akilah said. "Ma, you put your foot in the food?"

Amir shook his head at his sister's ignorance and Kenny laughed.

"It's just a saying," Amir said. "It means the food is slammin'."

"Oh."

We ate in the formal dining room, which was connected to the living room via a doorless opening. The men had wanted to bring their plates back to the living room in front of the tube, but I insisted we eat together as a family. I compromised by turning off the music so they could hear the game in the next room.

"Can we open our presents, now?" Akilah asked with a mouthful of peach cobbler.

"Girl, stop talking with your mouth full. You act like you're three," Amir shot back.

"Shut up, boy."

"I'm not a boy, I'm a man."

"Then act like one and stop arguing with your little sister," Kenny said.

"Little? Ain't nuthin little about her."

"Enough already you guys," I said. "Amir you only see your sister a few times a year, be nice. And Akilah don't tell your brother to shut up. It's Christmas, the season of family and love. Let's act like we love each other."

"I ain't no actor," Akilah said.

"What? You should get an Oscar for those shows you put on for Kenny so you can have your way," Amir said.

I cracked up. Finally somebody was on my side.

"Ma, why you laughin'? He ain't funny?" Akilah said with hurt in her voice.

"I'm sorry, baby, but he's right. You *are* a drama queen."

"That's OK, Kilah. He's just mad 'cause you got skills," Kenny chimed in.

"Yeah, skills to play you," Amir shot back.

Still laughing, I decided it was time for the scene to end. "OK, OK. If everybody's through with dessert, let's open the presents."

We moved to the dining room and sat around the tree. Akilah oohed and aahed over the outfits I bought her, but they didn't compare to Kenny's gift, a day in New York on a shopping spree. He bought her two $500 gift certificates to Saks Fifth Avenue and tickets to a Broadway play. Not that you could get all that much at Saks with a grand, but who gives that kind of gift to a 12-year-old?

Amir rolled his eyes when Akilah threw her arms around Kenny and planted wet kisses all over his face. "Daddy, you're the best!" she hollered.

It was the first time she'd called him "daddy."

The look on Kenny's face was priceless. I was upset that he hadn't bothered to discuss the gift with me, but I let it go. I didn't want to ruin his moment.

Amir wanted cash, and that's what he got. Together, we gave him a check for $1,500 dollars. We figured that would reduce the biweekly send-money-now calls he made from campus to maybe once a month.

He kissed me on the cheek and shook Kenny's hand. "Thanks, Ma. Appreciate that Kenny."

He handed us each a box. Mine contained a red sweater; Kenny's a blue one.

We thanked him. Then he threw Akilah a small, black velvet box. "Here, girl."

Her eyes lit up like the lights on the Christmas tree. "What's this?"

"It's a present, stupid. What does it look like?"

"Amir, what have I told you about calling her stupid?"

"Sorry, Ma."

Akilah opened the box and pulled out a pair of gold earrings.

"Wow. These are pretty, Amir. Thank you."

"You're welcome. Don't you have someplace to go now?"

"See, Ma. One minute he's nice to me and the next minute he's trying to get rid of me."

"Akilah haven't you figured out yet that your brother loves you and picking on you is the way he shows it."

She looked at her brother with amazement. "Really? You love me?"

"Duh. Now you know why I always call you stupid."

She smiled and almost knocked over the tree reaching over to kiss him.

"I love you, too, dummy," Akilah said after wrapping her arms around her brother.

"Yeah. Yeah. Yeah. Now go."

"Why?"

"I wanna talk to Ma and Kenny about somethin' and it's private."

"I have to give them their presents first."

Kenny smiled as he opened his tie and cologne and rewarded her with kiss. I got a pretty peach blouse and did the same.

"Sorry, Amir. I didn't know you were gonna buy me something so I didn't get you anything. I'll get you something tomorrow."

"Whatever. Take a hike, now."

With that, Akilah disappeared to her room, no doubt to call her girlfriends and tell them she was ready.

"You guys wanna open your presents to each other now?" Amir asked.

"No, we can do that later when we're alone. What's so important," I said.

Suddenly, Amir's nonchalance turned into nervousness. He looked down at his pants searching the fabric for answers, and then started wiping his hands on them.

I was getting nervous. "Amir what's the matter? You know you can talk to us about anything. Just let it out."

"I know, Ma. It's just this is harder than I thought. I don't want you to think bad about me or stop..."

"Stop what, Amir?"

"Lo..Loving me."

"Loving you? Man your mother could never stop loving you and neither could I," Kenny said, jumping to my defense before I had a chance.

"That's right. You know that, Amir," I said. "Why would you even say something like that?"

"I've got friends whose parents kicked them out the house and won't even talk to them anymore when they told them."

"Told them what? You're starting to scare me."

"OK.... OK. You know the date I told you I had later?"

"Yeah."

Beads of sweat began to trickle from Amir's temple down his cheek. He lowered his head and started tapping his feet.

"Well...It's... It's not with a girl that I met at school. It's...It's..."

"What!" Kenny said. "What are you trying to tell us?"

He exhaled loudly, and then drew a deep breath. "It's with a guy. My date is with a man."

Air struggled to fill my lungs and shock paralyzed my tongue. Still, I had to hold it together. I told my children I would always be there for them and now wasn't the time to abandon ship.

"Are you telling us you're gay, Amir? Just come out with it, please," I said as calmly as I could.

"Yeah, Ma. I'm gay."

"Gay? When the hell did you decide this?" Kenny snapped. "You weren't gay when you left here to go to college last year."

My chest was pounding inside my stomach. I closed my eyes. Purple, blue and red dots were dancing behind my lids. I grabbed my chest and told myself to breathe. Everything would be OK if I could just breathe.

"Kenny calm down and let him talk."

"I was gay then and I've always been gay. I've known since I was young."

"You're not old now," Kenny sniped.

The tension was getting thicker by the second and Kenny was making it worse. "Kenny, if you can't handle this maybe you need to leave. I want to hear him out if that's OK with you," I said.

"Fine. I'll be quiet."

"How young, baby?"

"I don't know, Ma. Eight or nine. I just knew I was different from the other boys. I didn't like girls the way they did. When I got to middle school, all the guys were trying to get in girls' panties. I wasn't thinkin' about 'em. I liked boys. I couldn't say anything 'cause I knew they would call me a faggot."

"What about the girls you dated?" Kenny asked.

"I only went out with them to get my boys off my back. They kept asking why I wouldn't give any play to all the honeys hollerin' at me."

"Have you... Have you ever been with another man, Amir?" I asked, needing but not really wanting to know.

"Yeah."

Tears were stinging at the corners of my eyes, but I fought them back. I reached for Kenny's hand. He grabbed it and held on tight.

"When you started doing that Internet dating stuff, I decided to check it out. I found some gay chat rooms."

"Oh my god, Amir. Do you know how dangerous that is?"

"Why is it dangerous for me, but not for you? 'Cause the people I'm meeting are gay?"

"No. 'Cause there are all kinds of liars and weirdoes on the Internet, gay, straight and otherwise."

"That's how you met Kenny."

"He's got you there," Kenny said.

"Anyway, I met some gay kids online. I didn't see any right away, though. I was too scared. But we chatted online, e-mailed, talked on the phone. I made some friends. Guys I could talk to who were goin' through the same thing as me. Eventually, I met this guy in person and we started going out. He was a senior at a different high school when I was junior."

I thought my heart would stop beating from the shock of what I didn't know about my own son. I was too busy to see his pain and loneliness.

"Why didn't you come to me? Didn't you think you could trust me with what you were going through?"

"I didn't know how you would take it," he said through tears. "Back in Connecticut, when we went to church every Sunday, the preachers taught that homosexuality was an abomination before God."

"You remember that?"

"Yeah. Plus Grandma Blanche is always talking about people with sugar in their tank burning in the lake of fire."

"Hmm. Hmm. With gasoline drawers on," I added.

"And that bishop...I forgot his name. He was runnin' a revival Grandma made me go to. Anyway, he was in the pulpit with two radios. He grabbed the plugs and tried to put them together, saying, 'you can't get electricity with two plugs or with two sockets,' talking about gays and lesbians. We were taught to hate homosexuals. For a while I even hated myself. And I didn't think you would support me."

Kenny stood up. "I'll be right back." He headed toward the kitchen, meaning he'd return with a drink.

I walked to the love seat and sat next to Amir, taking his hand in mine. "Don't you know that I would support you no matter what? You're my son. I just want you to be happy and healthy."

Amir's tears began to flow faster. "So does that mean you understand?"

"Yes and no."

"What does that mean?"

"I love you and I accept you no matter what. If you love men, I accept that. But I can't pretend to understand homosexuality, Amir, because I don't know anything about it. It's like expecting a white person to understand what it's like to be Black."

"Well, what do think about it, morally speaking, I mean?"

"I believe people have the right to live their lives the way they want as long as they're not hurting other people. I don't believe homosexuality is a choice. I think people are born that way, the same way they're born heterosexual. But it doesn't mean I get it. The attraction, I mean. The sex. That I don't understand."

"We love just like heterosexuals do. There's nothing to understand except it's two guys or two girls instead of one of each."

"You're 19. What makes you such an expert," Kenny said, sipping eggnog laced with cognac. I hadn't even noticed his return.

His question pushed the hot button on Amir's temper and he jumped off the couch. "Yo man, what's your problem? I'm sure you were bonin' girls at 19 and you knew how you felt about them didn't you? I'm an expert on how I feel, OK? And I don't have to explain myself to you anyway. You're not my father."

I stood up and grabbed Amir by the arm. "Calm down, baby. Sit back down."

"Nah. I don't have to take this shit. I'm outta here. I'll talk to you later, Ma."

Kenny backed off. "Wait, Amir. I'm sorry, man. Really. This is just a shock to me. I need some time to get used to it. I didn't mean to offend you. I'm gonna take a walk. You and your mother can finish talking alone."

He patted Amir on the back, got his coat from the hall closet and left. Amir sat back down.

"Are you OK?" I asked.

"Yeah. Yeah. It's cool."

"He's just shocked, Amir. He'll be fine. You guys will work this out."

"I know he's trippin,' Ma. But he needs to get over it. I'm not gonna come home on holidays if he makes me feel uncomfortable."

"This will always be your home and nobody is going to make you feel like you have to stay away."

Just then Akilah came bouncing down the stairs. "What's all the noise about in here? Why you yellin' at Kenny like that?"

Amir and I looked at each other, both wondering what to say. I shook my head letting him know now was not the time to share his secret with his little sister.

"None of your business, brat."

A horn blew outside, instantly taking Akilah's mind off the indignity her brother had just hurled, and giving us a reprieve. She looked out the window.

"That's Destiny and her mother," she shot over her shoulder. "We're going to the movies now."

She ran upstairs, grabbed her coat and purse and jetted out the door without so much as a goodbye. Relief washed over me temporarily.

"I gotta go, too, Ma," Amir said. "I'm supposed to meet my friend in half an hour. Are you OK with this? I wanted to tell you first because I'm not gonna live a lie anymore, trying to be someone other people want me to be.'"

That's it? He comes home, drops this bombshell and heads for his date as if all he said was he got an 'F' in one of his classes? What was I supposed to do? Tell him to have a good time?

"You're leaving *now*? 'Ma, I'm gay, gotta go,' just like that?"

"What do you want me to do?"

"Stay here and talk about this, Amir. That's what."

"What else is there to talk about? I'm gay. I'm attracted to men and I have a date with one tonight. I needed for you to know and I wanted you to understand and you said you still love me and you accept it, right?"

"Yeah."

"You sure?"

"Yeah. I guess I just feel like there should be something more. But I suppose you're right. There's nothing else to really say."

He put his hand on my shoulder. "You sure you gonna be OK with this?"

"I'll be fine. I'm just worried about you, that's all."

"Why?"

"It's tough being a Black gay man in America. You are not going to have it easy."

"It's tough being a Black man period. I'll be OK. I'm your son."

He grabbed his coat from the hall closet, hugged me, gave me a peck on the cheek, and left.

As soon as the door closed, I fell to the floor and curled myself into the fetal position. I'd always been liberal. Disagreed with the church's teachings on homosexuality. Had gay friends. But never did I imagine my own child would be gay. How was I supposed to feel about this? How was I supposed to tell Akilah and my judgmental mother?

I was scared for him. Scared of the life he'd have to live in a homophobic society. Scared he might contract AIDS. What was I supposed to do with this fear?

What goes around sure as hell comes back again.

I couldn't help but think that Amir being gay had something to do with the way I got revenge against Chauncey.

I'd arranged to have him unwittingly sleep with a man.

Danielle was a male prostitute who dressed like a woman and did a damn good job pretending to be estrogen-dominant.

When my accomplice and I taunted the homophobic Chauncey the next day with the revelation that he'd been bedded down by one of his own kind and we had it on videotape, he went berserk.

He attacked us. We fought back. I pushed him. He fell, hit his head on a table on the way down, and the next thing I knew, there was a pool of blood and he had no pulse.

I was charged with manslaughter, but Danielle came forward with a tape proving it was self-defense and I was exonerated.

Still, there were people who thought I should've been punished for setting the revenge plot in motion in the first place.

Was this my punishment?

I must've been on the floor a long time because the next thing I remembered was Kenny finding me there when he returned home.

He knelt down, helped me to the love seat and went to the kitchen. He came back with a brandy snifter half full of his favorite cognac.

"Here. A sip of this will help calm your nerves."

I gulped the liquid fire in one swig. It burned all the way down. So did the second and the third.

By the time Kenny helped me into our bed, my head was swimming, my body was numb and I was wishing Christmas Present had been Christmas Wasn't.

Twelve
Arianna

My mind could usually replay events like a video recorder. Once I gained consciousness, however, my memory started playing hide and seek.

With my phone numbers, home and cell.

The name of Akilah's school.

The name of the man who shot me.

I remembered hearing the name while I was unconscious, yet wide-awake I couldn't recall it without prompting from someone else. My body was the damn enemy. I felt like the Body Snatchers had planted me in someone else's carcass.

Not being able to recall information I knew I possessed was driving me crazy.

So was therapy. It was kicking my butt, but I was recovering movements, learning how to eat, drink and speak again.

Slowly, but surely.

My mouth was working well enough to piss off the hospital staff so much that some of the nurses refused to care for me.

Hell, even I was beginning to hate the woman staring back at me in the mirror.

So they called in Kayla Morton, a psychiatrist whose job was to help me stop being a bitchy ex-coma patient.

Kayla was a sista. She was petite and attractive with skin the color of maple syrup. Her chestnut and coral crocheted sweater and green suede skirt matched her earthy personality.

"Arianna, everything you are feeling is perfectly normal," she said.

I longed to wear real clothes. To be able to use the bathroom without help from the nurses. To be my independent self again.

"Nooorr-mal for who?" I slurred sarcastically. "Not me."

I hated to hear myself talk. Words dropped from my mouth like bricks. I sounded illiterate.

"Normal for a woman who was in a coma for a month. Don't you realize how lucky you are to be alive? You were shot twice. In very critical places. We didn't know if you'd ever regain consciousness or ever walk again. But you woke up and you're taking more steps every day. Soon, you'll be able to go home and get back to your life. You just have to learn to be patient with yourself and with the staff."

"I - don't - feel - lucky," I stammered.

"You're probably depressed. Dr. Balaji told you depression is common in people who've been in a coma, didn't he?"

I nodded.

She grabbed my hand.

"You will get through this a lot easier if you focus on the positives and your recovery and not the negatives. The staff tells me you have the nurses calling the police every day to get updates on your case. That's not a good idea."

"Why- not? I - need - to - know."

"I understand that. And when the police have some new information, I'm sure they will share it with you. In the meantime, you need to let them do their job, while you do yours. And right now, your only job is to get better. Be proud of how far you've come and don't get so angry when your progress doesn't go as fast as you want it to. Understand that it's going as fast as your body will allow."

♅♅♅

My body allowed me to leave the hospital three weeks later. Walking was a skill I hadn't yet mastered so I left in a wheelchair, my pill bottles in tow.

My first challenge was navigating the media.

Someone leaked my release date and there were several cameramen and reporters lying in wait as I emerged into the sunshine for the first time in eight weeks.

I was in the spotlight more than an actor on Broadway.

"Who do you think was behind your shooting?"

"Are you paralyzed?"

"Will you ever walk again?"

"Will you write a book about this?"

"Will you seek revenge against the man who shot you?"

I just gave them the hand and did my best to ignore them.

"My wife has no comment," Kenny said.

He'd had enough of being Mrs. Arianna Singleton and I knew this was probably the last straw, even though he didn't say anything.

I came home to find Kenny had bought a pullout couch for the living room so I could sleep on the first floor and not have to use the stairs. He had the first floor powder room turned into a full bath and hired a home caregiver.

Kenny went to work a few hours after I got home.

So much for a heartwarming welcome.

I'd noticed since I came out of my coma that he was uncomfortable being around me in my weakened condition. His eyes rarely met mine and he had little to say.

When I questioned him about it, he said he needed time to get used to my being dependent. Said he didn't know how to act or what to say. It was a role he'd never pictured me in.

Still, I couldn't believe he hadn't taken the day off to be with me on my first day back. This was his chance to be the strong one.

I guess he just wasn't up to the challenge.

I refused to feel sorry for myself, though. His behavior made me work harder to get back to my old self.

I decided to try making dinner.

The caregiver, Aretha, a fair-skinned woman with a short Afro insisted on helping but I sent her to the grocery store instead. The last thing I needed was another woman in my house telling me what to do.

The hallways of my hundred-plus-year-old house in Mount Airy were wide, so I had little trouble navigating them with my chair. I took only a little paint off the walls making my way to the kitchen.

As soon as I made it to the refrigerator, the phone rang. I wheeled myself to the counter where the cordless sat chiming and picked it up. At first, all I heard was breathing. "Are you going say to something?" I snapped. "Yeah, bitch. You got what you deserved," a raspy male voice said before hanging up.

It rang again. I ignored it and started my way back toward the refrigerator, determined not to let these ignorant fools get to me.

The rank smell of moldy Cornish hens with coagulated grease so thick you could cut it with a knife slapped my nose when I opened the refrigerator. The stinky meat, a half empty gallon of milk, condiments and butter were its only contents.

I had no doubt Kenny had been feeding my daughter a steady diet of fast food in my absence. It took me an hour to clean the fridge. By the time I was done, Aretha had returned.

I let her help with the grunt work, cleaning the chicken and greens, opening cans of peaches, straining the starch from the macaroni. The shit work my mother used to make me do when I wanted to help cook.

When I was finished, the kitchen table was piled with Akilah's favorites -- fried chicken, collard greens, macaroni and cheese, and peach cobbler for dessert. A home-cooked meal trumps McDonald's anytime.

The aroma of soul food floated through every room and left unmistakable evidence that the woman of the house was back.

"Ma! It smells great in here. Where are you?" Akilah yelled from the front hallway, when she returned from school.

"I'm in the kitchen, baby."

The bounce in her step as she pranced through the kitchen to greet me let me know I was indeed missed. Akilah wrapped her arms tight around me and squeezed my body like I was one of her stuffed teddy bears.

"I'm so glad you're home."

"Why? 'Cause I'm making your favorite foods?"

"Yeah, but not just because of that. I missed you. It's not the same when you're gone."

I smiled. "I know. The house stays dirty and nobody cooks. Did you and Kenny do anything besides eat out while I was gone?"

"Yeah. We went to the movies and he took me skating," she said, grabbing a chicken wing from the bowl, taking a bite and licking her fingers. "I spent this weekend at Grandma Mae's 'cause he had stuff to do."

"Stuff like what? And did you wash your hands?"

"No."

"Then keep them out of my food and wait until I fix your plate and eat the whole meal at one time, please."

Impatient, she washed her hands in the kitchen sink. "He had business out of town or something. You know how much I like your fried chicken. Can I just have one more piece?"

"No more until the mac and cheese finishes cooling down, which will be in about 10 minutes. Besides, it's too early for dinner. Did Kenny say anything about his plans tonight?"

"No. But I don't think he'll be late or anything lest he would have told me. Can I please eat now? I'm starving."

ɖɖɖ

I was reading "Don't Shoot I'm Coming Out," a book I'd had Aretha pick up for me while she was out, when Kenny came home from work. I'd heard of the book about a teacher who hid the fact he was gay to keep his job and now was calling on the Black community to stop oppressing gay men while I was in the hospital. I figured it might help me deal with Amir's homosexuality and help him deal with it, too.

Kenny snuck up behind me and planted a kiss on my cheek.

"What'cha reading?"

"A book about what it's like living as black gay man."

"Oh. Shouldn't Amir be the one reading that?"

"Sure, but so should we. It'll help us understand him."

"If you say so."

Kenny was wearing my favorite cologne. The scent wafted through the air after he'd taken off his coat. The fragrance sent shivers between my legs. I inhaled deeply and smiled.

He took off his olive green double-breasted suit jacket and sat in his recliner. He was handsome in his green striped shirt and sage tie.

"It's nice to have you home," he said, flipping through the mail and avoiding my eyes.

"I gathered that by the empty fridge and layers of dust on everything in the house."

He smiled. "What can I say? I gave the maid a few weeks off. Speaking of which, it smells good in here. Did Aretha cook?"

"No, I did."

"You? Should you be cooking so soon after getting out of the hospital? Arianna, I hired Aretha to help out, but she can't do that if you insist on doing everything for yourself."

"You know me well enough to know that if I can do it myself I will. But don't worry, I let Aretha help."

"What'd she do, take out the trash when you were done?"

I laughed. "No. I let her do a little more than that. Are you gonna have a plate? I did go through a lot of trouble to make the meal."

"Sure, you know I am. You want me to fix you a plate?"

"No thanks, I ate with Kilah. She couldn't wait for you. You know how she is about fried chicken."

A smile covered his face. "Yeah, I'm surprised she left any for me."

He stood up and headed for the kitchen. "Can I get you something to drink while I'm up? A pillow? Anything?"

"Actually, what I need is some tender, loving care."

He stopped and looked at me with question marks in his eyes. Surely I couldn't mean what he thought I meant.

"A back rub? Sure. Let me finish eating and I'll hook you up."

I winked. "A massage would be nice, but I had something a little different in mind. Something more intimate."

Kenny's smile quickly turned into a frown. "Arianna, please. You just got out the hospital today. I know the doctor did *not* say it was OK for you to have sex."

"He didn't say we couldn't have sex, either. And if I say I'm ready, who cares what some doctor says or doesn't say?"

"I do. We nearly lost you and I'm not taking any chances with your health. We can wait until we get the OK from Dr. Balaji."

"Kenny, I was in the hospital for two months. And I know my memory isn't the best these days, but I can't even remember the last time we made love before then. Are you telling me you haven't been climbing the walls?"

"I'm fine," he said.

"I'll bet you are. Who is she?"

"What are you talking about?"

"The woman who you've been fucking instead of your wife. I know you're cheating on me, Kenny. Who is she? Are you in love with her or is it just sex? Tell me what I'm competing against."

"Arianna, I am not cheating on you. Where the hell is that coming from? 'Cause I don't want to have sex with you the same day you get out of the hospital? That means I'm having an affair?"

"No. Because you *never* want to have sex with me, Kenny. Besides, I heard you talking to your mistress when I was in the hospital?"

"What?" he said looking perplexed.

"On the phone. She called you the day Detective Howard came by. You guys were talking about the asshole who shot me and as soon as he left, she called you on your cell. I heard you talking to her. You told her you couldn't see her 'cause you were taking Kilah to the movies."

Kenny plopped back into his seat, looking as if he'd seen a ghost.

"How could you have heard that conversation? You were in a coma."

"I heard just about everything that happened in my room including the doctor telling you that I could probably hear, remember?"

"Yeah, I remember him saying that, but..."

"But you didn't believe him. And that's why you never talked to me when you came to visit. But I'm sure you talk all the time to whoever it is you've been sleeping with."

"Arianna, that was Clay. He wanted to know whether I was making band practice that night."

"Kenny, do I have Boo-Boo the Fool tattooed across my damn forehead? I know the difference between how you talk to Clay and how you'd talk to a woman."

"Arianna, I am not cheating on you."

"Whatever, Kenny. I'm not going to argue with you. Men would almost rather cut off their dicks than tell the damn truth."

"Well, I can see you're not going to believe me no matter what I say."

"No, I'm not going to believe what you say. I believe what you do. And your actions tell me a lot more than your words ever could."

He shook his head and then resumed his trek toward his first love, food. Before he made it out of the living room, though, Akilah appeared from upstairs.

"Ma almost dying didn't mean nothin' to you guys," Akilah said, her voice startling both Kenny and me. "You just can't stop arguing. Why don't you just get a divorce like the rest of my friends' parents? At least then we'll have some peace around here."

"I'm sorry, baby. We need to work on keeping our voices down so we don't upset you with our nonsense," I said.

She turned and stomped back up the stairs.

Later that night, after Kenny had gone to bed, Akilah sat next to me on the pullout couch.

"Are you guys gonna get a divorce?" she asked me in an almost whisper.

I caressed her cheek. "I honestly don't know, baby. I won't lie to you. Things between us aren't good and they seem to just get worse. I don't know how much longer I can stay married if they don't get better."

"Then do something to make them better," she said, tears streaming down her face.

I pulled her face to my chest and held her in my arms. "Akilah, listen. No matter what happens between Kenny and me, you will always be number one for both of us. We will never stop loving you."

"But he's not even my real father. If you guys get divorced, I'll never see him again."

"Kenny is your real father. He adopted you and gave you his last name. He adores you, you know that."

"I know, but if you divorce him and he's mad at you, he won't want to be bothered with me."

"Has he stopped spending time with you, yet? Like you said, we haven't been getting along for a while now. That hasn't stopped him from being your father."

She didn't say anything.

"Well?"

"I guess."

"No, you know. Kenny will always be your father no matter what."

"That's right," Kenny said from the bottom of the stairs.

Akilah lifted her head from my chest and wiped her eyes with her hand.

"How long have you been standing there," I asked.

"Long enough. Can I talk to my daughter alone?"

"Sure."

Akilah followed him upstairs.

I grabbed a pillow from the couch, cradled it to my stomach and let my mind wander. Could I stay with a man who cheated on me just for the sake of my child? The old Arianna wouldn't. Is this what they meant by personality change? Or was I just too damned emotionally drained to make any changes in my life? Did I even know what the hell I wanted?

"Yes. A man I can respect, one with integrity who takes care of his body like I take care of mine, and accepts me as I am, flaws and all," I said aloud, surprising myself.

Then appeared an image of Randy Yates. He definitely fit the bill.

This sexy man had invaded my thoughts daily since the first afternoon we'd spent together.

᪥᪥᪥

I had just finished a 45-minute session on the treadmill at the gym. I turned off the machine and slid off backward. Sweat was dripping from my locs and stinging my eyes. My tight black and red spandex sweat suit was sticking to me like glue.

When I stepped off, Randy was standing there with a towel as if he were my butler.

"Go ahead. I haven't used it yet. Looks like you forgot yours."

I took the towel and wiped my face. The specimen before me was the color of tea and chiseled like a statue. His biceps bulged like a crotch with a hard-on and I could've sworn his pecs were winking at me.

His black dreads were shoulder length, slightly longer than mine, and his sexy smile sent shivers down my spine.

I usually saw him in the gym on the days I awoke before the sun and couldn't get back to sleep. He'd shown me a few pointers in the weight room and had asked me out a couple of times. I turned him down, but didn't mention I was married. I didn't know if he'd ever noticed my wedding ring.

The brotha was fine and seemed genuinely nice, a lethal combination for a horny sista who hadn't been touched in what seemed like a decade. I usually avoided him and temptation by coming in after eight. He was an early bird, got to the gym the minute the doors opened at 5:30 and was usually gone by 7:30. That day, I arrived around 11 a.m., and he caught me off guard being there so late in the day.

It was a shame I knew that much about this man's schedule.

As I stood there trapped in the lustful stare of his deep-set eyes, I knew if he asked me out again, I wouldn't be able to find the word "no."

"Thank you, Randy."

"Oh, so you remember my name?"

"Of course."

"Do you always remember the names of the men you reject?"

"I didn't reject you. I just turned down your offer for lunch."

"That's the same thing as rejection."

"If you say so."

I handed him back the towel and started to walk away.

"Thanks again."

"You're welcome. Why are you rushing off?"

"I'm done."

"Me, too. So is today my lucky day?"

"Huh?"

"That lunch date I've been trying to take you on. You game today?"

"I'm sorry, but I'm married."

"I know. I saw the ring. Did you take a vow not to eat lunch?"

A giggle escaped my lips. "So you're a comedian?"

"A teacher. You?"

"A writer."

"Technical, creative?"

"I used to be a reporter. Now I'm a novelist."

"Really. What's your book about?"

"Internet dating."

"Hmm. Interesting. Tell me more."

"Why not just read the book?"

"I'll buy your book, if you let me buy you lunch."

"What do you get out of the deal?"

"The pleasure of your company and hopefully some interesting conversation."

An hour later, I was dressed, refreshed, doused in Innocent, my favorite perfume, and sitting across from Randy at Sansom Street Oyster House in Center City.

The crab cakes on my plate were good, but I was more interested in knowing what Randy tasted like.

As he smoothly licked the taste of sea bass from his lips, I wondered how his tongue would feel tracing the erect circle between my legs.

The conversation flowed like a river, as if we'd known each other for years. He was 38 and divorced with two adolescents who were giving him and his ex-wife hell. She was a successful lawyer who grew tired of a husband who made less than half her salary. He declined administrative jobs that would have paid a lot more, preferring to stay in the classroom where he was more valuable to the students.

He loved his students.

Those hormonal middle-schoolers could drive the devil to drink, but Randy said he always could find a way to connect with them.

The eighth-grader who witnessed her father getting shot was one of his favorites. Despite the turmoil in her life, she had a light in her eyes he didn't want to go out.

He felt needed in the classroom.

I admired his choice. Not too many people -- men or women -- would choose kids over money and power.

He found my Internet dating experience interesting, but said he'd never attempt to meet people that way. Too much mystery, he said. He liked to know what he was getting upfront.

The weather was mild for a December afternoon. Parking was expensive and scarce in downtown Philly so after lunch, we bundled up and walked the three-quarters of a mile to Black Horizons Books at the Gallery at Market East so Randy could pick up a copy of my novel.

Pedestrian traffic in Center City was heavy as usual. The City of Brotherly Love had more than one and half million people and always looked busy.

We hurried our way through the lunch crowd and made it to the Gallery in about 10 minutes.

After he bought the book, Randy asked me to read a chapter. I declined, suddenly feeling shy and offered him a rain check. He wanted me to sign it, but said he would wait until after I'd read to him.

We weren't quite ready to part company, so we strolled through the huge retail complex in downtown Philadelphia window-shopping and people watching, admiring some and making jokes about others. I hadn't had that much fun or felt so relaxed in a long time. I wanted to feel that way again. So when Randy suggested we have dinner together later that night, I quickly agreed.

❈❈❈

I went to the grocery store before picking up Akilah from her tutoring session. She was struggling with math and went three times a week to one of those expensive learning centers. Earlier that week, she and I had gotten into it because of her smart mouth and we'd barely said five words to each other.

When I picked her up, she'd dropped the attitude and apologized for being disrespectful.

With the air between us much lighter, I headed over the Ben Franklin Bridge to New Jersey and took Akilah shopping at the Cherry Hill mall where we picked up the designer cell phone she'd been begging for and some new shoes.

Christmas was a week away and the older she got, the fewer surprises she'd find neatly wrapped under the tree. I'd learned with Amir it's better to just let them pick out what they want.

I was good at picking out clothes for her, though, and always managed to bring a smile to her face when she yanked my selections from glossy shopping bags. There were several outfits befitting a diva-wanna-be hiding in my trunk to be placed under the tree on Christmas Eve. Akilah was such a snoop. Leaving anything in the house was out of the question.

I bought Kenny a watch; a set of drumsticks hand-carved in Africa and a gift certificate to a music equipment store, hoping it would inspire him. Akilah got him a tie and a bottle of cologne.

When we came home from our shopping spree, we sat in the kitchen where I made Akilah a cup of hot chocolate and myself a cup of herbal tea.

My kitchen was cozy with walls the color of cornmeal, bordered with red and yellow flowers. I took advantage of the intimate setting and the relaxing liquids flowing through our veins and initiated a mother-daughter chat about communication and expectations.

Akilah agreed with everything I said, of course, because she'd just been blessed with that ghetto fabulous pink cell phone with a white rabbit etched on the back.

She was in such a good mood; she helped me make dinner and didn't whine when I told her I was going out.

Neither did Kenny.

Cornish hens, wild rice and green beans with almonds awaited him when he arrived home from work that evening.

The aroma of a home-cooked meal was all he needed to soothe whatever was ailing him when he walked through the front door mad at the world.

I greeted him with a kiss, a smile, a glass of wine and a dinnertime notice of five minutes. He returned the smile, sat back in his recliner and started pressing buttons on the remote control, trying to decide which of the 900 channels he would settle on for the night.

When I told him I was going out, he just said, "OK, baby. Have a good time."

Had he asked me with whom I was going, I would have lied.

He didn't ask, so I didn't have to.

I would have preferred having to.

ꗷꗷꗷ

Randy wanted to eat at Zanzibar Blue. Since Kenny and I had our first date there, I suggested Warm Daddy's instead.

The funky spot in Old City was my second favorite restaurant in Philadelphia after Zanzibar. It was known for its blues, and reminded me of trendy spots in New Orleans.

Unfortunately, I never made it there.

Halfway down the driveway, I discovered that someone had tried to make a meal of my rear tires, carving them up like a Thanksgiving turkey.

Bits of rubber were strewn about the driveway. A knife was sticking out of the driver's side wheel, its tip holding a yellow piece of paper.

HELL HATH NO FURY LIKE A BROTHER SCORNED! GET A LIFE, BITCH!

I stood there dumbstruck, holding the note in one hand and the knife in the other. My heart was skipping every other beat and my hands began to tremble.

It was 7. The sun had long since gone to sleep.

I was supposed to meet Randy at 7:30. No way was I going to make it.

I hid the knife, which I was careful to grab by the blunt edge of the blade to keep from cutting myself, under my jacket. I didn't want to scare Akilah.

When I went back in the house, she and Kenny were sitting at the dining room table. He was inhaling the flesh I'd baked while she was picking at her food and talking on her new cell phone at the same time. God, he let that girl get away with murder. Talking on the phone at the dinner table!

I was too upset to even bother chastising her. I told them I had a flat and I needed to call road service. Kenny offered to change the tire, but I told him I didn't like riding on a spare. I didn't tell him both tires had been massacred. He nodded and went back to chewing.

I threw away the knife, tucking it deep under the trash in the kitchen garbage can. No use keeping it. It's not as if the Philly police were going to investigate an act of vandalism.

After arranging for road service, I dialed Randy's cell. I tried to cancel, but he wouldn't hear of it, arranging to meet me at the service station. I told Kenny I was going to the station, then keeping my plans and would take a cab home later.

He just grunted.

I didn't want to tell him what happened because I knew that instead of sympathizing, he'd just tell me to shut down the Web site.

During the ride in the tow truck, I couldn't stop thinking about the vandalism. I was angry and scared at the same time. Though I figured the culprit probably wouldn't do me any bodily harm, the thought that someone with that much hatred was so close to me and my family was frightening.

It wasn't enough these tired men were dogging their women; they had the nerve to get pissed when someone called them on their shit!

I was in no state to be taking my ass on a date. I was worried and preoccupied for one thing.

Married for another.

I should've canceled. But I don't always do what I should.

Besides, there was nothing I could do about my situation that night.

As good a rationalization as any.

And given a choice between going home to Kenny and spending the evening with Randy, I chose Door Number Two. I'd try to put off worrying about slashed tires and haters until the next day.

Randy was waiting inside the auto repair shop when I arrived just before the place closed at 8. I arranged to pick the car up the next morning since they couldn't get to it that night and hopped in Randy's blue Honda CRV truck.

"Are you sure you don't want to postpone this dinner? I don't think I'm going to be good company tonight."

"No. I might not get another chance," Randy said, smiling.

He offered to grab take-out to eat back at his place. I hesitated at first. I didn't trust myself. That night I was especially vulnerable. But I thought about the snoring husband who likely awaited me at home and decided to take the chance.

Randy lived in a three-bedroom row house a few miles from the Philadelphia International Airport on the edge of the hood. His son and daughter both had their own rooms and he only entertained when they weren't visiting.

His home was neat and modestly decorated. A treadmill sat in the corner of the living room. Colorful abstract prints with hues of yellow, red, blue and green decorated the walls and dozens of books, mostly non-fiction works on race issues, history and education, lined the built in shelves in his living room.

There was no television.

"I don't have time for that idiot box," he said.

"But don't you need to know what your students are watching, keep up with what's going on in the world?"

"That's what reading is for."

He pointed to a magazine rack filled with newspapers and magazines on every subject from news and entertainment to architecture and geography.

"I'm impressed."

"Good," he smiled. "I've been trying to impress you for months."

I returned the smile. "What about your kids?"

"They don't watch TV when they come over here. I take them places and we read and listen to music. We play cards and board games, go shoot some hoops, stuff like that."

"And they don't whine and fuss about it?"

"Sure, at first. But they're used to it now and they admit they have more fun over here than at their mom's where they watch TV and stay on the computer all day."

He took my coat and invited me to the kitchen to help him prepare our plates with the vegetarian Chinese food he bought.

There was a granite top island in the center of the room with a sink and long counter where four wooden stools stood.

"This is nice," I said, rubbing the goose bumps that had suddenly appeared on my arms.

"I'm sorry. I like it cold. I'll turn the heat up for you."

He went back to living room. "Is 72 OK?" he shouted.

"Seventy-five would be better."

He laughed. "Seventy-five it is. How 'bout some music?"

"Sure."

"Any requests?"

'No, just put on what you like to listen to."

A few seconds later, Vivian Green's *What Is Love* was blaring through the house.

"You like?" Randy asked as he returned to the kitchen.

"Are you kidding? I love every track on this CD. I wish she got as much airplay as those damn rappers."

"She's tight, ain't she? You know she's from Philly?"

"Yeah, used to sing back up for Jill Scott. She's got another CD out now, but I like this one better."

"Ah, so you're up on your music."

"Yeah, good music. But what's up with your English?"

"I beg your pardon?'

I smiled, flirting without even realizing it. "You said, 'ain't.' Is that how you talk with your students?"

"Of course not. I'm versatile. I tell my students I don't mind if they sling that street slang as long as they can speak properly when they need to. That's the key. When in Rome..."

"Do as the Romans do," I finished for him.

"Would you like some wine? You look like you could use a drink."

"Sure."

I carried the plates, heavy with fried rice, spring rolls and mixed vegetables, while Randy carried a bottle of white wine and glasses.

We sat on the plush carpet of his living room floor, our plates on the coffee table, eating and listening to Vivian.

"This is how I like to eat. Do you mind? We can eat at the dining room table if you want."

"No, this is cool. I'm fine."

For several moments, Vivian's soulful voice was the only sound in the room. The silence between us was easy.

After dinner, Randy and I put away the cartons of Chinese food and sat on his living room couch, sipping from our refilled wine glasses.

In the middle of a sentence, he jumped up and pulled his copy of my book from a shelf. "You probably thought I forgot?" he said, handing me the book.

"No, but I was hoping you did," I said.

"Too bad. Start reading," he laughed.

I hesitated. I wasn't ready for him to know the book was based on actual events and someone had wound up dead. I wanted to keep things light. So I read a couple paragraphs from the funny chapter that described all the weirdoes I'd met online.

"Personal experience?" he asked when I finished reading.

"Unfortunately, yes."

Randy smiled. "So is that why you started your Web site. To get back at all the crazies you met online?"

"No," I said, surprised that he knew I owned the site.

"I'm surprised you asked me out considering most men think I'm nothing but a man-hating bitch."

"I'm not most men. Besides, I know there are a lot of bad apples out there. I happen to be one of the few without worms. So where did you get the idea?"

"I met a lot of women on my book tour and at book club meetings who would tell me they wished there was a site where sistas could warn each other about no good men like the characters in my book tried to do. So I made it happen. I use the site to promote the book and provide a public service."

"So you consider it a public service?"

"Yes. I do. And so do my subscribers. How did you hear about it?"

"Read about it in the *Press-Herald*. They ran a little picture of you with the story. I recognized you from the gym, so I read it. I didn't read the whole thing. Just enough to know you started the site after a bad experience."

Clearly he didn't read far enough to know how my bad experience turned out and I wasn't about to tell him. At least not right then. I wanted him to like me before finding out I'd sent a man to meet his maker.

"I'm really amazed at your attitude about this," I said.

"Don't get me wrong, now. I don't think you're going to change the world or anything. Men are not going to stop cheating. And women are still going to get involved with cheating men. But if your site keeps a few women from getting their hearts broken, I'm all for it."

I was starting to like this enlightened brotha more and more.

I smiled. "You're probably right. But at least I'll know I've done my part for womankind."

He laughed.

"I wish more men felt like you. The reason I had to put my car in the shop tonight was because somebody slashed my tires and left me a note letting me know he didn't share your views about ExposeHim.com."

"Are you serious? That's pretty scary. Are you OK?"

"Yeah, I guess. I was pretty freaked out, but there's nothing I can do about it tonight so I decided to come over here and try to forget it."

"Did you?"

"For a while, yes. Thank you."

"You want to read to me some more?"

"No. Not really. What do you do besides read when your kids are not here?"

"I spend time on my computer. Not dating, mind you. Researching stuff. Coming up with new things to do with my students. I keep busy."

"Play a lot of solitaire?"

"Nope. I do have some board games, though. I play with the kids all the time. I've got Scrabble, Monopoly, Taboo and Trivial Pursuit. What's your flavor?"

"Scrabble."

"Figures. Guess you think you're going to kick my ass 'cause you're a writer?"

"No. You're a teacher. You should know as many words as I do."

"I teach middle school," he said as he set up the board on the coffee table and took a seat on the floor across from me. "They don't exactly use a whole lot of big words in eighth grade. But that's OK. I've got the Scrabble dictionary memorized so you're in trouble Miss Author."

He was right.

I lost two games before deciding I needed to get home.

"You want a rematch?" Randy asked, gloating.

"I don't think so."

"Why not? I thought you enjoyed getting your butt whipped," he said, joining me on the couch.

"I don't enjoy getting beat, but I did enjoy your company. Maybe too much."

"How's that?" he said, scooting close enough for me to smell the fermented grapes on his tongue.

I scooted away.

"Because I'm very attracted to you, Randy."

"Why is that a problem?"

"'Cause I'm married. You know that."

"You're not happy, though."

"How do you know that? You don't even know me."

"Arianna, I don't need a Ph.D. in psychology and I don't need to know you for years to see that. If you were happily married, you would be home having dinner and playing Scrabble with your husband. Not here with me."

He leaned in to kiss me. I desperately wanted his lips to touch mine, but just before they did, I jumped up. Kissing Randy would've made me a cheat. I would've been no better than the men whose pictures graced the pages of my Web site.

Kissing him also would've made me no better than Kenny. I just wasn't ready to go there.

"I can't do this, Randy. I'm sorry. Can you call me a cab?"

"No."

"Excuse me?"

"I brought you here and I'm going to take you home," he said with disappointment in his voice. "No need for a cab."

"Oh. You don't have to do that, Randy. I don't want to put you out."

"It's not a problem. I would like to know one thing."

"What's that?"

"What did you think would happen between us when you accepted my invitation to come over here?"

"That I'd have a good time with you and I did."

"You knew I was attracted to you, right?"

"Yes."

"Did you think I might try to kiss you?"

"I honestly didn't think that far, Randy. This is the first day we've spent time together, so why would I assume we'd kiss? You knew I was married when you invited me over, too."

"True that. True that. Don't get me wrong, Arianna. I'm not blaming you for anything. I just want to make sure I understand where you're coming from. That we are on the same page."

"I don't even know what page I'm on, Randy. You're right, I'm not happy in my marriage. In fact, I'm miserable. But, I care about my husband, and I don't want to betray our vows. Plus, I have to think about my daughter and what a divorce would do to her."

He helped me put on my coat.

"I can respect that. The hardest thing about asking my wife for a divorce was leaving my kids behind. I mean I see them all the time. Every weekend and several days a week. I take them to my family reunion every year and I'm really involved in their lives. But it's not the same as being there every day. But I decided it was better for them to have two parents who loved them and lived in different places, than two parents who were driving each other and them crazy in the same house."

"That's a good point. Our house is so tense right now. Akilah hates it when we fight, and it seems like that's all Kenny and I do lately. I am sorry for leading you on if that's what you think I did, Randy. But don't you think we were moving too fast anyway? I mean we barely know each other."

"I guess. But some things just feel right."

"And sometimes we let lust get the better of us and justify it by calling it something else."

"I plead the Fifth on that one."

I smiled. "So are we cool?"

"Sure. I've been where you are now, so I can relate. If it's meant to be for us to hook up like that, we will."

"Can I use your bathroom?"

"Sure. Go out and take a right."

I peed and touched up my makeup. After redoing my face, I couldn't help but search Randy's medicine cabinet. There was nothing unusual. Shaving cream, a razor, and an unopened box of condoms.

I eased the door shut and returned to the living room.

"You ready?" he asked.

"Yeah. Are you sure you want to drive? I don't mind taking a cab."

"Let's not have that conversation again. Come on."

Randy parked three houses away from mine, just in case Kenny was up and looking, which I was sure he wasn't. He asked me whether we'd see each other again outside the gym and I told him I didn't know.

He asked me if I wanted to.

I responded, "Definitely."

He kissed me on the cheek. "OK. I'll take that for now."

Thirteen

Arianna

Randy had called a few times while I was in the hospital, during and after the coma, according to the nurses. I was still unable to talk then so I didn't get the chance to speak to him. He didn't visit, and I didn't expect him to.

The first couple weeks I was home from the hospital, I avoided calling him because I was afraid of how he'd respond to my answers to the myriad questions I was sure he now had about me.

What must he think about the constant drama that surrounds my life?

With Kenny and Akilah upstairs and out of earshot, I bit the bullet and called him. He was glad to hear from me and invited me over. I agreed to meet him the next day.

Climbing the few steps to his house that evening was one of the longest journeys I'd ever taken. I held my breath until I reached the door.

Randy came to the door shirtless, wearing silk pajama bottoms and a drowsy look.

"I'm sorry. I didn't mean to wake you. Didn't you remember I was coming over?"

"Hey, I'm sorry. I fell asleep and let the time get away from me. Come on in. It's good to see you. How are you?"

"OK for somebody who's seen the other side and lived to tell about it."

Randy laughed. "Have a seat. Can I get you something to eat or drink?"

"No thanks, I'm fine."

"I'm gonna get some water. I'll be right back."

I eased onto the couch and took a quick survey of my surroundings. Not much had changed since my last visit, except for the faint scent of marijuana in the air.

"Do you have any more weed?" I asked Randy when he returned to the living room with a bottle of water.

Again, he looked surprised.

"I can smell it. It's pretty hard to hide, especially when it's cold out and you can't let up the windows," I smiled.

"I didn't know you indulged," he said.

"I usually don't. But I could use a coupla tokes right about now," I said only half-jokingly.

"Tokes?" he laughed. "Nobody uses that word anymore. It's called a hit."

"I thought a hit was what people who snorted coke did."

"Weed, coke, whatever. You can take a hit of anything."

"You do coke, too?" I said, hoping the answer would be 'no.'

"Nah, of course not."

"Actually, I'm surprised you smoke weed. What about your students?"

"What about them? What I do on my own time is none of their business. This is how I relax from the classroom drama. I give my all to them every day. And I take care of me at night. Do you want some weed for real?"

"No, I don't want any. I was just feeling you out about your vice. We've all got them."

"What's yours?"

"It used to be cigarettes a long time ago. Now...Well, I guess it's masturbation."

Randy nearly choked on the water he'd just sipped.

"Too much information?" I asked, smiling. "I have been accused of being too direct."

"Yeah. Now I'm going to be trying to picture you doing that all night."

"Sorry. Let's change the subject."

"OK. I've been reading a lot of things about you in the paper since you got shot... How you...well....killed a man, for example. I guess I was supposed to know all his stuff already, but it did come as a surprise. Guess I'm not up on all the Philly gossip. Anyway, I'd like to hear about it from you. Care to share?"

"I take it you haven't read my book yet?"

"Yeah, but it's fiction. I didn't know how much of it was actually true and I certainly assumed the part where one of the major characters kills a guy was made up. That is, until I read the papers."

A half-hour later, I'd told Randy about Chauncey's death and my part in it. It was a story I was damn tired of repeating.

His tired red eyes stayed focused on me the whole time as if I was an episode of his favorite show, and he quizzed me relentlessly afterward.

My case never went to trial, but if it had, I was sure the cross examination couldn't have been worse.

Randy kept repeating himself. "Wow. Wow. That's deep. That's really deep. He just hit his head and died, huh?"

Since he was at such a loss for words other than those and I'd had enough, I decided to leave him with his shock and awe.

"Look, I'm going to take off. I know I've given you a lot to think about. If the situation were reversed, I'd probably be wondering whether I'd still want to be your friend. Just call me if you decide you want to see or talk to me again."

He finally stopped mumbling and looked me in the eye.

"I have to be honest, Arianna, you've got a lot of issues. A death on your hands, a guy trying to kill you, *and* a husband."

"So when all I had was a husband that was cool with you?"

"Sort of. I've been where you are in your marriage and I could tell you weren't happy. I figured it was matter of time before you were single again and I didn't mind being around when that time came."

"And now?"

"Your plate is too full. There's no room for dessert."

"And that's what you consider yourself?"

"We don't know each other well enough for either of us to even think I could be the main course."

"How about an appetizer?"

Randy laughed. "I need some time to think."

"So do I. Tomorrow I'm meeting my girlfriend at the office to decide whether to keep my web site going."

"Isn't that where you got shot?"

"Yeah. I'm scared about going back there but it's something I have to do."

"I admire your courage," Randy said. "Not many women would be able to do that."

"Thanks. I also need to figure out what to do about my marriage, whether you're in the picture or not," I sighed. "So as far as you and I are concerned, I guess if I hear from you I hear from you. If I don't, I'll know you couldn't deal."

He laughed again and shook his head. "You really are direct aren't you?"

"I just call it like I see it."

Randy was still shaking his head as I walked out the door.

Fourteen
Nicole

Arianna's hand was glued to the knob and she seemed paralyzed by fear, unable to open the office door when I arrived.

The word *BITCHES* had been sprayed over the black letters that spelled ExposeHim.com. Hate dripped from the sign in dried, red paint.

We were meeting to decide whether or not to get the Web site back up and running. I had been going through a lot lately and really didn't want to have this meeting at all. Then I figured I could use the distraction.

I told Arianna we should talk at her house or even a restaurant. She insisted on the office.

I didn't think she was ready so soon after being released from the hospital. She begged to differ, as usual.

Yet, there she stood frozen at the front door.

She didn't hear my car pull up across the street. I watched as she grabbed the knob at least a dozen times, hoping she'd give up and turn around. Truth is, I was scared to go in there. I could only imagine how Arianna was feeling considering the memories that building held for her.

She wasn't going to give up so finally I got out of the car and walked over to her.

"What are you doing here? You were supposed to wait for me," I asked, putting my hands on her shoulders. I could feel the tension easing from her body as she turned around and smiled.

"Damn, girl. You're really showing," she said.

My stomach, the size of a soccer ball, was between us. "I'm almost five months, I should be. Don't try to change the subject. Why didn't you wait for me?"

"The better question is why are you dressed like a child instead of a woman who's carrying one?" she asked, opening my coat to get a better view of my denim maternity dress. It was a jumper and underneath I wore a white and red striped blouse that had a red bow at the neck.

"Lorenzo bought it for me," I said in a near whisper, sadness washing over me as I reflected on my marriage. I couldn't let Arianna in on my pain, though.

"That's exactly why I don't let Kenny shop for me. I pick out the clothes and just let him pay for them."

"Too bad he can't buy you some tact." I didn't mean to be short with her, but sometimes Arianna didn't think before she opened her mouth and my patience was thinning because I'd been on such an emotional roller coaster.

"What is that supposed to mean?" she said, almost sounding hurt.

"It means you didn't have to crack on my outfit."

"Only a true friend will tell you the truth. Fake ones let you go out looking a mess."

"So you're saying I look a mess?"

"Girl, you know what I mean. Stop being so sensitive."

"I will. When you stop being so insensitive."

"I'm sorry. Really. I didn't mean to hurt your feelings."

"You didn't. So are we going inside or not?"

"Yeah. I feel like I've been standing here forever. I keep trying to open the door, but I can't."

"Isn't that why we agreed to do this together? You knew this was going to be hard on you. I don't know why you insisted on coming here. Me and Keisha could've handled anything that needed handling in this office."

"You and Keisha can't face my fears for me."

"Arianna, this isn't a fear that needs facing. You were shot in there and nearly died. It's natural for you not to want to go back inside. If it were me, I would never step foot in the place again. Heck, it wasn't me and I don't want to go in there. I'm only here because you feel like you have to be. Why is that?"

"Cause if I can't go in there, it means that Darryl Crump and whoever else tried to hurt me, wins!" she yelled, startling me. "I'm not going to be their victim for the rest of my life."

"All right. All right. You don't have to yell."

Arianna took a deep breath. "I'm sorry," she said. "I didn't mean to take my stuff out on you. It's just...I'm scared as hell of walking in there and it makes me so mad that I've given them that kind of power over me."

I could see how much this meant to her so I pushed all my negative feelings aside. I pulled her as close to me as I could with my stomach in the way and hugged her. "OK. Let's go in there and get your power back then."

"All right," she said, taking a deep breath. "I'm going to have to do it sooner or later. Might as well be now."

I opened the door. Air colder than the wind outside greeted us. Arianna flinched. I grabbed her hand. "You sure about this?" I asked.

"I'm sure."

Together we entered the building.

I flicked on the light switch. She jumped. Dropped my hand. Grabbed her chest.

My heart rate quickened. "You OK?" I asked.

"Yeah. Yeah. I'm fine," she lied.

I disengaged the alarm.

For a moment, we just stood in the reception area, silent. I could tell she needed the time to pull herself together.

Then slowly I began to walk past Keisha's desk and into Arianna's office, leading her by the hand like a child.

She dropped my hand at the doorway and looked intently at the floor. I could tell she was expecting to see bloodstains. She walked over to her desk. On it sat a brand new computer screen.

I had Keisha see to it there was no tangible evidence of the violence this room had seen.

"We had the place cleaned up and ordered you a new computer as soon as we found out you were out of the coma," I said, raising the window blinds to let in the sunlight.

Suddenly, Arianna screamed.

"No!" she shouted, covering hear ears. She turned and ran for the door.

Whoever this Darryl Crump was, he'd stolen my friend and I wanted her back.

"Arianna!" I yelled. She stopped dead in her tracks as if my voice had halted her legs. "You can do this. You already made it this far. You said you wanted to confront your fears, well let's get on with it then. I didn't drive my pregnant butt all the way here just to turn back around."

She turned around and managed a slight smile. "When did you get to be so big and bad?" she said as she slowly made her way back to the desk.

"I got big when I got knocked up. I got bad when I saw you running out of here like a scared little girl. I want to see you whole, back to the way you used to be."

"Like a little girl? Whatever."

"Why don't you sit down at your desk, I'll pull up a chair and we can talk about the future of ExposeHim.com."

She ran her hands across her jeans, giving the sweat to the denim, then traced the edges of her new flat screen monitor with trembling fingers.

"What's going through your mind?" I asked.

"I guess I'm half expecting Darryl Crump to jump out. The last time I was here, he shot my computer screen and I watched the glass shatter everywhere."

"Then what happened?"

"I hit him over the head with a paperweight Kilah made me in elementary school and tried to run away. That's when he shot me. You know I don't even think he was here to hurt me. He had no idea I would be here that night."

"So why do you think he did?"

"Maybe 'cause I hit him. I don't know. He told me to shut down the site. Then he shot the computer to make sure I would. I can't believe I almost died over a stupid Web site."

"Does that mean you want to keep it down," I asked.

"Do we still have our server?"

"Yeah. I didn't cancel any services from our providers. Just stopped taking new posts and new subscriptions."

"So what has Keisha been doing since I've been laid up, then?"

"Dealing with our providers, the media, our subscribers. Believe me, she's had her hands full."

"What do you think we should do?" she asked as she booted up the new computer.

"My feelings about this Web site were mixed from the beginning and they haven't changed. On the one hand, I'd hate to see us go out of business because somebody forced us out. On the other hand, after everything you've been through, do you still want to do this?"

"I don't know. I agree with you about not letting assholes run us out of business. But I'm tired of being in the spotlight. My kids have suffered. My marriage has suffered. And for what?"

"I understand. You know I can get another job anywhere. Besides, Lorenzo doesn't want me to work after the baby's born anyway."

"It's nice to have that option," she said.

"Yeah, I guess," I sighed.

"Is everything all right with you? We've been so consumed with all my drama; I haven't bothered to ask what's going on in your life. How's the pregnancy? Jamal? You and Lorenzo still happy with your decision to get pregnant so soon after the wedding?"

"Things are OK. I'm just tired, that's all. You know how it is carrying all this extra weight."

"Sort of. It's been a while."

"For me, too," I said. "I forgot about all the negative things you go through just *being* pregnant. Labor lasts a few hours, the pregnancy lasts nine months. Morning sickness, swollen feet, heartburn, hemorrhoids, peeing all the time..."

"Damn, girl. You got all that?"

"Morning sickness and heartburn. But I know the rest is coming. It did with Jamal."

"Whew! You couldn't pay me to go through it again," Arianna laughed.

"Yeah, I already told Lorenzo I've changed my mind about having another one. This is going to be it for us. So let's get back to ExposeHim. Shut it down, or keep it going?"

Arianna sighed. "You can be a little more objective than I can right now. What do you think?"

I'd been checking our e-mail from home and you'd think we were a charitable organization based on the response we'd been getting. I had to admit I was moved.

"After you got shot, all kinds of women sent get well e-cards and best wishes and a lot of them asked us to keep the site going. We got this one e-mail... Here I saved it."

I clicked open the company inbox and scrolled down until I found the e-mail that made me want to keep the site going.

"Read that," I said, pointing to it.

"Shit! I remember now!" Arianna shouted, startling me.

"Remember what?" I asked.

"The e-mail about..."

She looked up at me and stopped mid-sentence.

"The e-mail about who?"

"Nothing. Never mind," she said, eliciting my suspicion.

Clearly, it was more than nothing by the way she yelled.

"Arianna, what's going on? I know you've been having trouble with your memory lately and you've obviously remembered something important. Why don't you want to tell me what it is? Is it something scary from that night you don't want to talk about?"

"Yeah," she responded, way too quickly. "I don't want to talk about it. Let's get back to this e-mail, OK?"

I was dying to know what had her acting so weird, but I didn't push. Instead, I focused my attention on the screen and read again the e-mail that made me question whether shutting down the Web site was a good idea.

Dear Ms. Singleton,

I read about what happened to you and I wanted you to know how sorry I am. I hope you get better very soon and they find the person who did this terrible thing to you. You did not deserve it. I know a lot of people disagree with sites like yours, but I want you to know you saved my life. I'm 23 and I had been dating this guy for a few months and I really liked him. He's 27, good-looking and smart, had a good job and treated me nice. I've had bad luck choosing men in the past, so after the first few dates, I checked your Web site to see if there was anything about him there. There wasn't. I checked some of the other sites, too. Nothing. So I felt a little better about seeing him. Anyway, after a few months, he started pressuring me about having sex with him. (I decided not to get intimate with him right away after reading one of your articles.) When I thought I was ready, I asked him about his HIV status and he said he was negative. But I remembered another article you wrote on your Web site under the advice column where you said to assume everyone you meet is HIV positive and have them tested before you begin a sexual relationship. So I asked him to get tested. He agreed, thinking of course, that everything was OK. We decided to get tested together. Thank God, I came back negative. Unfortunately, he was positive. He was shocked and passed out in the clinic. I felt very bad for him and told him we could still be friends, but of course, I would never have sex with him. Although I doubt I would have had unprotected sex with him anyway, I'm so glad I took your advice and made him get tested. Condoms are not 100 percent effective and there's no telling what might have happened. Some people might say I should've known to have him tested anyway, but sometimes we women don't always do what we know we should when it comes to the men in our lives.

Reading the articles you write on your Web site to empower women really made a difference for me.

I hope you make a full recovery and go back to inspiring and helping other women like me.

Celia Grady

Washington, D.C.

"Wow," Arianna said after reading the e-mail. "If I give such good advice, how come my life is so screwed up? You know when I first sat down here and was looking at this computer, I was thinking about all the aggravation the Internet has caused me. I met Chauncey on the Net. This Web site has made somebody hate me enough to have me shot. I was ready to say to hell with this stuff."

"I know," I agreed. "Some people use new technology to take advantage of people. Some use it to help. I was thinking maybe we should stop letting women post the bad stuff about their men and keep the other stuff, like the advice columns, relationship tips and spy software. That way, we're still providing a service, but without the stuff that makes people want to picket and sue us."

"Not people, Nicole. Men."

"OK, men."

"Not just sue us, either. Hurt us. Well, me, anyway. God, I wish they would hurry up and find the man who was working with Darryl Crump. That shit is creeping me out. Somewhere out there is a person who wants to really hurt me. And I have no idea who it is. He could step up to me any minute and put another bullet in me. Or stab me like he did the tires on my car. Or hurt my kids. I keep getting these stupid crank phone calls. I'm so scared, I went out and bought a gun."

Hearing those words brought back the feeling I'd told Lorenzo I had that something bad was going to happen.

"What!" I shouted. "Are you crazy, Arianna?"

"No, I'm trying to protect myself," she shot back.

"There's gotta be something else you can do. Can't you hire security guards to watch the house?"

"I thought about that, but they wouldn't be with me all the time. What about when I leave the house like today? The person who's after me could be watching me right now. You have no idea how it feels to be in this position right now. You've never been shot."

"I know. I know. But buying a gun seems a bit extreme, Arianna. Especially, when you have a child in the house. People who buy guns to protect themselves usually end up accidentally hurting themselves or somebody they care about. It's never the bad guy who gets hurt. I say throw the thing away."

"Like I said, you've never been shot. You don't live in constant fear. I'm keeping the gun, now let's get back to business. I don't think your idea will work for our Web site."

"Don't say I didn't warn you. Why won't it work? It takes all the controversy out of it."

"That's the problem. The controversial stuff is what drew women to our site in the first place. The other stuff is gravy, a bonus for being a member. I doubt we'd get paying subscribers just to read my advice columns. Hell, I'm surprised anybody reads that shit, anyway. I'm no walking billboard for successful relationships."

"You don't have to be in one to know what one should be like," I said.

"Good point. But our site isn't really for women who are *in* relationships with cheaters. It's to keep women *out* of relationships with them. The women who come to our site are being proactive. And we want to encourage that, right? I mean most women do more research picking out a lipstick than they do on the men they're intimate with. Remember the reason we started this was to help sistas get accurate relationship resumes 'cause too many men doctor theirs up. Leaving out a wife or girlfriend here, a kid or two there."

Or worse, I thought.

Suddenly, my mind was no longer in East Falls, but back on my empty house in Bowie where I was dealing with my own demons that needed exorcising. My poor knees were carrying the burden of my extra weight since I'd been spending every spare moment in my prayer closet. I didn't want to share my problems with Arianna, though. She had enough to deal with so I decided to keep my new drama between God and me.

"Right, Nicole?" Arianna said.

"Huh?" My ears had stopped hearing her words when my mind went momentarily adrift.

"Where are you?" she said. "I said that we've talked ourselves into staying in business. Right?"

"Yeah, I guess so."

"OK, then let's get outta here. I'm gonna start looking for a new building tomorrow."

"But I thought you said..."

"I said I needed to face my fear and I did that. I don't want to have to stare it in the face every day, though. This place gives me the creeps. I can't work here anymore. It's time for something new."

With that we left and closed the door on Arianna's nightmare. Outside I gave one last glance to the building and suddenly, instead of seeing red paint dripping from the sign on the door, I saw blood.

I flinched and covered my mouth.

"What's wrong Nicole? Are you OK?"

"I...I...I think I just had a premonition," I said shaking.

"About what? And isn't that like devil worshipping or something? I thought you didn't subscribe to that garbage."

"No. Crystal balls and that stuff are from the devil. The Bible talks about the gift of prophecy so I believe there are people who God has blessed to be able to predict the future."

"Are you one of those people?"

"I never thought so, but lately I've been having feelings and just now I swear I saw blood on that sign."

"It's red paint, not blood," Arianna said.

"I know, but for a second it wasn't dry anymore and it was dripping like blood. I can't explain it, but I know what I saw."

"OK, then what does it mean?"

"I wish I knew," I said, suddenly even more scared. "I really wish I knew."

I thought I already was going through hell with my domestic problems. What I didn't know that morning was an even worse nightmare awaited me.

Fifteen
Arianna

My memory of the e-mail about Lorenzo resurfaced while Nicole and I were in my office deciding whether to keep ExposeHim.com alive.

The next day found me in D.C. with Agnes Jackson, a woman old enough to be my mother, who had become my confidante.

Agnes and my mother had one thing in common. They didn't take any mess. Agnes was an old-school sista who believed in telling it like it is.

So I called her immediately for advice.

She told me exactly what I didn't want to hear.

We were having lunch at Georgia Brown's, a popular restaurant in D.C.'s McPherson Square known for its "low country" Southern cuisine, better known as soul food.

Agnes' locs were wrapped in a bun and she wore a casual, soft black denim pantsuit with black high-heeled boots. Her tan camisole exposed a slight hint of cleavage and the neutral shades she used to paint her face gave her a warm glow.

She was hip for a woman in her 60s and I loved her laid-back style.

For appetizers, I lamented over the latest scenes of "As Arianna's World Turns." Agnes had visited me several times in the hospital, but it wasn't the time or the place for me to bring her up to speed.

I dropped it all on her at lunch.

Gay son. Mystery accomplice behind my attack. Attracted to a man who was not my husband. My pregnant girlfriend's husband on the down-low. I skipped the part about my own husband cheating. I already knew what to do about that. I just needed to stop procrastinating.

Agnes listened intently, sipping her Charleston She Crab Soup and peering at me from behind her designer black frames. She nodded here, shook her head there, but didn't express shock, surprise or any emotion resembling the two.

The waiter came with our food, black-eyed pea cakes and Ms. Brown salad for me, and grilled catfish for Agnes.

I'd monopolized the conversation for about a half hour with my drama, so after taking a few bites, I finally asked Agnes to speak up. She was, as usual, blunt with her advice and opinion.

A gay son? No big deal, she said.

"Just love him and don't worry about what other people say. If he weren't gay, they'd find another reason to talk about him. If he's happy, and you say he is, what else is there to worry about?"

Darryl Crump's accomplice? Be patient and leave it to the police. They'll find him in due time.

Randy skeptical about being with me?

"Can you blame him?" she said with raised eyebrows and a mouth full of fish. She swallowed and sipped her drink before continuing. "What would you say if he told you he killed some woman just because she cheated on him? A woman who wasn't his wife, who he didn't even claim to love? Besides, I told you before, leave that man alone. You have enough problems with your husband. You don't need to add another man to this mess."

"Mess? My life is a mess?" I stabbed my fork into my salad with a vengeance, stuffing the greens, apples, blue cheese and walnuts into my mouth as if they were being punished.

Agnes calmly took a sip of her Bloody Mary and then put her hand on mine.

"Arianna, what you have just described to me is a mess. You have to admit that. I'm not judging you, honey. Just making a statement of fact."

The warmth of her words combined with the comforting touch of her hand had an immediate soothing effect. I put down my fork and looked up from the plate I'd been staring into.

"You're right. It is a mess and I need to find a way to fix it."

"To fix *your* life, not Nicole's."

I sipped my wine and swirled it in my mouth, letting the fruity oak flavor bathe my tongue before sending it down to fulfill its mission of dulling my senses.

"She has a right to know, Agnes."

"But if you're not sure, then you shouldn't say anything. Hell, even if you are sure, you shouldn't say anything."

"Are you serious?" I said, shocked by her response. "Why on earth shouldn't I say anything? When Chauncey was cheating on her with me, she let me know."

"Exactly, and where did that get you?"

"It's not the same thing. Nicole isn't going to kill Lorenzo if that's what you're trying to say."

"No. What I'm saying is no good can come of it. Nicole will find out. She probably already knows. Most of us do. We just choose to play dumb. Ignorance is bliss and all that."

"But what happens when she finds out I knew and didn't tell her?"

"She'll thank you."

"I doubt that," I said with my mouth full.

"Arianna, trust me on this. When we take it upon ourselves to out our friends' men, all we are doing is forcing them to deal with something they're not ready to deal with. So they blame the messenger. Or they refuse to believe it. Or make excuses for the man. Anything to keep from having to make a decision to kick his ass out."

"I don't know. She's my friend."

"And I'm your friend. I'll tell you right now, if I saw your husband with another woman, I would not tell you."

"You wouldn't?"

"No. It's your marriage. Your business. And truth will out."

"Huh?"

"The truth always comes out. I'm just not going to be the one to give it to you. It's not my place."

"All right. You've made your point. Let's talk about something else. Is there any good news in the world?"

"Yes, I finished the manuscript and I've got an agent."

"What! Oh, my God, that's great," I said remembering the excitement I felt when I got an agent for my novel.

Her book was about the quirky ladies of a book club. Kind of a black Ya-Ya Sisterhood. She modeled the characters after some of the women in her group.

I was her editor.

And I was enjoying her work. Akilah and being Agnes' partner on the book were the few bright spots in my life. Her novel gave me the chance to lose myself in someone else's world.

"Congratulations, Agnes. I am so happy for you."

"Thanks, I'm pretty excited. Who would've thought an old woman like me would become an author this late in life."

"Please. You are hardly old. So give me the rest of the chapters so I can finish editing and you can get the complete manuscript to your agent."

Agnes smiled, reached into her duffel bag and handed me the document.

After leaving Georgia Brown's and promising to get back to Agnes in a week about her book, I opted to take her advice and not go to Nicole's.

For the time being.

Sixteen
Arianna

A loud banging noise was echoing through the living room as I entered the house after a morning of physical therapy. It was too early for Akilah or Kenny to be home. Startled, I went inside the hall closet, unlocked the box where I kept my new gun and nervously cradled the cold metal steel in my shaking hands.

Paranoia had been slowly suffocating my brain ever since the doctors sent me home. The investigation was moving too damn slow. I'd been seeing Darryl Crump in the closet, under the bed and in the back seat of my car.

Knowing he and his accomplice were free and not knowing when or if they'd strike again had me constantly on edge.

My phone had been ringing off the hook with the crank calls. Idiots breathing obscenities into the receiver and making threats such as, "The third bullet's the charm, bitch." I had the number changed twice. They managed to get the new one both times, so I just stopped answering the phone unless I recognized the number.

I was convinced Darryl Crump or his wingman was either making the calls or putting someone else up to it. I had always been afraid of guns, but I was afraid of this stranger more.

Trembling, I tiptoed toward the noise. My heart raced and my palms sweated. I should've called the police or ran back outside, but I wanted to be the one to put an end to the madness.

I was sick to death of being this asshole's victim.

The sound was coming from the kitchen. As I got closer, I called out. "Who's there? I've got a gun!"

A familiar voice hollered back.

"Arianna? Is that you? Did you say something?"

The voice was Kenny's. I lowered the gun to my side in relief, my hands still shaking, heart still racing. I took several deep breaths, and then entered the kitchen. Kenny was banging an ice tray against the counter, trying to get out the cubes.

A look of bewilderment covered his face when he saw me standing in the doorway carrying a Smith and Wesson.

"What are you doing home?" I asked.

"I live here. What the hell are you doing with a gun? I thought we agreed..."

"We didn't agree on anything. You said you wouldn't buy me one so I bought one for myself."

"Without telling me?"

"I didn't want to argue with you, Kenny."

"Great. As usual, you do what the hell you want to do, and to hell with what I think."

"Don't start that shit with me, again, please. I don't need your permission to protect myself."

"Whatever, Arianna. What are you doing with it?"

"You scared the shit out of me with that damn noise."

"OK, now that you know it's me, can you put it away please?"

I went to the closet to return the gun.

Kenny followed.

"What if I *were* a burglar or something, Arianna? Were you really planning to shoot me?"

"I don't know if I would've pulled the trigger, Kenny. Nobody can say what they would do until they are actually put in that situation. I wanted to scare you, well not you, but you know what I mean."

"Yeah, but what if I had a gun, too? Then what? You better believe a criminal is gonna know a lot more about using a gun than you do. So he's gonna have the upper hand. Just get rid of that damn thing."

"Nobody is going to ever have the upper hand on me again," I yelled, as memories of the fear I felt that night suddenly flooded my brain. "Ambushed once, shame on you. Ambushed twice, shame on me."

Kenny shook his head. "There is just no talking to you."

"Not about this Kenny. You've never been a crime victim. You've never been shot. Why do I have to keep reminding people about the violence I've been through?"

Tears erupted from nowhere and began trickling down my face. "You don't have some whacko calling you and making stupid threats. I'm scared, don't you get that? Every time I leave the house, I'm scared of what might happen to me out there. That I might never make it home again."

"OK. OK, calm down, baby," Kenny said in a soothing tone. "I'm sorry, I didn't mean to get you so upset."

He took my hand and led me to the living room couch.

"You're right," he said, wrapping his arms around me. "I have no idea how you feel. I wish I could do something to make you feel safe."

"There's nothing you can do except be there for me."

"Whoever this guy is, he's not gonna come after you, now, Arianna. There's been too much attention on you since the shooting. He knows he'll get caught. He's probably hiding out somewhere or he's left the country."

He lifted my head from his chest and looked me in the eye.

"I'm gonna do everything I can to protect you. I won't let anyone hurt you again. And I really don't think he's gonna try anything. Please try not to worry so much. I know it's hard, but try. For me?"

His words were nice, but did little to ease my anxiety. I nodded anyway to make him happy.

"I'll try," I said, burying my head deeper into his chest. "You know this is nice, Kenny. Us sitting here this close to each other, connecting. You supporting me. Why can't we be like this all the time? Or at least more often?"

Apparently I'd said the wrong thing because his response was to sigh, lift my head off his body and scoot over. "I don't know, Arianna."

"Why'd you move away?" I asked annoyed at the distance he was suddenly putting between us. "We can't have a serious conversation unless there's a wall between us? I'm not trying to argue with you,

Kenny. I want us to work through our problems and we can't do that unless we talk about it."

"I don't know what you want me to say, Arianna."

"I want you to explain to me why it is that we haven't been married two full years yet and we are always at each other's throats. I don't get it. I wrote a book. You didn't like it. I started a Web site, and you didn't like it. Couples have much bigger problems than that and manage to work it out every day. Why can't we seem to get past this petty bullshit?"

He raised his voice slightly.

"Because what's petty to you is a much bigger deal to me. Since we've been together, it seems like everyone in the world has questioned my manhood. I even started to question it and it's done things to me."

"What things, Kenny?"

"Made me bitter and resentful."

"Of me?"

"Yes."

"Is that why you barely touch me?"

"Maybe."

"We were really good friends, why the hell can't we make this marriage work better?"

"I honestly don't know. I love you, Arianna. I really do. But I guess some things you just don't get past."

"Like what? You act like we've got some insurmountable problems. Obviously you know something I don't. "

"I don't want to talk about this anymore..."

"Kenny..."

"I'm sorry. I have to get back to work."

He grabbed his jacket from the back of the couch where he'd laid it and made his way toward the door. His hand on the handle, he stopped and turned around.

"I really do wish I could go back and do things differently."

Seventeen
Arianna

My new office was in the heart of downtown Philly in a prime high rise building on Market Street. The space was a lot smaller, but I felt safer being in busy Center City. Keisha had a desk in a shared receptionist area, which was adjacent to a beautifully furnished waiting room. I created a new company, Triple A Enterprises, named for myself, Amir and Akilah and rented the space under that name. I was pretty sure the landlord wouldn't want ExposeHim.com as a tenant. I made the Web site a subsidiary of Triple A.

Calls to ExposeHim went to an automated answering machine, which Keisha monitored throughout the day. It was the best way to maintain contact with existing subscribers, and hide from the media, which still considered me news.

I was sitting at my new desk in my new office when I got a visit from an old acquaintance that managed to track me down.

It was shortly after lunch when I looked up to find Keisha escorting a petite, walnut complexioned sista into my office.

"Arianna, this is Miss Bailey. She says she has information that can help you with the Rodgers case," said Keisha, a fair-skinned, attractive woman with auburn hair.

Miss Bailey was about five-two with shoulder-length hair that was bone straight and cut into flattering layers. She wore a form fitting wool beige skirt suit with knee-high camel leather boots.

"Have a seat," I said, pointing to the high-back cream leather chair that fronted my desk.

She sat down and crossed her hands in her lap.

It wasn't until she was sitting directly in front of me and had my complete attention that I realized how familiar she looked. Then she opened her mouth to speak and I immediately recognized that Kewpie doll voice.

"I know I'm the last person..." she began.

"Janelle? I interrupted. "Janelle Carter?"

"It's Bailey. I go by my maiden name now," she said as if she were addressing her banker or a colleague instead of a woman she'd tried to send to jail.

I jumped up, reached across the desk and bitch-slapped her so hard she fell over backward in the chair. Her head hit the floor like the rock it was made of.

I rubbed my hands together, trying to soothe the sting the connection with her face left on my palm. She stumbled back to her feet, caressing the crimson handprint on her cheek with one hand, smoothing her clothes with the other.

"I don't give a damn what you go by," I snapped. "What the hell are you doing in my office? You've got a lot of nerve bringing your ass here."

Keisha ran inside. "Arianna is everything all right?" she asked, her eyes darting back and forth between a disheveled Janelle and me.

"Everything's fine, Keisha. Shut the door, please," I said, trying to sound as professional as I could.

Janelle was shaking. I could tell she wanted to hit me but didn't dare. I had been holding on to my hate for her for more than two years. Something simmering that long was a lot more potent than any angry feelings she might have caught in that single moment.

Our last face-to-face encounter took place at Chauncey's wake. Janelle was the woman he was going to marry even though he already had a wife.

Nicole and I had befriended her, even accompanied her to the clinic when she aborted Chauncey's twins. But she turned on us after he died, giving me up to the cops, telling them I'd killed him.

The Janelle I remembered was grossly overweight, had unkempt hair, and low self-esteem.

She was so pathetic, readers often took pot shots at the character I'd modeled after her in my book.

She inspired a spirited discussion at a co-ed book club meeting I attended in Philly.

"No woman can be that stupid," said Brandi, the woman who'd invited me to speak to the club. "I mean she was so pathetic. You made up a lot of stuff about her for effect, right? She wasn't actually going to marry that asshole was she?"

"Brandi, have you ever seen Jerry Springer or Ricki Lake?" asked Lance, a middle-age, mocha-colored brother with gray around his temples. "Triflin' brothas make their living off gullible women like her."

"Oh, please," Brandi said. "That's acting. That shit ain't real."

"Well, she's real," I said. "Real gullible and real needy and there are lots of women like her who will put up with a piece of man just to have a man. You just haven't met one yet, Brandi."

The rest of the group shook their heads in agreement.

Brandi turned to Lance. "So why do men take advantage of women like her?"

"Not just women like her, any woman?" I added.

Lance's response was simple. "Because they can. We, and I'm talking about men *and* women for my gold-digging sistas out there, do what we can get away with. If a brotha can stay out all night, come home and tell some lie and his woman lets him get back in her bed, why wouldn't he do it again? Grown-ups ain't no different from kids. If there are no consequences for bad behavior, we repeat it. Sistas have to start holding brothas accountable and vice versa."

The whole room erupted in a chorus of "Amen!" as if Lance had just delivered a rousing sermon.

The Janelle quivering before me, however, bore no resemblance to that woman Brandi's book club made fun of. She was slim, sophisticated and before I slapped her, confident.

I had to admit the bitch cleaned up well.

"Look, Arianna. I deserved that, so I'm going to let it go," she said picking up the chair. But I hope you got it all out of your system 'cause I didn't come here to fight you. But I will if you hit me again."

"Is that a threat?" I snorted.

"No. I'm just telling you I won't let you do that again without defending myself."

"You mean like I had to defend myself against those bogus charges because of you?"

"You have a right to be upset with me about that. That's why I'm here. I came to apologize and believe it or not I came to help you."

"How the hell can you help me? And why would you want to, considering a couple of years ago you were trying to get me locked up?"

"I was a different person then," she said quietly.

"You *look* different. I'll give you that."

"I'm different in other ways, too. I know what I did, reporting you to the police after you did nothing but help me was wrong, and I'm sorry."

"It took you two years to figure that out?"

"No. I figured it out a while ago. And I wanted to apologize. I just didn't think you cared whether or not I was sorry."

"I don't. So why are telling me now?"

"Because I know you want to hear what I have to say, now."

"Why would I?"

"Because it could you help win this case. Can I sit back down, please?"

We both took our seats. I couldn't help myself. I wanted to hear what she had to say.

"I'll ask you again. Why do you want to help me, Janelle?"

"To make up for trying to hurt you before. If I hadn't sicced the cops on you, you never would have been charged with killing Chauncey. You didn't deserve that. I was so consumed by jealousy of you and Nicole because I felt like he treated you guys better than he treated me even though I was the one spending all my money on his triflin' ass. I was angry with myself but I couldn't deal with that so I lashed out against you."

"Sounds like you've been getting some professional help," I said, softening up just a bit.

"Yes, I did. I took a long look at myself in the mirror, decided I needed to confront my issues and make some changes in my life. I started with the inside, and then worked on the outside.

"Nicole was able to forgive me. She told me I should talk to you, too, but I figured you wouldn't want to hear it."

"You've been in touch with Nicole?" I asked, anger rising in me again because I'd been kept in the dark.

"Yeah," she stammered. "For months, now. I've got a shop in Baltimore and one in D.C. in addition to the one in Richmond. I've expanded my business. Nicole and I get together for lunch every now and then when I come up North. She keeps saying she's going to tell you, but I guess she keeps chickening out."

"I guess so," I mumbled, pissed that Nicole had been keeping this huge secret from me. "Can we skip to the part where you can help me?"

She crossed her legs. "I've been following your career every since you got off that manslaughter rap in California. I know about your book and your Web site."

"And?"

"And I told a lot of my clients about the site. You know how women are. They tell their beautician about their men. When things are good and not so good."

"What's that got to do with this case, Janelle?" I was losing my patience.

"One of my clients is Eugene Rodgers' mistress. He's been telling her for months that he's going to leave his wife and every time that day comes, he says he has to wait a little while longer. They both have careers to think about, yada, yada, yada. Anyway, one day she comes in pissed, telling me she's done with him and she wants to pay him back for screwing with her life and all that. She asks me for the name of the site again. I had mentioned it a few times, but she forgot it. I gave it to her again and this time she wrote it down. I'm pretty sure she's the one who posted that information about him. I read it and I noticed it was anonymous."

"Yeah, I allow women to post anonymously as long as I can verify the e-mail address and some information. I e-mailed the woman who sent the post and she e-mailed me back with details about the guy and their relationship. But when I tried to get in touch with her again, after Rodgers filed suit, my e-mail bounced back."

Janelle nodded. "She's afraid of him. He has a lot of power."

"All I know is Eugene Rodgers is making my life hell right now," I sighed. "And I've got enough to deal with without having to worry about this lawsuit."

"I heard about the shooting," she said. "How are you by the way? You look good."

"Fine," I said.

"You know your site is making Eugene's life hell," Janelle said. "Everybody at my shop is talking about him. Once I told them about your site, all my clients were checking it out, posting information and sending pictures. It's like the new therapy for getting over a cheating man. Some of them check the site a few days a week to see if any guys they know or their girlfriends know have been added. When they saw Eugene on there, they had a field day."

"I thought he was chief of a *small* town," I said.

"A black chief of police? The size of the town doesn't matter. And neither does the wedding ring. Sistas got radar for a black man in uniform. Everybody knows him."

We both laughed at that one.

I couldn't believe I was actually sharing a light moment with the woman who wanted to see me behind bars.

And now was she trying to help me.

Her information would be the break I needed.

"So are you going to give me the woman's name?" I asked.

"Well, first I have to ask her if it's OK. I wanted to see if you would actually meet with me and accept my help before I talked to her. Like I said, she's pretty scared of Eugene. I will get in touch with her and call you in a couple of days."

I couldn't believe she set me up like that. Why the hell didn't she just come with the information? Why wouldn't I want it? I wasn't stupid enough to turn down information that could save my business and keep my life savings in my pocket just because it came from her.

But I was not in a position to be nasty about it.

"Can you get back to me as soon as you can?" I sighed. My stomach was churning at the thought of needing this heifer for something.

"Sure," Janelle said, standing up and walking toward the door. "By the way, I read your book. Did you have to make my character so pathetic?"

"Truth is better than fiction, Janelle."

"I see you still haven't changed, Arianna."

She frowned, shook her head and left.

Then I dialed Nicole.

Eighteen
Nicole

A lot had changed since I pushed Jamal into the world 12 years ago, and since Lorenzo had never had the privilege of witnessing the miracle of birth, I decided we should take classes.

I had just pulled up to the Anne Arundel Medical Center in Bowie to register the two of us for the birthing class and sign up Lorenzo for the Dr. Dad class, where he'd learn how to care for both me and the baby by experienced fathers, when my cell phone started chiming Kirk Franklin's "Looking For You."

His remake of Patrice Rushen's "Haven't You Heard," usually got my foot stomping every time the phone rang.

Not this time.

As soon as I saw Arianna's name in the caller ID, something told me she wasn't calling to shoot the breeze.

I was right. She skipped the preliminaries of a greeting and went right to her complaint.

"When were you planning to tell me about your new best friend, Janelle, heifer?"

"I'm fine, thanks for asking," I said sarcastically.

"Whatever. Answer my question."

I filled my lungs with air, then slowly released, preparing myself for this showdown. It didn't matter what I said. Arianna was not going to take lightly the fact that I'd been sympathetic to Janelle and she was going to be even madder that I'd kept it from her.

"I don't know when I was going to tell you and she's not my best friend."

"What the hell is she, then?"

"A friend I guess. No...more like an acquaintance. Whatever she is she's not my best friend. That's your job, remember?"

"Actually, I don't....

A hissing sound and then silence drowned Arianna's words. The call dropped. A few minutes passed and I thought I was temporarily off the hook.

Then, Kirk Franklin's voice was ringing in my ear again.

"Sorry, my damn phone has been acting up a lot lately. I think I need a new one. Anyway, if I was your best friend, Nicole, I would have known you were getting reacquainted with an old one."

"How *did* you find out, anyway?"

I'd asked Janelle not to tell Arianna that I'd had lunch with her a few times. I didn't like lying, and that's how I saw it. A sin of omission was just as bad as a sin of commission in my mind. I kept justifying it by saying Arianna was better off not knowing.

I should've known she'd find out. The Bible says what's done in the dark will be revealed in the light.

"She just left my office. She came here supposedly to give me some information she thinks can help with the Rodgers' case. And she just happened to let it slip that you and she have been hangin' out lately."

"I would hardly call it hangin' out, Arianna," I said, rolling my eyes as I finally turned off the ignition.

"What the hell would you call it, Nicole?"

I hated it when she talked to me like that, as if she was speaking to one of her kids.

"Look," I said sharply. "Janelle called me a few months ago and asked me to meet her for lunch. She said she wanted to apologize for how she treated us. I believe in giving people second chances so I met her. She seemed really sincere. Felt really guilty about calling the cops on you and had really changed her life around. I was impressed, quite frankly."

"Whoopie for her. Does that mean you had to invite her back in your life?"

"I didn't have to. I chose to, Arianna. I thought about what she was going through back then. The man she loved and had made a lot of sacrifices for. The man she thought she was going to marry and was the father of her unborn children, turned out to be a liar and a cheat. Then he winds up dead. Our feelings don't just turn off because we find out people did us wrong. She loved that man. She had all that stuff pent up inside, hurt, betrayal, loss and nowhere to let it go. So she lashed out at us."

"You mean me. All she did to you was act like a bitch. She tried to have me locked up."

"OK, she lashed out at you. But I could understand where she was coming from. I wasn't pregnant by the man, but I lived with him for two years and I thought I was going to marry him, too. It was pretty hard for me to get around the fact that you killed him, even though it was an accident."

I hadn't done it intentionally, but bringing up his death was always good for shutting Arianna up, at least momentarily.

After several seconds of awkward silence, I continued.

"If I could forgive you, I certainly could forgive Janelle. I didn't tell you, 'cause I knew how you'd react. You are not the most forgiving person in the world, Arianna. And I know what she did to you, or tried to do to you, was a big deal."

"Not big enough for you to kick her to the curb."

"Where would I be if Jesus kicked me to the curb for all my sins? Where would you be?"

"Don't start with that, Nicole," she snapped.

I should've known not to bring The Almighty into the conversation. He never carried that much weight with Arianna.

"See? That's why I didn't tell you. 'Cause of that attitude right there. I do have a right to choose my own friends, Arianna."

Silence again.

"Arianna? Arianna, are you still there?"

"Yeah, I'm here. Fine, you have the right to choose your friends. And I can't approve them. I mean hell, you and Candace are almost as tight as me and you and I can't stand her ass. I just never thought Janelle would ever be back in my life."

"She's not. She's in *my* life. I told her to talk to you, give you a chance to forgive her. But that was more for her sake 'cause I knew you wouldn't do it."

"What do you mean, her sake?"

"You know how they tell alcoholics to make amends when they're in recovery?"

"Yeah."

"Well, that's how Janelle felt. Like she had to make amends to get her life back on track. That's why she called me. And she wanted to call you, too. I encouraged her to do it so at least she would know she made the effort even if you shut her down like we knew you would."

"Damn, Nicole. You make me sound like a cold-hearted monster."

"No. Just a little inflexible and unforgiving at times," I laughed.

"Would you have been so quick to forgive Janelle if she had done to you what she did to me?"

"I don't know. I would've had to pray on it, like I did when she called me. And the Spirit told me to forgive her so I did. The question now is whether we're going to get past this, Arianna?"

"What do you mean?"

"Are you going to stop being my friend 'cause I'm not enemies with Janelle?"

She sighed. "Of course not. I can't lie and say that I'm well with this shit, but you're my girl. Just as long as you don't expect me and her to be in the same room together."

"Sounds like you already were."

"That's different. This was business. You know what I mean."

"Yeah. So was she able to help? What information did she have?"

"Not yet. She claims she knows who the woman is who sent us the anonymous **e**-mail about Eugene Rodgers. Says she has to talk to her first and see if she'll let her give me her name so I can contact her."

"Great. That's all we need. To verify that it's true and we're off the hook. Let me know how it goes."

"I'm sure your friend Janelle can tell you."

I rolled my eyes again. Sometimes I wondered why Arianna and I were friends.

"Just call me when you know something, wise guy."

Nineteen
Arianna

A week later, Janelle was back in my office with an offer. She'd help me win the Eugene Rodgers case if I sold her ExposeHim.com.

"Why on earth would I do that and why would you want it? You already have your own business," I snapped.

"I know," Janelle said with a smirk. I want *your* business."

"Excuse me?"

Janelle scooted her chair away from my desk and stood up, putting enough distance between us to keep from easily slapping the shit out of her again. She smoothed the pants of the fitted crimson suit she was wearing and ran her fingers through her perfectly coiffed hair.

"You heard me, Arianna. I want what you have. That's why I sent that e-mail to ExposeHim.com in the first place."

"What e-mail?"

"The one about Eugene."

"You sent it? You set me up!" I yelled.

She backed up closer to the door. "That's right. I did. And you might want to keep your voice down. You don't want the people in the other offices to hear you."

"Don't tell me what to do, bitch! What happened to the so-called changes you made in your life? Your desire to make amends with the people you hurt. This is your idea of amends?"

"I did change, bitch!" Janelle spat, her eyes on fire with anger. "Then I picked up a copy of your book. You made me look like a pathetic fool. Do you know how embarrassing that was for me? I'm sure my clients and the hairdressers in my salon were laughing like hyenas behind my back."

"For god's sake, Janelle..."

A knock on my office door interrupted me. "Ms. Singleton is everything OK in there?" Keisha asked, the concern in her voice audible despite the thick door.

I opened it but didn't let her in. "I'm fine, Keisha. Thanks for checking. I'm sorry for all the commotion."

I closed the door and turned back to Janelle.

"You sound like my husband," I said through clenched teeth, trying to keep my voice down. "I didn't *make* you look like anything. I painted a realistic portrait of the person you were. If that woman was pathetic then the only person you have to blame for that is yourself. You're obviously not that pathetic woman now, are you? And why the hell do you care what other people say about you? Shit! If I worried about that, I wouldn't be able to function. People talk about me all the time. And you went to all this trouble to set me up just so you can have my business? What does that accomplish for you?"

"Payback, Arianna. You know all about that don't you? It's the reason Chauncey's rotting in his grave."

"Payback for what? I've never done anything to you, Janelle. At least when I went after Chauncey, I had a reason."

"I just told you. That damn book! My kids were so embarrassed. My daughter around her co-workers and my son around his friends. Even my no-good ex-husband called to make fun of me."

"That's your fault, too, Janelle. If you hadn't called the cops on me and gave all those damn interviews to the media, nobody would have ever heard of Chauncey Cockfield, Arianna Singleton or you. The only reason anybody knew you were the woman I based your character on was because of *your* big mouth."

"So what. You didn't have to write a book about what happened in the first place. Just when I was getting my life back together after the mess Chauncey made of it..."

"You mean the mess you *let* him make of your life," I interrupted.

Janelle was seething. She was waving her index finger in the air like a teacher scolding a misbehaving student and shaking her head like an around-the-way girl checking her man. Her anger was sucking the air from the room.

She ignored my interruption and picked up right where she left off.

"Just when I was getting my shit together, I pick up a copy of that trash you called a novel and had to relive all that drama again. My kids didn't know I had an abortion. Now they do, thanks to your fucking book. How do you think that makes me look to them? You took sensitive and embarrassing moments in my life and told the whole world about them. You rocked my world and fucked with my kids. Now I'm going to rock your world and take away the things that matter to you."

"You mean you're gonna try. You think I'm just going to roll over and let you walk all over me. That's your style, not mine."

"You won't have a choice. If you don't sell me the Web site, you're going to lose it in court, anyway. Either way, I win. So you can either do this the easy way or the hard way. Sell it to me and you make a few dollars and save face."

"What do you get outta this? What are you going to do with the Web site?"

"I get to take something away from you first of all. And when I hold a press conference to announce that I'm the new owner of ExposeHim.com, I become the woman with the power, the one in control. I get to be the woman who makes these assholes mistreating women pay. Not the pathetic creature the world believes I am because of you."

All I could do was stare at Janelle. Finally, I walked back around to my desk, plopped in my chair and exhaled.

"That press conference is never going to happen, Janelle. You will never take away anything that belongs to me. Now get the hell out of my office."

She flashed a sinister smile. "But I already have, Arianna. I already have."

Twenty
Arianna

Twenty

Eugene Rodgers may have been holding the cards to my financial future, but he was not the man who'd put Darryl Crump up to breaking into my office.

That was the conclusion of the Philly police department after weeks of an investigation that had led nowhere.

Detective Howard had checked out every name we'd given him and even ones I hadn't. He looked into Chauncey Cockfield's family on the slight chance one of them had waited two years to seek revenge against me.

He even managed to get the names of some of the men who had protested outside my office.

Nothing.

He hit one dead end after another and I was beginning to think they'd never figure out who was behind my shooting.

I hadn't felt that helpless since my first husband Michael died. When I thought my world had slipped from its axis.

This was different. This was not some distortion of nature, like cancer. This was man-made. But like cancer, I had no control over it.

I wanted it to be Eugene. If he was locked up, his stupid case against me would go away and Janelle would have no leverage over me.

I couldn't believe I was in such a predicament. I just knew I had to find a way out. No way could Janelle win.

I wanted a drink. No, I needed a drink.

My nerves were frayed like the hem of an old denim skirt. Too bad alcohol was out of the question because of my pain medication.

The gym was calling my name. I'd always been able to release frustration by working out. My back injury prevented even that.

I turned on the radio in an attempt to get lost in someone else's misery and pain put to music. Instead of rhythm and blues, though, the DJ was prognosticating about the game that night between the 76ers and the Denver Nuggets as if he had a crystal ball.

He was predicting victory for the 76ers.

I'd been a basketball fan for years, but writing the novel and touring had kept me from seeing a game up close and personal for a long time.

I decided to brush the dust off my season tickets and see if he was right. Maybe bad boy Allen Iverson and Chris Webber could take my mind off all that was bothering me. Even if it was only temporary.

❧❧❧

Halftime found me at the concession stand in desperate need of a bottle of water. I'd screamed myself hoarse rooting for the Sixers and my throat was parched.

The line was long and not worth the wait, so I decided to relieve myself. As I headed for the bathroom, I saw a familiar face walking toward me, smiling.

"I thought that was you," said Randy, who was looking suave in a pair of brown corduroy ribbed slacks, a tan and brown sweater and tobacco colored square tipped leather shoes.

"I didn't know you were a fan. You here with your husband?"

"No. I'm by myself," I said, unable to keep from smiling back.

"Me, too. My son was supposed to come, but he's got a stomach virus and decided to go back to his mom's. Something's going around. Is there an open seat near you?"

"I think so."

"Mind if I join you? We can watch the second half together."

"Are you sure?"

"Why wouldn't I be?"

"Well, after the other day..."

"Arianna, you're not my enemy. We can watch a basketball game together can't we?"

"I have to go to the ladies room, first."

"Cool. I was going to get some nachos. You want something?"

"Some water if you don't mind."

"See you in a few."

Randy was waiting in the hall for me after I relieved myself, bottled water in hand. The seat next to me was empty and it was in a section better than his nosebleed seats so he joined me.

Randy was easy to be with. We talked about the drama surrounding Allen Iverson, his ghetto fabulous but devoted mother, how he liked basketball, but loved golf and wished more of his students were interested in that and other sports.

"Most of them think they're going into the NBA and they haven't got a shot in hell," Randy said. "They look at Iverson who's from the hood and think they can make it, too. All these kids have is hopeless hoop dreams. I try to tell them to have a Plan B."

"They'll figure it out," I told him. "My son used to say the same thing. He got mad at me for telling him he wasn't going to be the next Michael Jordan and accused me of not having faith in him and not supporting his dreams. I told him it was all right to dream, but not plan your life around a long shot."

"What's he doing now?"

"He's a sophomore at the University of Maryland. Hasn't decided on a major yet, though."

"That's great. My son is more interested in girls right now than school," Randy said.

I liked that his kids were teenagers. If we did hook up, chances are he wouldn't want any babies and our kids would be out of the house around the same time.

"His mom complains about the 'stank hoes,' as she calls them, calling her house all the time," he continued. "I told her it's going to be like that for a while, but we've got to keep him grounded and teach him what's important. I'm sure you know what I mean. You've already been though that phase with your son."

"Yeah," I responded dryly. *Not really*, is what I should have said.

And just like that my mind was in another place.

I don't know what Randy said next because my mind had already drifted back to the Christmas Day Revelation as Kenny and I had referred to Amir's coming out.

"Arianna? Arianna?" Randy called, trying to bring me back to earth.

"Huh?"

"What's the matter? I was telling you about an exhibit I saw in University City and you were in another world. What's up?"

"I'm sorry. I'm just going through a lot right now and it's not a good time for me."

"Your husband?"

"Him, my son, my health. They still don't know who was working with the guy who shot me.

"Damn! You really are going through."

"My friend Agnes would say, 'growing through.' You know, whatever doesn't kill you makes you stronger and all that. But I just can't see how all this crap is gonna make me a better person."

"I wish I could do something to help."

"Thanks, I appreciate that, but I just have to work through it. Let's talk about something else. What's the exhibit about again?"

"It's a showing of African art, prints, sculpture, dishes, all kinds of stuff. I was asking if you'd like to go see it with me."

"It sounds great. Does this mean you've decided you don't mind kicking it with this married lady with so much on her plate?"

"You know, Arianna, my hesitation about getting involved with you, even as a friend, isn't so much about that guy dying, although that's pretty bad, it was self-defense and you don't strike me as a murderer."

"You didn't seem so sure about that the other day."

"I was still in shock," he said.

"So what is it then?"

"It's the whole revenge thing. You went to a lot of trouble to get back at that guy. I mean I've heard of sistas who go all out, sugar in the gas tank, slashing tires, harassing the new girlfriend, even making trouble for a brotha on his job…"

"I take it your ex did one or more of the things to you?"

Randy laughed. "No. She can be mean, but she's way too saddity for that kind of shit."

"Oh. So she's better than the rest of us," I joked.

"No, but she probably thinks so. Getting back to you. What you did was extra. It was planned out for weeks, methodical. And based on what you wrote in your book, you weren't even strung out over the guy. And I got to be honest; it's got me wondering what kind of woman does that."

"So you'd feel better if I whipped out a knife and stabbed him in the heat of the moment?"

"Nah, but I could probably understand that better."

"You've got a point, but I'm not sure if I have an answer to that. I've thought about it a lot the past two years. The best I can come up with is I don't like getting played. I had a lot of bad experiences with men before my first husband. And I waited a long time after he died to start dating again. I met a lot of jerks. Then Chauncey came along and I thought I'd finally found someone who was worth my time getting to know. When I found out he was not only playing me, but half the East Coast, I was pissed. And maybe by getting back at him, I was getting back at all the other men who had done me wrong...and..."

"And maybe even your husband for leaving you at the mercy of guys like him?" Randy interrupted.

Words failed me. That thought had never even occurred to me. I pondered the idea, letting it marinate for a few moments.

"Arianna?" Randy asked, anxiously awaiting my response.

"Maybe," I said finally. "I just never thought about it like that."

"Well if you were working out some issues that had nothing to do with that brotha you only dated for a coupla months, I figure it must've been *something* serious."

"How'd you get to be so smart?"

Just then, the spectators were on their feet roaring about some play we had missed.

"What happened?" I shouted, trying to be heard above the fans.

"Dunno," Randy said, shrugging his shoulders. "I haven't been paying any more attention than you."

"Must've been a great play," I hollered. "So, how'd you come up with your diagnosis?"

He looked at me with a perplexed expression, and then realized I was picking up where we'd left off.

"Oh," he said, raising his voice above the crowd. "You know I've got a lot of kids in my classes who have lost a parent. Some of them to drugs, others violence, some AIDS. Their grandmothers are raising some of them. Some are in foster care."

The crowd calmed down and Randy's yelling was bringing us unwelcome attention.

I laughed.

He lowered his voice and then continued.

"The one thing these kids have in common is a lot of anger. They act like they are mad at the world. One of the guidance counselors explained to me they were angry at their absent parent. It's tough being mad at someone who's not around for you to yell at. Especially, when you blame them for leaving you alone in the world. She and I, the guidance counselor, got a couple of shrinks to volunteer a few hours a week to come in and counsel these kids. It's not like anybody at home is addressing their needs so we do the best we can."

"I think that's great," I said. "That you guys would go to all that trouble to help kids who the other teachers probably dismissed as behavior problems."

"It's part of the job," Randy said, trying to be modest.

"No it's not, but it's good to know there are men like you who think that way," I said, feeling myself falling under his spell.

"You know some people say losing a spouse is worse than losing a child," he said.

"I hope I never have to find out. It was definitely the hardest thing I've ever had to go through."

"Even compared to getting shot?"

"Yeah, I think so."

"Damn. People go through heartbreak all the time, but I guess it's really different when the person dies. You know you'll never see them again."

"It is. I've had a relationship end when I didn't want it to, and it hurt like hell. But you always know that person is still around. You can still try to reach out to them if you want. Call them or write a letter or e-mail. Arrange to *accidentally* run in to them. But death is so damn final. There's no going back."

"So you agree with my assessment, then?"

"I think you might just be right, Randy. You just saved me a couple thousand dollars in therapy," I laughed.

"That means the exhibit's on you then."

I smiled. "Sure. My treat. And I'll take that as a 'yes' to you wanting to see me."

"I think we'd make good friends. We have a lot in common and I'd like to start there. Taking things slow and see where they go..."

Iverson dunked on the Raptors' Charlie Villanueva. The crowd was back on its feet sending their loud excitement into the air.

Randy and I decided to join them and watch the rest of the game knowing it would not be our last chance to talk.

Twenty-one
Arianna

Amir came home for spring break the next day and hell started breaking loose.

When my son canceled his trip to South Beach to spend time with his recovering mother, neither of us had any clue his visit would unearth a secret.

I was in my room going through photographs from Nicole's wedding that I'd finally gotten developed and enlarged. Her birthday was coming up and I had bought a sterling silver frame and was trying to decide which picture to put in it and give her for a present. She still hadn't shared with me what was bothering her so I just went along with her everything-is-fine attitude.

If she was going to pretend her marriage was all good, so was I.

"Whatcha doin' Ma," Amir said, standing in my doorway wearing jeans two sizes too big and an urban label blue and red shirt two men could fit inside.

"I'm going to give Nicole one of these pictures as a present."

He sat down on the bed next to me and started picking through them. Suddenly, the color faded from his face and he looked as though he'd seen a ghost.

"Amir what's the matter?"

Silence.

"Amir, honey, what's wrong? Talk to me," I said, my voice getting louder.

"This guy is Nicole's husband?" he mumbled.

"Yeah, why?"

"I know him."

"Really? How?"

"I met him at a punk bar."

"What the hell is that?"

"A gay bar, Ma," he said, as though I should've known.

My mouth opened liked I was in a dentist chair awaiting an exam. "Lorenzo is gay?"

I slammed the picture frame on the bed and jumped up. "That lyin' ass mutherfucker."

"Damn, Ma. Chill. You just got outta the hospital, remember?"

"I know, but this shit pisses me off. You're telling me he's on the down-low?"

"Word is he's bi."

"As in bisexual?"

"Yeah."

"I didn't know he went both ways when I first met him. Later, I heard he got married. But I had no idea it was to Nicole."

He shook his head in disgust.

"How well do you know Lorenzo, Amir?"

He lowered his head and started rubbing his hands on his pants, the same way he did when he told Kenny and me he was gay.

I slumped back to the bed with the realization I wasn't ready to hear this truth.

Amir hesitantly gave it to me anyway.

He and Lorenzo had a brief relationship. A few dinners, the movies. And yes, they'd had sex.

Lorenzo called things off between them when he learned Amir's age. My son could pass for damn-near 30 and Lorenzo had assumed he worked at the university and hadn't realized he was a student. Amir didn't bother to tell him until they'd been seeing each other for several weeks.

That's when Lorenzo moved on to Damon.

Amir never told Damon about himself and Lorenzo. Figured there was no point. They weren't exactly friends, just acquaintances who shared a sexual orientation and talked shit at the gay bars when they ran into each other there.

Damon did confide in him that Lorenzo was "confused," not sure whether he wanted to live life as a gay or straight man. Damon had managed to get himself sprung and "confused" was his definition for bisexual.

Amir was grateful he'd never caught feelings for Lorenzo.

Words failed me.

The thought of my son in bed with my best friend's husband brought mental snapshots I didn't want to see. It made me queasy. I swallowed hard, trying to hide my uneasiness.

"You OK, Ma?" Amir asked.

"Yeah. This is just a lot to take in."

"How do you think I feel seeing those wedding pictures? First you and Nicole sleep with the same man and then me and her do. This shit is crazy."

"I know," I said, grabbing at my chest. "It's almost incestuous."

"Huh?"

"Nothing. I just can't believe this, that's all. How 'bout you? I mean, you said you weren't in love with him, but..."

"I don't give a damn about Lorenzo, but I like Nicole. I don't know her well, but she's a nice person and I feel bad for her."

Suddenly, the lights went on in my brain and everything hit me at once.

The scene I witnessed outside the church between Lorenzo and Damon. And the e-mail I was reading just before Darryl Crump tried to send me to meet Jesus.

He lives in two worlds. In his other life, ...

Amir and Damon were in his other life.

"Is Damon light-skinned, about five-ten, with curly black hair?"

"Yeah. How'd you know?" Amir asked with eyes as wide as half-dollars."

"I saw him and Lorenzo arguing outside the church the day of the wedding. Lorenzo said something about him being in a mentorship program he runs, but I knew something else was going on. Damon was mad as hell. Obviously, because Lorenzo was getting married."

I shook my head. Did Nicole know about this? Is this why she was talking in code that day we went to the office?

I put my face in my hands. "What the hell am I gonna do? Nicole does not deserve to have to go through this shit again."

"Why do you have to *do* anything?"

"'Cause Nicole is my friend."

"So you don't need to get in her business, Ma. This is between her and her husband."

"Are you serious, Amir? What if you were still seeing him? Wouldn't you want me to tell you he was married?"

"I don't know."

"Well, I know Nicole would want to know."

"It's my business, too, and what if I don't want her to know?"

That had never even crossed my mind.

For a moment, the room was silent as I contemplated what he said.

"Amir, you're not making sense. Why did you tell me if you didn't want me to tell her?"

Amir exhaled. "I don't know. I guess I want her to know about him, just not about me."

"Why, Amir? You didn't do anything wrong. He did. I thought you weren't trying to hide your homosexuality anymore."

"I'm not. I'm just not used to people knowing, yet.

It's one thing telling you. It's another thing telling strangers. I gotta get used to it. And being out is not the same thing as everybody knowing my business. Especially, this."

"Nicole is not a stranger, Amir."

"I know. How about you tell her Lorenzo is bisexual without telling her about me and him. Tell her about him arguing with Damon and how you got that e-mail Damon probably sent."

I put my hand on his shoulder. "All right, Amir. I won't tell her about you and Lorenzo but can I tell her what you told me about him and Damon dating? That e-mail means nothing and neither does that argument. I need to tell her something concrete."

"Fine. It's not like she's gonna step to Damon and tell him she got the information from me."

"Are you sure you're doing all right?" I asked.

"I'm cool. Nicole's the one you really need to worry about."

Amir kissed me on the cheek and left, saying he was going to visit friends.

I went to the kitchen and poured myself a glass of ginger ale to calm my stomach and to think about what, if anything, to tell Nicole.

Twenty-two
Arianna

I hated that my first time in Nicole's new house in swanky Montgomery County was for such a lousy occasion.

Her home was gorgeous. Four bedrooms on the second floor, each with its own bath. A nursery for the baby, a room for Jamal, an office for Lorenzo and, of course, a master bedroom for the happy couple.

The living room was huge, decorated with Victorian style cherry wood furniture. The kitchen was modern, stainless steel appliances everywhere, a huge marble countertop island in the center with a double sink.

That's where we settled after Nicole gave me the grand tour.

Though she smiled like a Stepford wife as she narrated the tour, I could tell something wasn't right. I didn't ask, though, 'cause I knew whatever it was didn't compare to the bomb I was about to drop.

She poured me a glass of orange juice and threw some packaged cinnamon buns in the oven.

"That's why you're blowing up like that. You're hooked on the doughboy. You know how fattening those things are?" I said, searching for anything to talk about besides my intended subject.

"Yep. And I don't care. I love 'em and while I'm pregnant, I'm going to eat 'em. I'll work it off after the baby comes."

The aroma of cinnamon wafted through the kitchen as Nicole droned on about something I wasn't paying any attention to.

I got up and checked on her buns. They were done.

I grabbed her potholders from the stove and retrieved the treats from the oven.

I felt like a hypocrite, but I couldn't resist. I got two saucers from her cabinet and put a bun on each and put them on the table in front of our seats.

"Oh, but they are so fattening," Nicole said sarcastically.

"Yeah, but *I'll* work it off tomorrow."

"You keep talking junk and *I'll* take it from you," she said, reaching for my bun.

"Whatever," I said, laughing.

Not quite ready to talk about Lorenzo, I told her first about Janelle's blackmail.

"You're not serious."

I just looked at her. Like I would make this shit up?

"I don't believe this. She told me she was sorry for what she did to you and then turns around and does this? What are you going to do?"

"I hired another private detective. Even though she says *she* sent the e-mail, I believe the affair is real. This time we're going to find Eugene's mistress. Janelle already gave us the best clue."

"What?"

"Her salon. The one in Richmond. When she first came to see me she said Eugene's mistress was a client of hers. Something tells me she wasn't lying about that part. Janelle didn't just make the stuff about him up out of the sky. And since she's been so busy following my career as she calls it, she has to know we've been sued before. Hell, Eugene might even be in on it with her."

Nicole's eyes widened. "Don't you think that's a little too Machiavellian for Janelle, Arianna?"

"No I don't. At first I didn't think she was that damn smart. But, why would she post anonymous information about a man unless she knew he was going to sue me? If the whole point of her doing it in the first place was to get back at me?"

"Maybe it all just fell in her lap that way and she decided to take advantage of his lawsuit."

"Nicole, what is it going to take for you to believe the worst about this woman? She is blackmailing me. She says she wants to take away the things that are important to me. That needy, pathetic woman we met and tried to help a couple years ago doesn't exist anymore."

"I'm beginning to wonder whether she ever did," Nicole sighed.

"Oh, she did. We women are strange creatures. We can be smart as hell in some areas of our lives, but dumb as a box of rocks in others. She owned her own business when we met her, remember? Stupid people don't become business owners. Janelle was only stupid when it came to men. And unfortunately, we only knew *that* Janelle. We never really got to see the savvy side. Now we're seeing it up close and personal."

"I'm going to talk to her."

"What good is that going to do?"

"Well, maybe I can soften her up, get her to back down. She's not mad at me. She's mad at you. Maybe I can run interference."

"Feel free to give it a try, but I doubt it'll work. That woman has got a hate-on for me like you wouldn't believe. You didn't see her in my office. If she had handled Chauncey's ass like she called herself doing me, he wouldn't have been able to walk all over her."

"So what are you trying to say about me?"

"Oh, don't start with me, Nicole."

For a few moments we just sat there at her kitchen table licking our sticky, frosting-coated fingers in silence. Nicole and I had come full circle. We met because she had discovered her man was cheating on her and decided to share the news to keep other women from experiencing her pain.

Now I was there to deliver her the same kind of heartbreaking news.

It was news I didn't want to broadcast. Lorenzo wasn't her Mr. Right Now. He was her husband, the father of her soon to be born child. And she was crazy about him.

I did not want to be the one to tell her he was no good.

I eased into it by telling Nicole about Amir's homosexuality. I expected shock and questions. Lots of questions.

I got silence.

I waited. Still, she said nothing.

Then, I studied her face. I could see in her eyes that she was hiding a secret of her own.

"Nicole what's going on with you? You haven't said a word. Asked me any questions. Nothing."

"I was letting you tell your story, that's all," she said in a near whisper. "I feel bad for you, Arianna. I know you want your son to be happy and that's going to be hard for him living that life."

"I know. But he has to be true to himself. And I think society is becoming more open to homosexuality."

"Then why are so many men still lying about sleeping with each other?"

"I said *becoming* more open. We have a long way to go. We've been here 400 years and white folks still ain't figured us out yet. Homos are just really beginning to fight. I told you about Amir, Nicole, because he told me something about Lorenzo that you need to know."

Slowly, she put down the glass of juice she'd been nursing, got up and walked toward the stove where she drew a deep breath. "About his sexual preferences?" Nicole asked matter-of-factly. "I already know."

"What?" I said, jumping up from the table and knocking over my glass.

"Damn!" I shouted as the cool liquid soaked through my brown wool pants and into my skin.

Nicole grabbed a dishtowel from a kitchen drawer and handed it to me. "Use this," she said.

I wiped the juice from my pants leg and the chair.

"What do you know and how long have you known?"

"Let's go sit in the living room," she said.

A half hour and several hundred words later, Nicole was weeping on her couch as I held her like a baby.

A few weeks after I was shot, Lorenzo made a confession.

Apparently, he knew his secret was about to be exposed and he wanted to be the one to tell his wife.

Lorenzo, indeed, was bisexual.

He was dating Damon when he met her, and ended their relationship a couple of months before he and Nicole walked down the aisle. Damon didn't take it well and kept threatening to out him.

He wasn't on the down low, according to him. He had always been bisexual and didn't feel the need to make a choice.

Until Nicole.

The one thing he'd always struggled with was reconciling his sexuality with his religion. Then God brought Nicole into his life.

She was special. The one who made him decide to live life as a heterosexual, settle down and get married. She was the woman God had chosen for him.

Lorenzo and Damon were intimate during the first few months of his and Nicole's courtship. That's why he didn't sleep with her. He wanted their wedding night to be the first time they made love. It would be the first night of his new life.

He loved her. He loved Jamal. He loved his unborn child and wanted to be a husband and father.

He begged for forgiveness. Told her it's what God wanted her to do.

Forgive him, that is.

He'd never been unfaithful once he made her his wife and never would be. He'd made that vow to God and himself and intended to keep it.

He hoped she would never find out about his other life, but Damon was turning out to be a fatal attraction and wouldn't leave him alone.

He found out about ExposeHim.com and posted Lorenzo's picture and his dirt.

Only none of us actually got the chance to see it thanks to Darryl Crump.

Still, it was only a matter of time before Nicole found out. She needed to hear it from him.

She listened. She screamed. She cried.

She kicked him out.

She didn't tell me any of it because she thought it was for my own good, given my health.

I knew better. She was ashamed. First, Chauncey. Now Lorenzo. I'd warned her about Lorenzo and she hadn't listened.

Now she was a mess. Five months pregnant and living in a new home that her new husband picked out without the new husband.

Jamal Jr. was confused as hell, but she didn't know how to deal with him because she hadn't come to grips with the situation herself. She sent him to stay with his father until she could figure out the rest of her life.

Now was no time for I-told-you-so's or being judgmental. I just tried to be supportive.

"Do you still love him?" I asked when she finished sobbing.

"Of course," Nicole said, lifting her head from my chest. "I can't just turn off my feelings. That's the hard part. If I didn't love him, this would be a whole lot easier."

"Do you believe what he said about being faithful during the marriage?"

"I don't know. He lied to me practically the whole time we were dating, so how can I believe anything he says?"

"You can't believe what he says. I'm asking you what your gut tells you."

"Since we've been married, I've had no reason to doubt him. But I don't trust my gut. My gut told me Chauncey was the love of my life. It told me Jamal would be a good husband and father. I never got to find out about the husband part and he's only stepped up in the fatherhood department since he found a new woman."

"He stepped up because he grew up, period. It takes some men longer than others. Some never get there at all. Just be happy he did. Amir's father is still in the wind."

"I guess."

"And Lorenzo is about to be a father. You have to take that into consideration. If he's committed to you and this child, don't throw that away lightly."

Nicole couldn't believe her ears.

"What? Are you telling me to take him back? The woman who once said she wouldn't let a man get away with playing her like PlayStation to get in her Xbox?"

"Why do you always bring that up? That man wasn't my husband or the father of my child, either. Believe me, it's different when you're married. Otherwise, I would've been long gone from Kenny. And, no, I'm not telling you to take him back. I'm just saying think long and hard about whatever you decide to do."

"Believe me I have been," Nicole said. "I've realized that we tend to make decisions based on emotion. Men do it based on logic, what makes sense. I kicked Lorenzo out because of how I felt."

"He deserved it," I said. "What else were you supposed to do? He lied to you and he cheated on you."

"I know. I'm just saying that I think sometimes we would be better off if we acted like men. So, I'm taking this time while Lorenzo is gone to really think about what I want and what I need, not just how I feel. And I know I don't want to be a single mother again."

"Yes, that shit is for the birds," I said.

"Lorenzo is a good provider, and he treats me great. Before I found out about this, I was happy. If he's going to be a loving and involved father, and good to me, is it worth throwing all that away because he lied?"

"Only you can answer that, Nicole. I'd make him pay for lying to me, though. You know me. No way should he get away with this bullshit with just a few days in a hotel or wherever the hell he's staying. I know you're not into payback, but you need to make his ass squirm a little.

"Then, if you want, you can let him come back and do the daddy thing. Pay the bills on this big-ass house and take care of you and Jamal. But I don't know if I could do the wife thing. As far as conjugal duties are concerned, I mean."

I damn sure couldn't do it, because Lorenzo had slept with my son, a detail I was purposely leaving out. Not only had I promised Amir I wouldn't tell; if Nicole was seriously contemplating taking back the jerk, she'd certainly change her mind if she knew.

No way could she handle it.

"A lot of women have forgiven their husbands for infidelity and gone on to have strong marriages," Nicole said. "If I do take him back, at least this time I'll know exactly what I'm getting. They'll be no more bombshells."

"I guess. And the reality is there's a 90 percent chance the next one will cheat, too. And he won't be the father of either of your children and not likely to help with them."

"I know. I think if Lorenzo had cheated with a woman this would be a little easier. But he had sex with men. I just don't know if I can get past that."

Twenty-three
Arianna

On the way back to Philly, images of Amir and Lorenzo flashed through my mind like a slide show.

I wondered if men who were lovers showed affection the same way with each other as they did with women. Did they kiss, hug and hold hands?

Clearly they loved just as deeply considering the way Damon was acting over Lorenzo. And were just as romantic. I read in my book by the gay teacher how he met his significant other and it was like something out of a fairy tale. Eyes meeting across a crowded room, followed by a timeless love connection.

I hoped Amir would find a love like that. Even if it was with a man. Just not a confused man like Lorenzo.

Was I making the right decision keeping their relationship from Nicole? Should she try and make her marriage work with a man who might decide one day he'd rather be with another man?

My head, heavy with confusion, was bobbing up and down as I navigated the interstate in the darkness. To avoid killing myself or someone else, I pulled into a rest stop.

I lay back in my seat, turned up the heat and closed my eyes. A short nap and I'd be ready to hit the road again.

Or so I thought.

I didn't wake up until five hours later to the ringing of my cell phone.

"Ma, where are you?" Akilah yelled. "I've been calling you for hours."

"I'm sorry, baby," I said wiping the evening duck butter from my eyes. "What time is it?"

"It's 11. I haven't heard from you all day and I'm starving."

"Where's Kenny?"

"He's gone. The least you could do if you're not gonna cook for me is leave me some money so I can order a pizza or something."

"Look. I understand you being upset, Akilah, but you are not going to talk to me in that tone. Do you understand me?"

I didn't hear anything.

"Akilah, did you hear me?"

Still nothing. I looked at my phone. The call had dropped. Why the hell didn't cell phones have dial tones like land lines?

I called her back, forced to repeat myself.

"Look, young lady. You need to watch the way you talk to me, understand?

"Yeah," said Akilah, anger still wrapped around her tongue.

"Excuse me?"

"Yes, I understand."

"Where's Amir?"

"I don't know. He left a long time ago and I haven't seen him. He didn't tell me where he was going."

"OK. I got caught up and lost track of time. I'm still in Maryland so I won't be home for a couple of hours. There's a twenty-dollar bill in my underwear drawer. Use it to get yourself something to eat, then go to bed and I'll see you in the morning."

"Fine."

"Kilah?"

"Yeah."

"I'm sorry if you feel I've been neglecting you. It's not intentional. You do know that mommy loves you right?"

"Yeah, I know. I'm sorry for yelling. I love you, too."

"Goodnight."

❂❂❂

By the time I made it home, I'd come to a decision: Keeping Amir's secret was the right thing to do.

If not for Nicole, for him.

It was a small favor, the least I could do considering what I'd put him and Akilah through.

Amir had never really gotten over all the teasing they received when the drama with Chauncey played out in the newspapers and on TV. They had it hard for months.

I changed their schools and the fact that Amir's last name was different than mine helped him remain anonymous.

He wouldn't admit it to me, but for a long time he was embarrassed to have me for a mother. He had a fit when I wrote *Busted* because he thought he was in for more teasing. We dodged that bullet because the few friends he had who actually took the time to read and knew about the book were impressed his mother was an author.

Still, he wanted little to do with the people in my life who reminded him of what I'd done and what he'd been through because of it. So he and Nicole had never really connected.

By the time I got home, everyone was asleep.

I wanted to talk about my horrendous day, but Kenny's voice had lost its ability to soothe me and his arms no longer provided comfort.

So I didn't bother waking him.

My back had healed enough for me to make the trek upstairs to our bedroom, but I chose the living room sofa where I could drift off to sleep without the disturbing sound of his snoring.

Not long after my head hit the pillow, I was knee deep inside a nightmare. When I awoke, funky with perspiration and my heart break-dancing inside my chest, all I could remember was a bleeding body on the floor and a gun in my hand. I couldn't make out the face or the identities of the other people in the room.

The nightmare felt damn real.

I couldn't help but wonder whether this was what Nicole's premonition was about.

Twenty-four
Arianna

The next morning, I called Kayla Morton.

I needed help figuring out the mess of my life and when we met in the hospital, I felt like she was someone I could trust.

She graciously agreed to take me as a patient, and fit me into her busy schedule that day.

Two hours on her couch and I'd spilled it all. My gay son who also was the lover of my best friend's husband, and my nightmares that felt more like premonitions.

There was Kenny. And somewhere in the middle of the madness was Randy.

Kayla couldn't solve any of this for me, but she could listen with an objective ear and help me sort it out for myself. I'd come to the conclusion that was worth the money.

Just talking with her helped me realize once and for all that though I loved Kenny, I was never truly in love with him. Gratitude was a poor substitute for passion. And intimacy can only be achieved through communication, something my relationship with Kenny was sorely lacking.

I saw her four times that week and she helped me see Kenny was a stand-in for my dead husband. I'd dated so many losers, including Amir's trifling father, that when Michael Singleton came along, I thought I'd struck gold.

He gave me love, affection, security and passion in abundance.

And he gave me Akilah.

When cancer took him from me, I thought I'd never find anyone like him again. Until Kenny.

He was honest, dependable, reliable and had a good heart.

So like so many women, I settled.

Once again, I let the man choose me, instead of vice versa. He was a good man; he just wasn't the man for me.

How could I walk away from a man who had been so good to my children and me? How could I take away the only father Akilah had ever known? Even before we were married, he spent a lot of time with her and they'd become very close.

Kayla suggested Kenny deserved better. Even that I deserved better, too.

We also talked about Randy.

I'd also seen him several times that week. The time I spent with him gave me an escape from the realities of home.

Procrastination had always been one of my strong suits.

Since I'd become especially good at it in not dealing with my crumbling marriage, Kayla advised me not to pursue a relationship with Randy until I did just that.

"Don't you think you have enough going on in your life?" Kayla asked. "You are still healing mentally and physically from your attack. The police have yet to find the person behind your shooting. Soon, Darryl Crump's trial will start. Your marriage is in trouble, and you're running a business."

"That's exactly why I like having Randy in my life," I told her. "He's like a refuge from my storms."

"Don't you mean he makes a great hiding place?"

"What do you mean by that?"

"Arianna, Randy is an escape for you. He is to you what alcohol is to a drunk, or crack to a crackhead. Instead of dealing with issues, people use those things to medicate themselves against them. In your case, Randy is your drug of choice."

"That's bullshit. I'm dealing with my issues by coming here and talking with you."

"Yes, talking with me is helping you to confront your problems. But you don't actually deal with them in here. You do that by the actions you take once you leave this office. We talk about your marriage, but you are still in it and unhappy. That's because you haven't *done* anything about it, either to make it better or to end it. That would be dealing with it."

"OK, I guess you got me there, but what's wrong with having a friend? It's not like Randy and I are doing anything."

"Yet. We both know you want to. And so does Randy from everything you tell me."

"OK. But being friends first is not a bad thing. I'm not breaking my marriage vows."

"If that's how you see it. But it's the *first* that bothers me. That suggests there is something else coming beyond friendship and you haven't sorted out your last friendship turned romantic relationship yet."

She was right. Ending things with Kenny meant admitting I'd failed at yet another relationship, something I wasn't quite ready to do.

Randy was like a ray of hope that one day, perhaps, I'd get it right.

And I wasn't going to give him or that hope up.

Besides, Kenny couldn't have cared less what I did.

For the most part, when he was home, he was too tired to be bothered with me. He always seemed stress about something he refused to talk about. The free time he did have, he spent with Akilah.

So I spent what time I didn't devote to Akilah with Randy.

And when I left him, I usually needed a few minutes with one of my products from EbonyLadiesofPassion.

Twenty-five
Arianna

Ebony Ladies of Passion was the other Web site I owned. I'd started it shortly after my meeting with Agnes' book club. I got the idea listening to the middle-age women openly talk about their libidos and unmet needs.

Most of the women were in their late 40s; a few were older, somewhere around Agnes' age, which she refused to tell exactly.

The discussion with her book club was nothing like the one with Brandi's group. These sistas had no sympathy for any of the "characters" in my book, least of all me.

Though they said it was a good read, they blamed the women for being duped by Chauncey, saying they should have known better. Should have seen the signs.

"What man do you know falls in love after two or three dates?" said one.

"And if he wasn't' bringing home the money, then he wouldn't have no home," said another.

"And what was you so hot and bothered about," Agnes asked me.

"I beg your pardon?"

"All he got from you was a piece of tail, that you enjoyed mind you, and you go out plottin' some elaborate scheme to pay him back."

"A waste of some good dick if you ask me," said Ruth, a bronze sista with a head full of twists and a mouthful of cake.

I opened my eyes so wide you could see my brain. This was not the response I was expecting.

"So if a brotha dogs you out, you just say, 'whatever,' and keep on stepping?" I asked indignantly.

"Yes," Agnes said calmly. "Revenge is not your responsibility. People reap what they sow. That man would have gotten what was coming to him without your help."

I flashed back to when Nicole quoted the Bible, telling me, "Vengeance is mine saith the Lord." I imagined she'd mature into a woman a lot like Agnes in **20** years or so. Agnes was genuine and I knew she and the others didn't mean any harm, but they had put me on the defensive and I didn't like being there.

"So, you're telling me I should've done nothing? Chalked it up to another lesson learned?"

My words were sharp, but Agnes' response was blunt.

"That was one option," she said. "Or you could've played his game."

"Meaning?"

She sipped some coffee, and then returned the cup to the cocktail table, clasping her hands in her lap.

"There was a scene in the book where the main character – you -- fucked the shit of him just to get her rocks off even after she found out what a no-good-nigga he was. Did that really happen?"

"Yes."

"Then why not keep doing it? He was using you for sex and enjoying your company. Why not do the same thing to him? Enjoy him *and* anybody else you want to spend time with, too."

"Hello?! I heard that," Ruth said, wiping crumbs from her mouth. "I am as faithful to the man I'm with as he is to me. I don't trip off a nigga playin' the field. I give him the benefit of the doubt, first. But if I find out he's messing around, I just act accordingly."

"So you don't mind sharing?" I asked.

"Chile, please. Most of us are sharing," Agnes said. "Some women accept it. Others are in denial. And a lot of women just choose to be alone."

"Which category are you in?"

"Single, free and loving every minute of it."

"That's OK for Agnes. Me, I got my needs," Ruth blurted.

"Hmm Hmm," most of the other dozen women in the room chimed in unison.

"I do, too," Agnes said. "So I make occasional booty calls – on my terms only -- and I keep plenty of batteries. I don't have the time or the energy for relationship drama."

I burst out laughing. God knows I was no stranger to self-pleasure, but I hardly expected a woman Agnes' age to admit she indulged. Hell, most women I knew who were my age acted as though masturbation was still something taboo that only white girls were freaky enough to do.

"What are you laughing at," Agnes said, smiling. "I know you get your freak on. You wrote about it in this here book."

With that, the discussion strayed completely off course and the book club quickly became the Celibate and Hating It club.

Even the four married women in the room admitted not getting it as much they would like. Ruth was definitely the biggest freak in the group. She complained about most vibrators being white or pink when she preferred brown or black. And she didn't like the way the men who worked in sex toy stores looked at her when she patronized them.

I told her I bought my supplies discreetly off the Internet.

She said she'd try it, but then went on to bitch about the lack of porn geared to women.

"I need a little stimulation," she said. "But I get sick of these movies that show the man going down on the woman for 30 seconds, and then the woman giving him head for 30 *minutes*. Like that's going to do something for me. The camera cuts off his face, moves down and all I see is her mouth wrapped around his thing for half an hour."

"The whole sex industry was designed for men, Ruth," I said. "Some men are just figuring out that we actually like sex and it's not all about them."

"You ain't never lied."

Agnes grabbed some cake plates from the cocktail table and took them to her kitchen. I picked up a few coffee cups and followed her.

"Girl, what are you doing? You are an invited guest. I don't want you cleaning up."

"It's OK. I don't feel much like a guest, anyway. I feel like one of the girls."

Agnes smiled as she gently placed the china in the sink. "I'm sorry. I don't usually let the discussion veer off track when we have an author visiting. But during our meetings, after we finish discussing the book of the month, we talk about some of everything. You know how we women are."

"Yes, I do."

"Do you usually rip the authors a new one like you did me?"

Her smile quickly disappeared.

"Is that how we made you feel? We didn't mean to. We only invite authors whose work we like. But we do give what we think is constructive criticism and we discuss our opinions on the theme."

"I was just kidding. I did feel a little sting but I'm over it."

"Good. You know we didn't talk about how killing your lover made you feel. I know it was an accident, but how do you handle something like that?"

There was something about Agnes that made me feel I could trust her. "Can this just stay between you and me?"

"Sure, honey."

"I'm thinking about seeing a shrink. I guess I've been in denial for the most part, but my husband finally convinced me to deal with it because I've been having nightmares off and on for the past couple of years."

Agnes put her hand on mine.

"There's no shame in that, Arianna. Why do so many black folks think it's OK to see a doctor for your body, but not for your mind? I've seen a counselor and I ain't ashamed to admit it."

"Did it help?"

"Sure. It helps to have someone to talk to. You can't always talk to your friends or your family. Half of them will either spread your business or judge you."

"I know that's right. I couldn't even get sympathy or understanding from my own mother."

"I gathered that from the book. She seems like some piece of work."

"That's as good a way to describe it as any, I guess."

"Well, I hope it works out for you. Are you going to write another book?"

"I'm not sure. I need to do something, though. But if do I write one, will you read it and invite me back?"

"You're welcome to come back even if you don't write another one."

On the two-hour train ride back to Philadelphia, I couldn't stop thinking about Ruth, the other women and their "needs." Leaders of the women's movement were so busy trying to stop the exploitation of women who obviously didn't mind being exploited in the porn industry; it never occurred to them there might actually be female consumers who wanted equal treatment.

And who would've thought demands for diversity in entertainment included multicultural sex toys?

With all the subscribers I had for ExposeHim.com, I figured more than a few of these single ladies were spending lonely nights at home. I also was sure that though they preferred the touch of a real man, sometimes they, too, had to settle for plastic.

And who better to meet their needs than a woman who knew exactly what they were going through?

I thought about what the women in the group said. They were sexually frustrated and needed stimulation, but were tired of vanilla vibrators and frontal nudity for men only.

More sistas than would actually admit it were pleasuring themselves. Unless they were willing to spread eagle for any Pookie or Ray-Ray who came along, many had no other option.

I could provide them with a place they could visit from the privacy of their own homes and get their rocks off. Hell it was the No. 1 reason men visited the Internet.

I'd call my new venture, EbonyLadiesofPassion.

After getting Akilah off to school the next day, I wrote my business plan and did research.

I decided what would appeal to women was a combination of sensuality and lust, emotion with animal passion. My site would provide intellectual material including a regular women's health feature with information on sexually transmitted diseases, breast and ovarian cancer, fibroids, exercise and other issues related to black women's health and fitness.

I'd provide phone sex by Barry White-sounding men who could talk the ladies moist. Videos geared toward women where the men would spend 30 minutes between their legs instead of vice versa. The sex would include erotic massage, sensual foreplay, and kissing in addition to the traditional straight up banging featured on male porn sites.

And of course, sex toys in every shade of brown and black would be a huge feature.

Spreading the word about the site would be easy. All I had to do was create an ad and put it on ExposeHim.com, which was getting more than a hundred thousand hits a day.

Of course, I didn't tell Kenny about my new venture. There was no way he would ever understand. I knew he'd see it as an announcement to the world that he wasn't satisfying me in bed.

Even though it was true, that was not my intention. I wanted to provide a service to my sistas in need and make money. Period.

I'd just pay a few bucks extra to keep my information private with the domain registry service. That way, the only people who'd know I owned the site would be the ones I wanted to know.

During the following week, I purchased the domain name, hired a Web site designer and Web master, set up a deal with two sex toy distributors to provide products catering to African Americans and make them available online at my Web address.

I set up a 900 line and through an ad in the women-seeking-men section of the *Press-Herald* classifieds, hired five brothas with velvet voices who could speak orgasms into existence.

The content was set, except for the articles. Months of going without had left me with no inspiration. I spent an entire morning at the bookstore and left with copies of *Playboy* and *Penthouse,* books on black erotica and how-to-write-sex-scene articles. They littered the floor of my home office.

I had digested every word, yet still had no clue what to write. I'd been staring at my computer for hours trying to pen my first erotic story for EbonyLadiesofPassion.

Finally, I gave up, gathering all the books and magazines and stored them in my secret hiding places, the shoeboxes in my closet, and prepared myself some lunch, peanut butter on rye with a soymilk and strawberry smoothie.

I took my food to the living room where I popped my Teddy Pendergrass Greatest Hits in the CD player hoping to get inspired.

Then a spark hit me in the middle of *Turn Off the Lights* when Teddy started begging to be rubbed down in some burnin' hot oil and then promised the object of his desire a special treat.

I remembered the scene I'd written for my novel describing in graphic detail how I'd used Chauncey for sex. I'd fucked the shit out of him and had him calling *my* name.

My editor deleted it with her red pen, saying it was gratuitous sex readers wouldn't care about. I didn't agree, but she was the boss, so I reduced the scene to a few sentences for the book. The ones Agnes referred to when she told me I should've kept him around as my sex toy.

I saved the scene on my laptop, not wanting to discard my hard work in an electronic trash bin. I searched the electronic folder with my documents and found it under the file name "ChaunceyFucked."

For the story, Arianna became Diamond and Chauncey was Derrick.

Diamond stared at Derrick. She decided the lying cheat was good for one thing – pleasing her in ways that showerheads and whirlpool jets couldn't. Why should she deny herself his services one last time?

She licked her lips.

"How about impressing me with your real skills? hat you can do under the covers."

Derrick smiled, releasing the tension trapped in his muscles, and scooted close to her. "Are you trying to seduce me?"

She slid her hands between his legs, grabbing his crotch. "No. I'm straight out asking for it."

She straddled him and whispered in his ear.

"Fuck me."

Diamond dismounted him, stood up and headed for the stairs. Derrick followed. He sat on the bed and watched as her shirt came off one button at time. She put her hands between his legs and squeezed hard.

Her shirt fell to the floor followed by her bra. Diamond's heavy breasts sat boldly atop her chest like scales in perfect balance. Her nipples were like Hershey's kisses, round chocolates with an erect tip. Firm, yet sweet candies that melted to the touch. They commanded his attention and he marveled at them. She fed him her breasts, putting them in his mouth one at a time while she held his head close, stroking his baldness.

He feasted on the brown treats like a suckling baby. She watched as his cheeks puckered and his tongue glided around them like a lollipop, each lick sending warm tingles and liquid desire to her center. Her heart began a marathon and her lust was released in short breaths as her lungs tried to keep up. She took away his appetizers long enough to strip off her jeans and thong, leaving them with her shirt in a heap on the floor. His clothes came off as he moved to the center of the bed. She grabbed a condom from the nightstand drawer and ripped open the wrapper with her teeth, leaving it at the top of the bed. She straddled him, dangling her breasts above his face. He grabbed them and picked up where he left off, sending shivers through her. He pulled her face to his and tried to kiss her. She thought about the other places his tongue had been. "No kissing tonight."

His eyes got that cue ball look again. "I'm not sure I like you like this, Lady Diamond."

She grabbed him, stroked him, and felt him grow between her fingers. "Why not hold that thought. Make up your mind when we're done."

She covered him with the condom then rocked her hips back and forth allowing his swollen flame starter to kindle the small, erogenous orifice in the heart of her jungle. She teased herself, raising her level of anticipation. She put his throbbing head inside, igniting a five-alarm fire. It raged out of control as he held her hips and guided her on their ride to the other side of the moon. She grabbed his ass and rode him like a champion thoroughbred on a race toward the Triple Crown.

The liquid desire flowing between her legs allowed him to smoothly navigate her delicate terrain. She moved faster as he lifted the weight of her body, the friction raising the temperature between them to volcanic levels. A howl of pleasure escaped from his lips. "Uhhhh!" It was a deep, throaty sound that traveled from his scrotum and landed in her ear. It made her move faster. He let go again. "Uhhhh! Shit!" He couldn't help himself. His eyes usually remained open like a camera capturing every scene for the photo album in his mind. Mental snapshots his ego could recall. That night, those snapshots were hers. She watched as he struggled to maintain his machismo behind his tightly closed eyes. There were no words. No ego-stroking questions about his ability to please. The only sounds in that room were grunts and groans that bounced off the walls. Noises he wished he could hold on to but couldn't.

Diamond liked being in control. Having the power to make Mr. Cool lose his cool.

"You like that, baby?" She panted out the words looking for his approval. "You like the way I fuck you?"

Silence.

She rode him harder, allowing him inside deeper. He touched walls she didn't know existed. "Shit!"

She repeated the threat he'd given her many times before. "Tell me you like it or I'll stop."

He whimpered, his eyes still closed. "You know I like it, sweethaart."

"How do I know if you don't tell me?"

She slowed down, taking control from his strong arms.

His eyes opened. "Don't stop."

She looked down at him as she moved her hips slowly, just enough to keep the blood flowing to his penis and give herself a second wind.

"Why. Because you like it?"

"Yes. I like it?"

"You want me to keep fucking you?"

"Yes.

"Then say it."

"Say what?"

"Tell me to fuck you."

"Fuck me."

She picked up speed. He let her go and grabbed the sheets.

"Say my name." She demanded. "Say my name. I want to hear it. If you like the way I fuck you, let me know."

"Damn, Lady Diamond. You're fucking me like a man."

Their magic ride came to a screeching halt as she stopped and pulled herself off him.

"Don't stop. What are you doing? I was just about to cum."

He sat up and reached for her waist.

"Say my name."

He whispered it. "Diamond."

She eased him back inside. "Say it louder."

"You're not going to have me screaming like a bitch in here."

"Just say it louder."

"Diamond."

She yelled. "Louder."

He yelled back. "Diamond."

She jerked the upper half of her body up trying to escape the intensity of the flames that threatened to consume her. He wouldn't let go. She threw her head back and gave in, making a face that said she couldn't take any more, but couldn't stop either. The volcano erupted. "Aaaaaaaahhhhh!" Diamond screamed so loud she scared herself.

When her breathing returned to normal, she got up and put on her robe and walked over to the side of the bed where Derrick lay.

She bent over and whispered in his ear, "Get out."

He jumped.

"I beg your pardon, Lady Diamond. Did you say something?"

"Yes, asshole. I said get out. You're dismissed. Your services are no longer required."

I laughed at the memory of Chauncey's reaction to the shoe being on the other foot, me using him. I decided to incorporate the scene in a short story for the Web site about a woman scorned.

I was feeling pretty satisfied with myself until I realized I hadn't had sex that good since that night.

For that reason, I kept a supply of products from EbonyLadiesofPassion hidden in my bathroom closet.

Unfortunately, when Kenny found out about them, he snapped.

Twenty-six
Arianna

April was around the corner and so was my libel trial. Janelle called to tell me her blackmail offer expired in a week. She also took great pleasure in letting me know that despite the fact my private detective had located Eugene's mistress, the woman was a friend of hers and would not testify on my behalf unless Janelle told her to.

I called my business lawyer and had him draw up the sale papers, then ignored my doctor's orders and went to the liquor store to buy a bottle of tequila.

Janelle having power over me was too much to deal with.

I could take my chances in court, but losing could wipe me out. Several plaintiffs had won multi-million dollar libel suits against newspapers. I didn't have big corporation newspaper money, but if Eugene Rodgers won, my home, both my Web site companies, my life savings including the royalties from my book sales and the money from my first husband's life insurance policy were at stake.

Reluctantly, I decided to surrender.

School was out for one of those inexplicable teacher workdays so after helping her pack an overnight bag, I dropped Akilah off at a friend's for a sleepover.

Then, I finally went to the wireless store to have my cell phone repaired. They couldn't fix it, but offered me a buy-one-get-one free deal on an upgraded phone with a camera. I had them switch Kenny's line to the second phone.

Then, I went home and got busy with my bottle.

By the time Kenny arrived from work, I was several miles past buzzed, a few exits shy of plastered. Sober enough to be horny, laced enough to beg if I had to.

As soon as he walked through the door, I draped myself around him. "I'm tired of fighting, Kenny. Can we put our differences aside long enough for you to make love to your wife, tonight? Please?"

Surprisingly, he didn't push me away with one of his myriad excuses. He kissed me with as much passion as he was capable.

Every fiber of my being told me something was wrong. That another woman was getting the affection that used to be reserved only for me. But I needed to be kissed and held, even if it was lie.

"I'm going to pour myself a drink and I'll meet you in the bedroom," Kenny said. "By the way, my cell isn't working, did you forget to pay the bill?"

"Oh," I said, remembering my trip to the store. "I had to get a new phone and since it was free, I got you a new one, too."

I reached in my purse and handed him the razor thin black phone.

"It's nice, thanks. But how are we going to tell them apart?" he asked.

"We'll put our names on the display screen like we did with the old ones."

I went upstairs, turned off the ringer on my cell and put it on the nightstand.

After a scalding hot shower, I slid my naked body under the covers and waited. There is nothing spontaneous or romantic about waiting to get laid. Kenny's minute was more like 30, and by the time he joined me in bed, the mood had long since gone and I was nearly asleep.

I wrongly assumed he would use his tongue to bring back my desire. Instead, he relied on his middle finger. I lay there staring at the ceiling while he rubbed my clit out of obligation, frustrating the shit out of me. He didn't even have the consideration to moisten his dry digit.

I moved his hand away from me. "I'm ready," I lied just to get it over with.

Kenny climbed on top of me, stuck in his dick and rode me until he came.

At least one of us was satisfied.

He kissed me on the cheek, rolled over to his side of the bed and fell asleep. Once I heard him snoring, I slipped on a silk nightshirt, went to the bathroom and put Mr. G to work. The chocolate, 7-inch, ribbed G-spot vibrator was my best seller on EbonyLadiesofPassion. I was sitting on the toilet, leaning against the porcelain back with my legs spread wide open, the vibrator humming me to orgasm when a naked Kenny stumbled into the bathroom half asleep and flipped on the light.

"What the fuck!" he said when his brain registered what his eyes had observed.

Mr. G fell to the floor and I was shocked upright. Words would not find their way to my mouth and embarrassment flooded every pore.

"Damn!" Kenny said. "I've never been enough for you have I?"

"It's...it's not that, Kenny. You came. I didn't. I just..."

"You just wanted what I couldn't give you. Did you use that when you were with Chauncey and your other men?"

Kenny stormed out and slammed the door, forgetting to pee or whatever he'd come in the bathroom to do. When I got the nerve to come out, he was getting dressed.

"Where are you going this time of night?"

"Out."

"No kidding. Out where?"

"Out anywhere. I need to think."

"And you can't do that here?"

"No. I can't. Can you do me a favor while I'm gone?"

"What?"

"Get rid of that thing you keep in the bathroom. I don't want to accidentally find it one day."

"Are you going to rid of your porno movies?"

"That's not the same thing and you know it. You're hiding a fake dick in the bathroom when you've got a real one right here."

No he didn't. That was it. I didn't give a damn about sparing his feelings anymore.

"I do?" I sneered. "You know at first, I was embarrassed when you walked in on me masturbating, but now I don't give a fuck. You know why? Because you made it all about you, as usual. What about me? What about my needs? You haven't gone down on me in months. When we do have sex, your idea of foreplay is five minutes of manual stimulation, which by the way is not fucking stimulating. You penetrate me while I'm dry as the Sahara desert and instead of taking your time and letting me get moist, you plunge away until you get yours, roll over and fall asleep.

"When was the last time I came? You can't answer that question because you don't know and you don't give a damn. All you care about is busting *your* nut.

"If I walked in on you masturbating after we'd just made love, I would ask you what I could do to please you. I would want to know what I was doing wrong. But not you. No... you get jealous of the other men I've been with who haven't got a damn thing to do with us. We were the only two people in that bed tonight. And you weren't a damn virgin when we met but do I constantly throw other women in your face? Did you fuck them the way you fuck me or am the only one who gets the wham-bam-thank-you-ma'am treatment?"

Kenny snatched me.

The next thing I knew I was lying face down on the bed with my nightgown hiked above my head, my legs spread eagle behind me and Kenny's face buried between them. His tongue was stroking my clit while he fingered my ass and vagina, a move he no doubt learned from his porno collection.

"Is this how you like it," he yelled, slapping my ass with his free hand. "Whose pussy is this, huh? Whose pussy?"

His words were angry, not passionate.

Kenny had never been verbal during sex, except to tell me he loved me. The most he did was moan and groan. I was usually the loud one. It was me who yelled the four-letter words.

He pulled his finger from ass and replaced it with this tongue. He then inserted three fingers into my vagina, thrusting them in and out hard.

"You like that?" he said.

I did, but I couldn't admit it. I tried to pull myself away from him, but he pulled me back.

The man tossing my salad was a stranger and I didn't know quite how to react. He was making me feel damn good, but at the same time I wondered if what was happening to me was rape.

My mind could not agree with my body. Lovemaking was not supposed to be like this. And whatever this was, I was not supposed to enjoy it.

"Stop it, Kenny," I moaned. "This isn't right."

"You don't want me to stop," he said entering me. "This is what you wanted. I'm gonna make you cum. You wanna cum don't you? Don't you?"

He plunged himself inside me over and over with his thumb inside my ass keeping time to the rhythm of his dick. Anger had brought out a side of Kenny he probably didn't even know he had.

I didn't want to come. Not like this. But I couldn't help myself. I grabbed the first pillow my hand came across and covered my mouth.

"AHHHHHHH!!!!!" I screamed.

The contractions of my vagina sent Kenny into an orgasmic spasm.

"Yes! Yes! Yes!" he yelled before collapsing on my back.

I crawled from underneath him to catch my breath, pulling my nightshirt around my waist. He lay there panting, fully clothed, his penis poking through the slit in his boxers and unzipped pants.

WHACK! I slapped the shit out of him.

Kenny jumped up, his head swirling. "What the fuck...?"

"I'm not your whore," I yelled. "I'm your wife."

He massaged the red skid marks my fingers had left on his face.

"I thought that's what you wanted. I read your story!" he yelled.

"What story are you talking about?"

"The one you left open on your laptop. Diamond and Derrick fucking the shit out of each other. I know that was you and Chauncey. I remembered the short version of the scene in your book. I thought you liked it rough."

I jumped up and went to slap him again, but he grabbed my wrist.

I snatched my hand from his. "I don't like it rough, asshole. I want passion, not angry sex. You just raped me, Kenny."

"You're my wife, I can't rape you."

"I don't think the cops would agree with you if I called them."

"You wouldn't? You came for God's sake so you must've enjoyed it. How is that rape?"

"For future reference when I say, 'no,' I mean 'no.' And what the hell were you doing reading my shit?"

"I was doing you a favor by turning off your laptop. When I went to close the file and I saw his name...well I couldn't help myself."

"What you read was a scene my editor deleted. It was fiction," I lied.

"Fiction or not, it was how you wanted it to be and you know it."

"Get the fuck out of here, Kenny."

"And go where?"

"I don't give a shit. Wherever the hell you were going when I came out the bathroom. To the bitch's house you really wanted to fuck tonight."

He zipped his pants, grabbed his jacket, snatched what he thought was his phone from the nightstand and slinked out the room.

Twenty-seven
Nicole

Janelle was sewing a weave track on a client's head when I walked into her shop, *Styles by J on* West Pratt Street in Baltimore's Carrollton Ridge neighborhood.

The shop, a few miles from the Inner Harbor, was decorated in neutral colors with a dark wood floor, contrasted by muted gold walls. Each station had a tall full-length mirror and brown leather chair.

Theater-type lights hanging from the ceiling lighted up the place. Prints featuring images of women getting glamorous, such as Kevin A. Williams' *Pamper Party*, donned the walls.

Women with towels and shower caps wrapped around their heads impatiently flipped through magazines as they awaited their turn to be rinsed, blow dried, curled, crimped, weaved or braided.

One was reading Arianna's novel.

I was sure Janelle was none too pleased about that since she claims the book was the reason she was blackmailing Arianna into selling her ExposeHim.com.

That's why I was there. To try and talk some sense into Janelle. She had agreed to meet, but warned me I didn't have much of a chance in changing her mind. I decided to try anyway.

"Hi, Nicole. Let me finish with this client and we can talk," Janelle said when she looked up from the woman's head and saw me standing at the receptionist's desk. She directed the woman at the desk to show me to her office.

"Wait for me in there and I'll be in as soon as I can, OK?"

I strained to smile in her direction and nodded.

Janelle's office was nothing like her neatly appointed salon. Papers and envelopes took up every inch of her huge mahogany desk that wasn't occupied by her computer tower and monitor. Hair supplies covered almost the entire floor. In the midst of the mess on her desk were framed portraits of her adult children and a picture of her and Chauncey.

Startled, I reached for my chest. I hadn't laid eyes on that man in two years. I picked up the bamboo-framed picture of him and Janelle on a merry-go-round at some amusement park and stared at his face.

The evil in his eyes and that sneaky grin were so obvious to me now. How I could not have seen it when he shared the same bed with me, I didn't understand.

Just as I couldn't understand how I didn't know something was amiss with Lorenzo. He was working overtime at persuading me to take him back. And I have to admit, I was warming up to the idea.

God, help me, I loved him. What I felt for Lorenzo was a deep and abiding love based on more than a physical attraction and unrealistic expectations about romance.

I put the picture back in its place. Chauncey was history and he no longer had any power over me. I said a quick prayer that his soul wasn't burning in the lake of fire. His untimely death was more than enough punishment for his sins.

As I was returning the picture, I noticed a CD on Janelle's desk with Arianna's name written in black marker. Attached to it was a sticky note with the words, "Cut at 28:09."

Nervously, I picked it up, removed the note and placed it in the CD drive of Janelle's computer.

I walked to the door and peeked out. "She'll be with you shortly," said the receptionist, a pretty, fair-skinned young woman with microbraids similar to mine. "She said give her another 15 minutes."

"OK, thank you," I said, grateful for the time to spy.

Spying was so unlike me, but I needed to know what was on that CD. Janelle had it in for Arianna and if there was anything on that CD that could help my friend, I was going to do something even more out of character: steal.

There was only one document on the CD, a video file. My hopes faded. I couldn't imagine a video could help with the lawsuit. I decided to play it just in case.

I was horrified by what I saw in only the first two minutes and couldn't keep watching. I stopped the CD from playing, ejected it from the computer and stuffed it in my purse.

My heart racing and hands shaking, I practically ran from Janelle's office and headed straight for the door.

"Nicole," Janelle hollered. I kept going. I couldn't look at her. She ran after me. "Nicole! I thought you wanted to talk."

I threw the words over my shoulder as I raced to my car. "I gotta go, Janelle. I'm sick. We'll talk another time."

Arianna definitely needed to see what was on that CD and I was going to make sure she did.

Twenty-eight
Arianna

It had been two days since Kenny fucked me like a 20-dollar whore and I hadn't seen or heard from him since.

While he was gone, sleep eluded me as frustration tossed me left and anxiety turned me right in our bed. As much as I detested his snoring, I preferred the noise to the empty space beside me.

Little did I know I'd be sleeping alone in that bed permanently.

I came home after a Friday morning of physical therapy to find Akilah sobbing in her bedroom.

"What's the matter, honey?"

"Kenny's leaving. He said he can't live here anymore."

"Did he say why?"

"Just that you and him would always be friends and that he would always love me and be a part of my life."

"You believe him about that, don't you?" I asked wrapping my arms around her. I couldn't believe Kenny was leaving, let alone that he would do it without talking to me first. Why on earth would he announce it to a child first?

Akilah laid her head in my bosom.

"Yes, but I don't understand why he has to leave. If you guys are friends, why can't you get along?"

A long sigh escaped my throat as I tried to come to grips with Akilah's words.

"'Cause friends don't necessarily make a good married couple. Some people are meant to be friends only. Some people are meant to be married. You need to be friends to be married, but you don't have to be married to be friends. Do you get that?"

"No."

"Maybe when you get older."

"You always say that."

"'Cause it's true."

"Well, I'm never gettin' married. People either die or get a divorce. All my friends' parents are divorced. And Ma, please don't get married again."

"I wasn't planning on it," Akilah. "But that doesn't mean marriage isn't for you."

I squeezed her tightly. "You know that Kenny and I will always love you no matter what, right?"

"I guess."

"I'm going to talk with him. You gonna be OK?"

"Yeah."

I kissed Akilah on the forehead and walked slowly toward my bedroom.

I wanted to cuss Kenny out for making a decision to leave and telling my daughter before even discussing it with me. Another argument, however, was not what Akilah needed to hear.

It certainly wasn't what I needed after the week I'd had. So I simply accepted the inevitable.

"Where are you going?" I asked, leaning against the doorjamb, arms folded tightly across my chest.

"My mother's for right now, until I get my own place," said Kenny, talking into his suitcase.

He was packing in a hurry as if he had a plane to catch. He hadn't even taken off his trench coat and was still dressed in his work clothes, a charcoal gray suit and white shirt.

I wondered when he slipped into the house to get his work clothes and noticed for the first time that he'd lost more weight. And it wasn't the healthy kind of weight loss.

Kenny was stressed. And it was over more than just me.

"Did she give you a curfew or something?" I asked. "What's the rush?"

"I just want to make a clean break, Arianna. No drama. I was hoping to be gone by the time you got back. I have to get back to the office."

"A clean break? This is more like an escape. I don't hear from you for two days, and then you come home in the middle of the afternoon and pack your shit. No warning, no nothing. When were you planning on letting me in on your decision to walk out on me?"

"I'm not walking out on you, Arianna. I'm leaving a marriage that doesn't work. We both knew this coming, so it can't be a surprise. Especially after the other night."

"That you would do this without discussing it with me and that you would tell Akilah? That does come as a surprise, Kenny."

"I had to tell her because she came home and saw me packing. I forgot she had a half-day at school today. I didn't tell you ahead of time...because...I just didn't want to argue anymore. I was going to call you."

"That's the coward's way out and you know it."

"You're right. But you're just as much a coward as me."

"How so?"

"You want out of this marriage as much as I do, and you haven't had the guts to say it. At least I'm finally doing something. We're miserable and we're making Akilah miserable. It's time for one of us to admit this marriage is a failure and get out while we still care about each other."

"So you still care about me?"

"Of course, I do, Arianna. I've made some mistakes. Some pretty big ones and so have you. But we've gotta move on."

I sat on the bed. I was numb. Even anger couldn't take shelter inside me.

"Look, Kenny. I am as much to blame for the failure of our marriage as you are. More."

Astonishment gripped his face. "What?" he asked.

"Yes. I can admit when I'm wrong. I never should have married you. We ruined a great relationship by trying to be lovers. I loved you, but not like a wife should love a husband."

"You think I don't know that? I thought your feelings would change in time, but they didn't. And as the months went on, I started to resent you, especially because I'd given up my chance to have kids of my own."

"I know. You deserve a woman who loves you the way you love her."

"The way you loved Michael."

"Yes. But you've never been competing with the ghost of a dead man except in your own mind."

"Then who have I been competing with?"

"No one. Why the hell are you so insecure?"

"Then who is Randy?"

For a second, I stopped breathing. How the hell did he know about Randy?

He read the question on my face and answered before I could ask. "I took your cell phone by mistake when I left the other day. He called several times. Left a couple text messages. Said he was looking forward to spending more time with you."

I couldn't think of anything to say.

"You gonna explain?" he said.

"When you explain the hang-ups I got from someone who called several times the night you left."

"How the hell can I explain that?"

'Cause you know damn well it was the person you've been fucking. We never had the chance to put our address books in the new phones so her name didn't come up, but I know it was her and so do you. So who is she?"

Finally, he allowed the outrage smoldering inside him to fully ignite. He threw several pairs of socks in the suitcase and slammed it shut.

"Don't turn this around on me when you're having an affair."

"Actually, I'm not, but is that really why you're packing up to leave?"

"No. But after seeing those messages, I figured why wait."

"I haven't been unfaithful to you, Kenny. Randy is just a friend."

We both were struck by the irony in that statement. Kenny gave me a look that actually frightened me.

He leaned against the mahogany dresser, folding his arms across his chest. "Who is he?"

"Does it really matter?"

"Yes it does, to me."

"A teacher I met at my gym."

"How long have you been seeing him?"

"I don't know. A few months I guess. We just hang out. It's not like I'm seeing him like you think I am."

"That doesn't matter to me. You're spending time with him. You have feelings for him. Despite what's happened between us I can't stand the thought of you being with another man."

"Are you serious?" I said, struck by his nerve. "Why is it that men think it's OK for them to plant their dick in any willing pussy regardless of whether or not they've got a ring on their finger or made a commitment to a woman, but when a woman does the same thing it's some unforgivable sin? You are such a fucking hypocrite. You can't stand the thought of me with another man, but it's OK for you to cheat on me? And don't stand there and tell me again that you're not seeing somebody else, Kenny, 'cause we both know you are."

"OK, you're right but it's only because I always felt like I wasn't enough for you."

"Justify it any way you want, Kenny. You broke our marriage vows. I didn't."

"You just said..."

"I said I had a friendship. I never kissed him and I certainly never fucked him. Can you say the same?"

He sat on the bed and sighed, looking at the floor.

"I didn't think so. Who is she?"

"It doesn't matter."

"There you go again with your bullshit double standard. A few minutes ago, you insisted on knowing who I was seeing and you slapped the shit out of me when I told you. You finally admit that you're fucking another woman and now you're telling me it doesn't matter who she is?"

"Because I just realized you were right. It doesn't matter does it? I don't know this Randy from a hole in the wall and you don't know the woman I'm seeing. They are people who are filling the roles in our lives we should be filling for each other. I don't love this woman. I turned to her because I thought she could give me something you couldn't."

"What's that, Kenny?"

"She made me feel special. More like a man."

"And I didn't do that for you?"

"No Arianna, you didn't."

"What does Randy do for you?"

"He talks to me, Kenny. Something you stopped doing."

"So how serious is it between you?"

"I don't know... Like I said, we're friends."

Kenny reopened his suitcase and finished packing with less animosity. I watched in silence, caressing my face and wondering about this unnamed woman. Or was he right? It didn't matter who she was.

Like he said, our breakup was inevitable.

Still, my gut told me there was more to this sudden split than Kenny was letting on. And though I knew it was best for both of us, my heart fell to the pit of my stomach when he walked out the door, suitcases in hand.

No sooner than he'd left, jazz started humming from my cell. Boney James' version of *Grazing in the Grass.*

I was hoping it was Randy, but I recognized the Philly police station number instantly and knew it was Detective Howard.

"Hello, detective. How are you?" I sighed.

"Ms. Singleton, we've had a break in your case and we'd like you to come down to the station so we can ask you some more questions. Can you come by tomorrow afternoon?"

"Can't you just ask me now?"

"Not really. We're still gathering information but we think we'll be ready for you tomorrow? How is three o'clock?"

"I guess it'll have to be fine."
Finally, some good news.

Twenty-nine
Arianna

Kenny's departure made me a free woman.

With one less thing on my get-my-life-in-order to-do list – one major thing - a 20-pound weight had been lifted from my shoulders.

The good part was since I didn't break up with him, there was less guilt. The bad part: I was alone.

Even though I often felt alone with Kenny right there in the house, his physical presence was in some way comforting. His leaving created a void much bigger than I'd expected.

I tried to pretend all was right in my world as I prepared dinner, but my mind wouldn't stop wondering. What's life as a single woman going to be like this time? What does Detective Howard have to tell me tomorrow? I was long on questions, short on answers.

I called Akilah down for dinner. We ate in silence, the slurping of strings of spaghetti the only sound in the kitchen. Akilah went straight to her room after she finished eating.

She needed time to grieve for the family she was losing, so I left her alone.

I drew a hot bath and tried to soak away my own anxieties. I filled the bathroom with candles, poured a glass of white wine and settled into the bubbles. As I ran the washcloth across my chest, my fingers accidentally touched my nipples. The arousal was instant. I began to caress myself, gently rubbing my hands across my breasts, my belly and between my legs.

Then I stopped. Damnit, I was tired of pleasing myself.

Spring was here. The first quarter of the new year was almost over. And the only person I'd made love to was me.

I wanted a hand other than my own to touch this body. And since Kenny left me, why shouldn't I give someone else responsibility for my orgasm?

I finished bathing, smoothed oil over my skin, dabbed my favorite perfume in all the right places, and put on makeup.

Then, I slid into a peach, satin negligee. I put on my coat, and checked on Akilah. She was already asleep. I kissed her gently on the cheek and headed for Randy's.

My horny ass was driving so fast, I almost wound up dead meat on the Schuylkill, or as natives called it the Sure Kill Expressway.

Outside Randy's house, I checked my makeup one last time and gently knocked on his door. Waiting in the cold, the frigid air whipping between my legs, I couldn't wait for Randy to answer. To take me to his bedroom and fuck the aftertaste of Kenny, Chauncey and ever mistake I ever made from my mouth.

He came to the door wearing blue and white striped pajamas and a perplexed look on his face.

"Fuck me," I said, grabbing him by the back of his neck and covering his mouth with mine. I thrust my tongue down his throat and wrapped my arms around his strong back.

I'd wanted to surprise him.

Bad idea.

He didn't return the kiss.

Instead, he pried my hands off and pushed me away as if I were a stranger.

"What the hell are you doing here?" he whispered between clenched teeth.

Behind him, I noticed four shock-filled eyes staring me down. Two belonged to his daughter, the other two his son. Embarrassment sent blood rushing through me like champagne flowing from an uncorked bottle. There wasn't a mirror in sight, but I knew my face was lobster red.

Randy shut the door behind him and joined me on the steps.

"Why would you come here without calling first, Arianna?" he said, anger and confusion stamped on his face.

"I'm so sorry, Randy. I had no idea your kids were here. I..I..don't know what else to say. I swear I'll never bother you again."

I turned around and jetted down the stairs like a runaway slave being chased by white men.

The ride home from Randy's was a lot slower than the journey there. It was difficult to maneuver traffic through the tears streaming down my face as I reflected on the fact it was the second time I'd been rejected that night.

Thirty

Arianna

The rhythms of Boney James pulled me from a deep slumber where a nameless, faceless man was having his way with me and I was enjoying it way too much.

"Arianna, wake up," said the frantic voice on the other line.

"Who is this?" I asked, only partially awake.

"It's Nicole, girl. Are you OK?"

"Yeah, why?"

'Cause you sound funny."

"'Cause you woke me up, damnit. And for once, I was having a good dream. What time is it, anyway?"

"It's eight o'clock."

"You know I don't get up before nine on Saturdays. What's up?"

"I'm coming up there today. We need to talk."

"Didn't we just talk a few days ago?"

"And?"

"So why are you driving all the way up here? What's new that you can't tell me on the phone?"

"I'll tell you when I get there. Is Kenny home?"

"No, Kenny doesn't live here anymore."

"What! Since when?"

"Since yesterday, but I don't want to talk about that right now."

"It's just as well. I'll be there around ten."

"Nicole…"

She hung up before I got to ask her again what the hell she was coming up for. Whatever it was, I knew it was nothing good.

I forced myself out of bed, took a shower and got dressed in a pair of jeans and a sweatshirt. Went downstairs and made a pot of coffee instead of my usual tea. I'd drowned my sorrows in an entire bottle of wine the night before and the fermented grapes were still sloshing through my veins.

The tart black liquid assaulted my tongue on its way down, beating the caffeine to the punch in jarring my drowsy senses awake.

After downing two cups and reading the paper from cover to cover, I awakened Akilah for praise team practice. If I didn't get her up, she'd sleep until noon. Like mother, like daughter.

The praise dancers rehearsed every other Saturday at 11. Thankfully, one of the dance team leaders was picking her up in the church van so I didn't have to drive her.

When the woman came to get her at ten-thirty, Nicole still hadn't arrived.

I made a fresh pot of coffee.

Sipped and paced. Sipped and paced.

Questions darted through my mind as if they were racing each other to an imaginary finish line.

Had Nicole discovered the truth about Lorenzo and Amir? Had she talked with Janelle? Was she bringing me good news? And what about Detective Howard? What did he have to tell me when we met later that afternoon? Was this nightmare my life had become finally coming to an end?

❦❦❦

Nicole arrived shortly before 12 saying traffic was hell on ninety-five. She neglected to mention, however, that she was bringing company.

With her when I opened the door was Agnes. I didn't even know they knew each other.

My jaw was open so wide when I saw them together, I could fit a fist in my mouth. I didn't need extra sensory perception to let me know their visit would not be a pleasant one.

"What's going on?" I demanded. "When did you two meet?"

"We met at the hospital while you were still in the coma," said Nicole, pulling the top of her curve hugging raspberry sweat suit over her partially exposed baby belly. "She was coming and I was going. I recognized her from what you told me about her."

"Why didn't you tell me?"

"I didn't think it was a big deal. We talked for little while in the hallway and exchanged numbers. We figured since we didn't live that far from each other, and both of us were so close to you, we should get to know each other. We said we were gonna do lunch, but we never got around to it, so that's probably why I never mentioned it to you."

The gray clouds I'd felt hanging over me from the moment Nicole's call had pulled from my sleep were quickly turning black.

"OK, so why are you getting together now? I've got a bad feeling about this. Agnes what did she tell you to persuade you to drive up here?"

"That you needed your friends. So I'm here."

Despite her casual appearance in jeans, a baby blue sweater, and short-heeled black boots, Agnes looked more serious than usual. This was definitely cause for concern in my book.

"Where's Akilah?" Nicole asked.

"Praise dance practice, why?"

"Good. 'Cause what I need to tell you and show you, she shouldn't be around for. Let's sit down."

We went to the living room and took seats, me and Agnes on the love seat, Nicole on the couch.

Nicole pulled down her top again and cleared her throat. Then she leaned forward, her elbows on her knees, her hands in the praying position.

"There's no easy way to say this, Arianna, so I'm just gonna come right out and say it."

"Say what?"

"Kenny is having an affair..."

"That's what you got me all worked up for," I interrupted. "Girl, I figured that out a long time ago."

But that's not all. I don't think you know *who* he's been sleeping with. If you did, you definitely would have told me."

"Who?" I asked. Unlike the night before when I failed to press Kenny for a name, now I was suddenly anxious to know.

She took a deep breath before almost whispering, "Janelle."

I just knew my ears were playing tricks.

"What did you say?"

"Janelle Bailey Carter."

"What the hell are you talking about, Nicole? Kenny doesn't even know Janelle. He never met her."

"He didn't meet her back when we were dealing with all that Chauncey mess, but believe me he knows her in the biblical sense now."

"How do you know? Did Janelle tell you?" I asked, laughing at what I thought was a lame effort by my nemesis to use Nicole to get to me. "She just made it up. She told me she was going to take away everything that was important to me. She started with the business, now she wants me to *think* she's stolen my husband."

"Didn't you say he left you yesterday?"

"He did?" Agnes said in disbelief.

"Yeah, I forgot to tell you about that part on the way here," Nicole said, looking at Agnes.

"Yes, but not for Janelle," I said, defiantly.

"I don't know if he left you for her, but he's definitely having sex with her," Arianna. "I saw it."

I twisted my face.

Nicole pulled a CD from her purse.

"Janelle videotaped it. I got this CD from her office. Actually I stole it," she said, looking ashamed.

"What does it have to do with Kenny and Janelle's supposed affair?"

"I went to Janelle's salon to try and see if I could get her to end this stupid case against the company. She was busy with a client so she asked me to wait in her office. I found this CD while I was there. It had your name on it so I put it in her computer. I didn't watch much of it, 'cause frankly, I just didn't want to, but I saw enough. It's her and Kenny together, sweetie. Intimately."

Nicole got up from the couch and walked over to me.

"Now if you don't want to watch, I will completely understand. But I wanted you to know that I saw it and it proves what I'm trying to tell you."

I reluctantly took the CD, my eyes darting between Agnes and Nicole.

Then I got up and headed for the stairs to go to my home office.

"Arianna, are you sure?" Agnes asked.

I just nodded my head.

Neither of them followed me. I didn't expect them to. If Kenny and Janelle were fucking, it wasn't a visual I wanted to experience with them.

❉❉❉

"When are you going to leave her?" Janelle panted from underneath Kenny's body.

The bed, comforter and matching green curtains with roses screamed that they were in a hotel. Kenny was planting kisses on her body, first her neck, then her stomach, where he lingered for a while.

My stomach began to churn.

"Soon, baby. Soon," Kenny mumbled between kisses.

"You've been saying that for a while, Kenny. When? I'm tired of meeting you in hotels for sex and having to wait for you to sneak to Maryland to see me."

The lamp on the nightstand next to the bed cast a dim light on their bodies. Kenny was wearing a pair of black, silk boxers. The satin peach nightshirt clinging to Janelle's frame had been pushed up over her breasts.

Clearly the light was left on for the camera, I thought. Since my name was on the CD, she obviously had made this porno movie just for me.

"I know. And it's almost time," Kenny said. "Just be patient a little while longer.

His head and lips moved from her stomach to her thighs, and then to between her legs. Janelle let out a loud moan.

Knowing your husband is cheating and seeing it up close and personal are two very different things. My stomach quivered as my shaky legs carried me to the bathroom.

Coffee and wine was all I'd consumed in the past twelve hours. A combination of the now-rancid liquids lurched from my stomach to the toilet as I held my head over the bowl.

I'd emptied my stomach and was sitting against the toilet wiping my mouth by the time Agnes and Janelle made it up the stairs.

"Are you OK?" Agnes said. "We heard you throwing up."

"You'd throw up, too, if you just saw your husband eating another woman's pussy when the best he can do for you is rub your clit like he's trying to start a fucking forest fire with the friction."

"I tried to warn you," Nicole said.

"Really, Arianna," Agnes said. "Why the hell are you watching it? Why would you purposefully torture yourself like that?"

"Curiosity," I said lowering my head as tears poured from my eyes. "Seeing is believing. I don't know. I guess I just needed to see for myself. I don't get it, though. How could he? How could he cheat on me with *her*?"

Nicole struggled to sit her round body next to mine and then wrapped her arms around my shoulder.

"It's OK. You're gonna get through this. We're gonna help you."

"Thanks," I said.

I got up and dragged myself back toward the office. "You're still gonna watch it?" Agnes asked with anger and incredulity in her voice.

"I wanna see if they say anything else about me other than when is Kenny leaving me, which was last night. I don't want to watch them fucking, but I do want to hear them talking."

"We'll wait out here," Nicole sighed.

When I got back in the room, Kenny was pounding Janelle like a chef tenderizing a steak.

I fast-forwarded, my eyes averting the screen, with the exception of intermittent glances, to make sure I didn't go too far ahead.

Finally, I'd reached a point where their bodies were separated. Janelle was sitting on the bed, while Kenny stood buttoning his shirt. I clicked the play button with the mouse.

"You've got to get him off my back," Kenny said.

"I've tried, Janelle responded. "I gave him more money and I told him since he was going down no matter what, there was no sense in all of us going down. He was pissed, saying we dragged him into this and he wasn't going down by himself. I don't know what to do."

"Yeah, that's what he said to me, too," Kenny said. "He's been hitting me up for money almost every week and threatening to call my wife and tell her everything if I don't give it to him."

"We can't let that happen," Janelle said.

"No kidding!" Kenny snapped. "I don't know how I let you talk me into this shit in the first place."

Janelle stood up, clearly angry. "I didn't put a gun to your head, Kenny. In fact you jumped at the idea when I first brought it up."

I stopped the video. What the hell were they talking about and who was this man who threatened to tell me about it?

I held the mouse on the rewind button on my computer screen until I saw Kenny rolling his big ass off Janelle, damn near gasping for air. It was about 28 minutes into the sordid video. Damn, I was lucky to get 15 minutes of Kenny's loving.

What I heard next nearly rocked my world.

When the video stopped playing, my body was trembling with rage. Angry tears rolled down my face and thoughts of homicide raced through my mind.

I snatched up the computer monitor. Threw it to the floor with the might of my anger. Shattered pieces of beige plastic littered the office floor.

Nicole and Agnes came in running.

"What's wrong with you!" Nicole demanded.

"Have you lost your mind, chile?" Agnes added.

"No! But somebody's about to lose and it damn sure ain't gonna be me," I shouted.

"Thanks for bringing the CD, Nicole. And Agnes, I appreciate you driving all the way here, but I gotta get outta here."

"And go where?" Agnes insisted, as she and Nicole followed from the office as I stomped across the hall to my bedroom.

"Anywhere!"

"That means you're going to see Kenny and I won't let you," Agnes said, grabbing my arm. "Not like this. You're too angry. Too upset. You need to calm down before you do something you'll regret."

"I already have. I married his ass. Before that, I let a snake into my life who's done nothing but bring me drama ever since. That would be your friend, Janelle, Nicole," I said, giving her an icy look.

"Look, Arianna. Obviously I made a mistake giving Janelle a second chance, but if she was out to get you, there's nothing I could've done to stop her. My befriending her had nothing to do with her sleeping with your husband."

"I know. I'm sorry. That was uncalled for."

"What else did you hear on that CD to make you so angry?" Nicole asked.

"The short version: My husband and his mistress were the ones behind my shooting."

Nicole and Agnes stared at me awestruck.

"I heard them on that video talking about how Darryl Crump was blackmailing them to keep their names out of it."

"That must be the part she meant to edit out," Nicole said. "There was a note attached to the CD with a specific place to edit."

Then she covered her mouth as another realization hit her. "Oh, my god. That's why his name sounded familiar to me when he got arrested. When Lorenzo and I bought the new house, Janelle told me she had a cousin who could do handy work and any repairs we night need. His name was Darryl Crump."

"He's handy all right," I said. "With a gun."

Suddenly, the weight of this new reality was too heavy to bear. My assailant was no longer a mysterious stranger. It was the man with whom I'd been sharing my bed, my home, my life.

I slumped into a heap on my bed.

Nicole and Agnes sat on either side of me, both trying to give me comfort.

"I can't believe this!" I hollered. "My own husband tried to kill me! My own husband! Now I know why he's been even more distant with me since I came home from the hospital. What he meant when he said there are some things you can't get past. He wasn't talking about something I did to him, but what he did to me!"

Nicole held me as I sobbed, overcome by a range of emotions I couldn't identify. My crying jag and self-pity session lasted about half an hour.

Then a desire I was all too familiar with took over.

I wanted revenge.

Thirty-one
Arianna

Images of Kenny's lips against Janelle's body flashed through my mind as streams of hot water splashed against me.

Agnes and Nicole had persuaded me to take a second shower, hoping my anger would dissipate enough to at least delay any revenge plots I might be contemplating. I agreed because I felt dirty after watching them together. Pleasuring each other at my expense. Him kissing her in ways he hadn't kissed me in what felt like forever.

Every time I closed my eyes, I saw them together. And I heard them. Trying to get away with damn near murdering me.

No way in hell were they going to get away with this shit!

I stepped from the shower, snatched a towel from the oak towel bar and furiously dried off.

Lotion, deodorant and perfume from the vanity.

Lipstick and mascara, too.

Panties, bra, a pair of socks from the dresser.

Red sweater, a pair of designer jeans, and red leather boots from the closet.

Damned if I wasn't going to look good. My insides were mush, but no one was going to know that looking at the outside.

I was heading into my walk-in closet when I heard a cell phone. At first I didn't recognize the ring. Then I remembered it was the generic one that came with the phones when I bought them a few days before.

Kenny had again forgotten his cell.

I went to the dresser and picked it up.

Let's celebrate your freedom! Got us a room at the Marriott. Champagne is chilling in room 339. Key in your name at the front desk. Let yourself in. See you soon. Wear those silk boxers I like!

The words from Janelle's text message shot through me like daggers.

I threw the phone at the wall, shattering it. Went back to the closet. Grabbed a red purse, red suede jacket and the gun I'd locked away there after nearly shooting Kenny in the kitchen.

He wasn't going to be so lucky this time.

I jetted downstairs.

"That shower did the trick," I said, the words rushing from my mouth. "I feel much better, but I still need to clear my head, so I'm gonna go for a drive. You guys can go back home. I'll be fine."

"You are so full of shit, Arianna Singleton," Agnes said. "You are up to something. What is it?"

"Nothing, I just need to get out of this house and figure out my next move. It's not every day a girl gets the kind of news I got this morning. I can't think here, that's all."

"Let's go to the police station, Arianna," Nicole said. "That should be your next move. You can't do anything about Kenny yourself. And you shouldn't try. If he paid someone to shoot you - my god, just the thought of that gives me the chills – but if he did do that you have no idea what he's capable of. This is a matter for the law."

"Fuck the law. That bitch and my husband deserve far more than what the justice system will give them."

"Hmm. Hmm, like I said you're up to something. Where are you really going, Arianna?" Agnes asked.

"To find my husband," I sighed, knowing I couldn't fool either of them.

"To do what?" Agnes asked. "Yell, scream and curse him out? What good is that going to do? Nicole is right. You need to call the police."

"The police probably already know. The detective handling the case called me yesterday and told me to come in this afternoon 'cause he had some news to give me. And if they do know, I want to get to him before they do."

"But what if they don't know?" Nicole asked. "The longer you wait to tell them, the longer Kenny and Janelle have to get away. You said he rushed out of here yesterday. He could be in a different state or a different country, already."

"He's not. They're together and I know where," I said.

"How do you know and what do you have against telling the police?" Nicole shouted.

"Because once they get involved, I won't get a chance to talk to him," I shouted back. "There will be detectives, lawyers, reporters. This is going to be a circus when it gets out that it wasn't one of those assholes on my Web site, but my own husband who had me shot. I...I just need to hear him tell me that he did it. And I need him to tell me why."

It wasn't until I finished ranting that I realized I was shaking and my face was covered with tears.

"All right, I can understand that," Nicole said. "But do you really think he's gonna talk to you if you find him? What if he tries to hurt you?"

"He's been living in the same house with me for weeks since the shooting. If he wanted to do something else to me he would've done it by now."

"Not necessarily," Janelle said. "Things are hot right now. He wouldn't take a chance on getting caught."

"Kenny should be a helluva lot more worried about me," I said.

Just then Akilah came bouncing in the door from dance practice.

Damn!

"Hey Miss Nicole," she said.

"Hey baby, how you doing?" Nicole said, planting a kiss on my daughter's cheek.

"Kilah, this is my friend, Agnes Jackson," I said.

"Hello, Miss Jackson."

"Call me Miss Agnes, sweetie. Your mother said you were at dance practice. How was it?"

I could tell Agnes was stalling.

"It was great. I get to be the lead dancer next week. Ma, where are you going looking all sexy?"

"I need to go out for a little while. You'll be OK while I'm gone, right?"

"Why can't I come?"

"'Cause you'll be bored. How 'bout I take you to Ashley's? You can hang out with your friend, while I hang out with mine."

She smiled. "I'll call and tell her to ask her mother."

While Akilah was in the kitchen, I resumed our conversation.

"Why are y'all trying to stop me? You know damn well if the shoe was on the other foot, you'd be doing the same thing," I said trying to keep down my voice.

"No I wouldn't," Nicole said. "And friends don't let friends act a fool."

"I'm not acting a fool. I just found out my husband paid off the man who shot me and has been fucking my worst enemy. How am I supposed to react to that? Calm, cool and collected?"

"Of course not," Nicole said. "You're shocked, pissed, hurt and probably feeling a bunch of other things you have every right to feel. And what you need to be doing is sitting in here with us letting it all out. Cry if you need to cry. Scream, throw a fit, whatever."

"I did that already, upstairs. What I need now is to see Kenny. I need to talk to him. Find out what would make him do this. He's my husband for god's sake. We had problems, but nothing that would make him want to hurt me like that. I need to understand this."

"All right," Agnes said. "But if you go, we're going with you."

"That's right," Nicole said.

"Fine," I relented.

"Ashley's mom said I could come over," Akilah announced as she headed back to the living room. "You ready, Ma?"

"Yeah, baby. Let's go."

"You guys can ride with me," Nicole said. "We'll drop her off first."

"But..."

"But, nothing," she said. "You're not going anywhere without us."

Nicole drove. Agnes and Akilah sat in the back. Me in the front passenger seat.

Ashley lived around the corner. The two minutes it took us to drive Akilah there were awkwardly silent.

"Where do you think he could be?" Janelle asked as soon as Akilah slammed the car door shut.

"He said he was going to his mother's, but do me a favor and take me by the office first. I need to check on something there."

"I can't believe you're thinking about work at a time like this?" Nicole said.

"Really," Agnes added sarcastically.

"It's not work, it's personal. I just need to pick up something."

It occurred to me as we were driving Akilah to Ashley's that unless Janelle had another way of reaching Kenny, he didn't see the text message, so he didn't know to meet her at the hotel. That meant she was there by herself.

Waiting on her ass-whupping from me.

Normally, I don't advocate stepping to the mistress. After all, Kenny was *my* husband. He was the one who took vows. Janelle never promised to honor and cherish me. And I never gave myself to her. But this was different. She wasn't some innocent victim here. Some woman who Kenny lied to and never told he was married so he could get in her pants. She went after him with the sole purpose of hurting me.

And she was in on whatever plot they cooked up that got me shot. Hell, she probably came up with it since the shooter was related to her crazy ass.

It was time she got hers.

"I don't believe this," Nicole said as we pulled up in front of my office building. "Lorenzo would kill me if he knew I was any part of this craziness."

"Lorenzo? I said with wide eyes. "When did y'all get back together?"

"A few days ago, but that's another story for another day. Right now we're dealing with your drama."

"Hold that thought, I said as I hopped out of the car. I used my key to enter the building, then went out the back door and jogged the three blocks to the Marriott.

Before going inside, I whipped out my cell and called Detective Howard.

"Hello detective. Does what you have to tell me this afternoon involve Janelle Carter?"

"As a matter of fact it does, how did you know?"

"That doesn't matter. You can find her at the Marriott in Room 339. But she won't be here long 'cause she knows you're on to her so you need to come get her right now."

"All right, I'll send a unit right away. Ms. Singleton..."

"I have to go, detective. I'm sure I'll be talking to you later."

The ride to the third floor felt like the longest elevator trip in history. Outside the room, incense tickled my nose. I pressed my ear to the door and heard jazz playing softly in the background.

Janelle was certainly setting a romantic mood.

Too bad her date was going to be me.

I unlocked the door with the key I'd had the attendant at the front desk give me by convincing him I was Janelle and had locked myself out.

The stunned look on Janelle's face when she saw me standing in her room instead of Kenny was priceless.

I walked up to her, balled my hand into a fist, reached back and landed a hook right across her nose.

"Shit! I hollered, pulling my hand back in pain.

She stumbled back onto the bed, blood dripping down her chin.

"That's for fucking my husband!" I shouted.

"And this is for those fucking e-mails you sent to set me up with Eugene Rodgers," I said as I clocked her again.

She tried to get up and come after me.

I grabbed her, knocked her back on the bed, and followed with a punch to the gut.

"And that's for paying your cousin to shoot me!"

Janelle grabbed her stomach and hollered in pain.

Before leaving, I stood over as she lay in the bed groaning and gasping for breath and spit in her face.

The police were walking into the Marriott as I headed out.

Thirty-two
Arianna

Nicole had turned off the engine and she and Agnes were waiting impatiently when I jogged back to the car.

"What the heck took you so long?" Nicole asked.

"Better yet, why the hell is your hand bleeding?" Agnes shouted from the back seat.

"I cut myself trying to open my desk drawer," I lied. "I forgot the keys to my desk and didn't want to ask you to drive me all the way back home to get them."

"Hmm Hmm," Agnes said.

"Where to now?" Nicole asked, clearly exasperated by the events of the day.

"Nicole, you can take me back home and I'll get my car. I know you must be tired. Carrying a baby is hard enough work, you don't need to add my drama to your stress."

"Whatever, Arianna. Stop trying to get rid of me and tell me where we're going."

"Fine," I snapped. "Let me call his mother and see if he's there. In the meantime, just start driving."

"How do I do that with no destination? I don't know which way to go."

"Nicole, just start driving, head south. Who cares, we can always turn around."

She rolled her eyes, let out another sigh and started the car.

I knew if Kenny wasn't at his mother's and hadn't left town, he was either at Max's or Clay's, the guys in his band.

Mae said she hadn't seen her son in more than a week, so I pointed Nicole in the direction of Clay's house. The band practiced there because he was single and they could keep up all the noise they wanted there. Kenny liked to practice there alone sometimes to escape whatever was bothering him.

My instincts were right.

As soon as we pulled up, I saw Kenny's car parked across the street.

Clay answered the door wearing his jacket.

"Arianna. Ladies," he nodded as he made his way past us and down the stairs.

"You leaving because of us?" I asked.

He turned around. "When three sistas roll up at my door for one man, it's time to make ghost," he said, smiling. "Go easy on my man. He's really down about this breakup."

"He's down about more than that," Nicole mumbled under her breath.

"Is that what he told you?" I asked.

"Yeah, more or less."

"Sorry you had to get involved in our problems," I said.

"It's cool," he said. "Kenny's my boy. He can stay here until you two work things out. I'ma let y'all handle your business. I'll talk with you later."

Clay's house was immaculate and drab. Hideous country style upholstered furniture in shades of brown and tan filled the living room and den.

Tan curtains hung from the living room windows, and fudge colored carpet covered the floor.

A basketball game was blaring from the 60-inch monstrosity of a television that damn near took up the entire length of one side of the living room.

Rows of shelves filled with albums, 45s, and CDs covered the opposite wall. And tucked in a corner was an eight-track player and old-fashioned stereo.

In the middle of the room, looking as out of place as Lil' Kim in Bible study, was Kenny, dressed in a velour running suit with a rapper's name emblazoned on the front, a cognac-filled rock glass in his hand. It was too damn early for alcohol, but under the circumstances, I wasn't surprised.

"Arianna, why did you bring them over here?"

"Hello to you, too," Agnes said.

He nodded in her direction.

"I don't mean to be rude, ladies, but Arianna's and my marriage is really none of your business," he said.

"Do you really think they came over here to talk about our marital problems?" I asked. "They're here to keep me safe from you."

A look of distress covered Kenny's face. He got jittery; the ice cubes in his drink clanking. "What are you talking about?" he said, sipping from his glass.

"About you paying Darryl Crump to shoot me," I said, trying, at least for the moment, to keep my anger in check.

His eyes bulged from their sockets like an erect penis. He took another sip of cognac, as if to gird himself for what was to come, and then sat on Clay's ugly sofa.

Kenny put his head in his hands and breathed deeply.

"I'm waiting, Kenny," I said.

"What do you want me to say?" he asked, when he finally looked up at me.

"So it *was* you?"

He leaned into the couch and exhaled as if he'd been waiting forever to unload. "Yes. Yes, it was me," he sighed

"Why, Kenny! How could you do this to me?"

Tears filled his eyes.

"He wasn't supposed to shoot you, I swear. Just vandalize your office, destroy your computers, stuff like that. I would never do anything to hurt you like that."

"Oh. So you wouldn't hurt me physically. Just mentally, emotionally and financially? Gee, thanks, I'm grateful. Why, Kenny? Why?"

"And where does your little slut, Janelle fit in, huh Kenny? You're not only fucking the woman who tried to put me in jail, but you were in cahoots with her on this plan to screw me out of my business?"

"What?

"Don't pretend to be shocked, Kenny."

"I am! What do you mean Janelle tried to put you in jail?"

"Now you wanna play dumb like you don't remember the heifer who went to the cops and told them I was a murderer?"

Kenny searched his mind for clarity.

"I thought that woman's name was Carter?"

"It was. She's going by her maiden name now. Bailey. You mean to tell me you honestly didn't know they were the same person?"

"I swear I didn't. I met her at Zanzibar Blue. She was there with a friend and she flirted with me. Started coming in a lot when the band played."

"Made you feel like a real man did she?"

"Well....Yeah. She made me feel like I mattered. Like my feelings mattered. And yes, she made me feel like a man when I was with her. Not a substitute for one."

"Does it matter that she was only using you to get back at me? That she hated the way I made her fat ass look in my book just like you did so she went after you? Who's idea was it to have me shot? Yours or hers?"

Kenny shook his head in disbelief.

"Arianna, I told you nobody wanted to have you shot," he said almost pleadingly. "You weren't even supposed to be there, remember? All I wanted to do is get you to shut down that damn Web site. It was making my life miserable."

"Why didn't you just tell me?" I shouted.

"I tried over and over. You just kept telling me you were providing a service and the hell with what I wanted."

"That's not true. You never told me how bad things were for you. You just made it sound like you were taking some ribbing from your friends. How the hell was I supposed to know how miserable you were? And that's your excuse for nearly having me killed. This is bullshit!"

He stood up and slammed his drink on Clay's coffee table. Agnes and Nicole, who had been standing against the music wall behind me, rushed over and stood by my side.

"How many times did I ask you to shut it down?" he shouted. "You wouldn't listen. First it was your damn book. Then your male-bashing Internet service. It was getting to the point I hated to show my face in public. Everybody pointing at me and whispering. Calling me whipped, punk, Mrs. Singleton. You have no idea what it's been like for me.

"I paid that asshole to tear shit up, period. I was hoping after you got that note, it would scare you enough to give up that damn site. You never even mentioned the note that night and it sure as hell didn't stop you. I didn't know what else to do so..."

I snapped.

Anger, shock and disgust crashed inside me, exploding into a cocktail of rage. I reached inside my purse, pulled out the gun, disengaged the safety and pointed the barrel in his face.

Kenny backed up, lost his balance and fell on the couch.

In unison, Nicole and Agnes shrieked, "Oh, my God!" as though they were the soprano section of a choir.

"Put that damn thing down, Arianna!" Agnes demanded, grabbing my bicep.

There were four people in that house and fear leaked from the pores of each one, filling the room and robbing the oxygen.

"Arianna, please," Nicole pleaded. "This is crazy..."

"Kenny will be the only one to get hurt," I said, interrupting her and yanking away my arm.

"I can't believe you sent me that note! And slashed my tires? Who the hell have I been living with these past few months?"

"I was just trying to get you to shut it down," he said.

"By scaring the shit outta me? I lost weeks of my life and I might be in pain forever because of you and that bitch. And yesterday you had the nerve to say you still cared about me? What the fuck would you do if you hated me? Huh, Kenny? Would you have pulled the trigger yourself instead of being a fucking punk and paying somebody else to do your damn dirty work!

"How 'bout if I shoot you now? Huh. We'd be even then right? A bullet for a bullet?"

I got in his face and pointed the gun at his temple.

"Oh...wait a minute. I got hit with two bullets, so that means I need to shoot you twice."

"Arianna, stop it!" Nicole shouted.

"Really, Arianna," Agnes said. "Shooting him won't solve anything."

"She's right," Nicole said, her voice a few octaves higher and agitated. "It won't give you back those weeks you spent in the hospital. It won't take away your pain, physical or otherwise. The only thing you can do is and try and forgive him and move on with your life."

"Forgive him! Why the hell should I forgive him!"

I was shaking and crying.

Kenny was shaking and crying.

Agnes and Nicole were just shaking.

I moved a few steps away from him. "Stand up!" I yelled.

He followed my order.

"You took the easy way out," I continued. "Sending me notes. Hiring criminals to do your dirty work. You need to take your punishment standing up like a man. And you still haven't answered my question. Whose idea was it to hire Darryl Crump?"

"Janelle's," he said, rubbing his temples. "I mentioned to her that I wished I could find a way to get you to shut down the site and she suggested we vandalize the place to scare you. Her cousin Crump is an ex-con who's done some minor burglaries and shit and she said he'd do it for a couple thousand. I didn't think anybody would get hurt, so I went along with it. She set everything up. I had no idea she even knew you. Really, I didn't. If I had known who she was I swear I never would have gotten involved with her, Arianna. Please believe that."

"And you don't need to do this," he said, wailing like a bitch. "I'm gonna go to jail. That's the real reason I moved out. I thought I could keep you from finding out. But Crump's been blackmailing me. I drained my 401K and gave him all the money I had and he keeps coming back for more, saying he wants to make sure he can pay for his lawyer and his family is taken care of. I even started embezzling from some of the accounts at work. I don't have anything else to give, so I knew it was only a matter of time before he dropped a dime. I didn't want to be there when you found out or when the cops came to arrest me. I didn't want Akilah to see me taken away in handcuffs.

I was gonna run away, leave the country. But, I don't have enough money to go anywhere, now. And I didn't want to live my life like that."

"Oh, but living it as a liar and as the man who put your wife in a coma was all right with you?" I said.

"Of course not. I've been consumed with guilt for so long now I don't remember not feeling like this. I could barely look at you in the hospital. The doctors told me to talk to you, but I didn't know what to say. Why do you think I've spent so much time away from the house since you got out? I couldn't face you."

"So now what? Am I supposed to feel sorry for you?" I said, lowering the gun to his chest.

"No, but you could put the gun down. I know you hate me right now, and I don't blame you, but you're not a killer."

"Oh, so now I'm *not* a killer. This from the man who takes every opportunity to throw my past in my face."

"We all know that was an accident," Nicole said. "Will you please cut this out. If you don't put down that gun, somebody is going to get hurt and you know you don't want that to happen. Remember what I told you when you wanted to go after Chauncey? Vengeance is the Lord's. It's not yours. Kenny's going to pay for his crime. You have to let it go."

"She's right," Agnes said. "Remember what I told you? Revenge is not your responsibility."

I was soaking in theirs words; letting them dance around my heart, prick at my emotions. The anger bubbling inside me was beginning to recede as I listened, and for once, took heed.

But just as I was about to lower the gun and stop the madness, Kenny reached for it, seizing the opportunity my distraction had given him.

He grabbed my arm. I tried to snatch it away.

We struggled. I pulled. He grabbed.

My index finger still arched around the trigger.

More pushing, pulling, screaming, crying and then *POP!*

The gun went off.

Kenny and I looked at each other. His brown eyes were glazed in fear. My heartbeat echoed loudly off the cream-colored walls, beating to the rhythm of an African emergency drum call.

Agnes' shrieks signaled to Kenny and I that neither of us had been hit. I dropped the gun and turned around. Nicole was on the floor bleeding.

Thirty-three
Arianna

Agnes and I took turns pacing the floor of Temple University Hospital's emergency waiting room as Nicole underwent surgery to remove the bullet from her abdomen.

I was on my fourth cup of coffee when Lorenzo arrived. Nicole had been under the knife for five hours.

Lorenzo wouldn't look at me. He wouldn't talk to me.

I'd given him the short version of the day's events when I called earlier to tell him his wife had been shot. It was the hardest phone call I'd ever made. He was less than sympathetic, blaming me.

Had it not been for me, he said tersely, his wife would've been safe at home decorating the nursery, the first event they'd planned together since he moved out.

Not long after Lorenzo arrived, Pam and Candace showed up, both with attitudes as big as Pam's waistline. Lorenzo apparently had filled them in, so they, too, acted as though they'd been frostbitten.

Nicole's brother Mark was out of town and trying to find a flight back.

Despite the fact we all loved Nicole; the waiting room was divided. Me and Agnes on one side. Lorenzo, Pam and Candace on the other.

It was a long-ass afternoon that turned into a long-ass night.

When the emergency room doctor, a short, balding white man, finally emerged from the operating room shortly after 10, he was not bearing good news.

Nicole's womb had become a tomb and she was hanging on by the grace of a higher power.

When the doctor, who had the bedside manner of a skunk, made this announcement, red, yellow and blue spots dotted the blackness that suddenly appeared before my eyes. I gasped for air, and then felt Agnes' arms around my waist, keeping me from hitting the floor.

Pam and Candace were busy trying to comfort Lorenzo. Their efforts were futile. He was inconsolable.

Still, I think I cried harder than him, and his tears flowed from a place so deep only God could find his way there.

After we all gained our composure, Lorenzo provided the final sting of the night by insisting that we go home and telling me not to bother coming back.

He told the staff not to allow me in Nicole's room for the remainder of her stay.

I ran to the parking lot as fast as my back pain would allow. I searched frantically for my car for several minutes until I realized it wasn't there.

Nicole had been our chauffeur for the day and her car was still at Clay's. An ambulance had taken her to the hospital and the police, who arrived with the paramedics, had driven the rest of us.

They also arrested Kenny.

Agnes showed up in the parking lot just about the time I realized I was stranded, saying she'd called a cab and it was on its way.

We rode to my house in silence. I could hear her thoughts, though. They roared through my mind like thunder: Nicole's baby would be alive if it weren't for me.

Since she drove from Maryland with Nicole, I offered to let her spend the night. She declined, saying she'd have the cab take her to the train station.

It was shortly after 11 when I walked through my door. About 12 hours had passed since I left. It seemed like a lifetime.

I plopped on the couch and called Amir. Told him to come home and pick up his sister from Ashley's on the way. I called her parents and apologized ahead of time for the late pickup but told them it couldn't be helped.

I needed time to regroup. Prepare to tell my children the news that was bound to be splashed on television for the next few weeks.

In the meantime, my bed was dialing me 911.

I answered the call immediately.

When consciousness found me a couple hours later, my children were hovering over my bed requesting an explanation for why they'd been dragged home in the middle of the night.

Once again, they would have to endure the invasion of strangers into our lives.

᙭᙭᙭

Telling Akilah the man she'd come to love as her father was responsible for putting me in a coma nearly broke me. I watched helplessly as the fire inside her died. Followed by her precociousness and sass. Then her spirit.

The only things left were pain, anger, sadness and confusion.

The perplexed expression on her face as I tried to explain the unexplainable would forever be seared into my memory. No explanation I could provide helped her make sense out the nonsense I'd just fed her.

All I could do was hold her as she sobbed. First for the loss of Kenny. Then for the loss of Nicole's unborn child. I'd thought of giving her the news in doses, but figured a one-shot deal was best.

As I provided the only comfort to her that I knew how, Amir stormed from the house blinded by rage. He wanted to kill Kenny.

At first he was shocked. Then anger took over.

For once, I tried to be the voice of reason. To make my son see that revenge was how we'd found ourselves here in the first place.

My words fell on stubborn ears.

Like mother, like son.

I didn't bother going after Amir because Kenny was locked up, safe from my son's wrath. Besides, there was no way they'd allow him visitors at that hour.

While Nicole was in surgery, Detective Howard came by to tell me Kenny and Janelle's involvement in my shooting was indeed the news he'd planned to give me that day.

Crump was planning to use the money he'd extorted from them to jump bail. He didn't know the cops were watching him, hoping he'd lead them to his accomplice.

They nabbed him at the Amtrak station, heading for Canada. He finally ratted out Janelle and Kenny.

The questions the detective wanted to ask me were about their motive. I told him about the affair I'd just learned of.

"Why didn't you call us when you found out instead of taking matters into your own hands?" he asked.

I had no answer for him other than temporary insanity.

He explained that Kenny and Janelle would spend the weekend in jail and be arraigned Monday. I asked, no begged him, to keep the news of Nicole's shooting and Kenny's arrest quiet for as long as possible to protect Nicole's privacy. Mine, too.

To my surprise, he agreed. Said he would see to it the desk sergeants gave only scant details to any media inquiries for the next few days. I think he felt sorry for me.

God knows he had reason to.

Thirty-four
Arianna

Amir and Lorenzo came to face to face again under the worse circumstances.

They'd run into each other in the parking lot of the police station where Kenny was awaiting his fate. Apparently, Lorenzo had the same idea as Amir. He needed to lash out at someone. Since he'd banned me from the hospital and I wasn't available, Kenny was the next best target.

Amir also had gone to the jail to give Kenny a piece of his mind. Neither of them got in, of course.

Their chance meeting brought another truth to the surface Lorenzo wasn't yet ready to deal with.

That Amir was my son.

He wasn't aware of the single degree of separation between himself and me until that night. When he and Amir shared their mutual disgust for my husband.

Amir wanted to confront Lorenzo about lying to Nicole about loving men as much as he loved women. The time wasn't right.

He felt bad for his former lover and offered him a shoulder. Lorenzo accepted.

Amir came away believing Lorenzo wasn't the monster we'd made him about to be, but a man who truly loved his wife and was grieving deeply over his unborn child.

His eyes never left the floor as he recounted their chance meeting. And it wasn't shame or guilt about their relationship.

No. His shame was for me.

My son couldn't look me in the eye because like everyone else, he believed I was the cause of Nicole and Lorenzo's loss and their pain.

It didn't matter that Kenny was the intended target of my anger. Nicole and her family were the accidental recipients.

Amir said he was still angry at Kenny, but after seeing Lorenzo's pain, he realized hurting him was not the answer.

He went upstairs and came back down with his overnight bag.

I reminded him he was supposed to take his sister to the movies the next day. Akilah needed the distraction.

He needed to get away more.

He left me in tears, and even more guilt-ridden, if that were possible.

Could I blame him, though?

If I could walk away from my life, I would have. But I was stuck with me everywhere I went.

So I crawled in bed. Turned off the house and cell phones, the TV, everything. The silence and darkness coupled with my gloom was eerie. Almost like being back in the coma.

Too bad almost doesn't count.

֎֎֎

Sunday morning found me in church seeking absolution. It was the only way I could think of to deal with the guilt and shame that threatened to swallow me whole.

Akilah opted not to go, and I was in no mood to force her, so I went alone.

I had no desire to run into my mother-in-law so I went to the church in Wilmington where Kenny and I were married. He had been a member there when he lived in Delaware and I'd visited a few times.

The pastor and his wife were a young couple, early 40s and progressive. They had ministries for everyone, young, old, married and single. You could wear whatever you wanted, including jeans, and the music was bumping.

I jumped on Interstate 95, headed south and made it just in time for praise and worship.

I'd let church dogma and bullshit keep me away so long, I'd almost forgotten the good things about going to church, like getting caught up in the spirit. I clapped and danced away my blues, at least temporarily.

During the altar call, I prayed for forgiveness and divine guidance from my seat on the last pew. I didn't want to get in the prayer line with the regulars. I also prayed for Nicole, the spirit of her dead child and Lorenzo.

I could've done without the check-yourself-before-you-wreck-yourself-and-go-to-hell sermon, but the rest of the service was worth the hour-long drive it took to get me there.

A sense of calm had washed over me by the time I left. My day got a little brighter still when I listened to the voice mail on my cell. Randy had left a message while I was in church with the ringer turned off.

Hey Arianna,

Look, I'm sorry about last night. It's just my kids were here and I certainly wasn't ready for them to witness that performance you gave last night. That doesn't mean I don't want to see you again. You just need to call before you come over next time. Call me so I know you're all right. I'm worried about you.

His second message made me blush.

Oh yeah. If my kids weren't here, I would have definitely taken you up on your offer. Whatever you were wearing under that coat sure looked sexy. I hope I get another chance to see it.

I was glad Randy didn't want to end our friendship. I wished I could've headed straight to his place and find the solace I so desperately needed after everything I'd been through the preceding twenty-four hours. But I had to get home to Akilah.

Thirty-five
Arianna

To my surprise, Detective Howard and his partner were waiting for me when I pulled into my driveway.

With a warrant for my arrest.

I couldn't believe I was headed down this road again.

"Ms. Singleton, I know this is a bad time for you, but I'm afraid I have to place you under arrest for criminal homicide of an unborn child."

I must have passed out because the next thing I remembered was Detective Howard kneeling over me waving a handkerchief in my face and his partner, a short white guy with red hair and red freckles trying to console a hysterical Akilah.

"Mommy are you OK?" Akilah cried, looking down at me.

"Yeah, baby. I'm fine," I said trying to assure her as I lifted my head from the ground.

"I thought you were in a coma again."

"No sweetie, I just fell. I'm fine."

As I pulled myself up, I noticed blood trickling down my face. I reached up to find the source. It was a gash in my hairline.

"You hit your head when you fell, Detective Howard said. "We'll get that treated before we take you in. Do you remember why we're here?"

"Y-e-s," I said, uttering the word one letter at a time.

"Do you have someone you can call to watch your daughter, ma'am?"

"No officer, I don't. My mother lives in Connecticut and her father...stepfather...Kenny is in jail, remember?"

"What about your in-laws, a friend, a neighbor?"

"My outlaws are out of the question. I don't have anyone I trust who lives in Philadelphia. I have a brother, but he lives in D.C. I could call my son, but he's in Maryland and it'll take him a while to get here."

"Why don't you do that, ma'am. Otherwise we'll have to call social services and she'll end up spending the night in a foster home. Your son should be here by the time they finish up with you at the hospital."

"The hospital?"

"We have to take you there to get that cut treated. Department policy."

"Mommy, what are y'all talking about?" Akilah asked frantically.

"I have to go with the detective, baby, and I don't know when I'm gonna be able to come back home."

"Is he arresting you for killing Miss Nicole's baby?"

Damn. Akilah just put the shit out there. Even Detective Howard was stunned by her awareness *and* her bluntness.

I lost it. Tears cascaded down my face like Niagara Falls and groans of sorrow escaped from the depths of my bowels. Somehow I was able to mutter the word "yes" through my hysteria.

I grabbed Akilah. We both were crying and shaking furiously. Detective Howard and his partner stood nearby looking pained. Pity, however, wasn't going to fix my situation.

We went inside the house where I called Amir. It hadn't yet been 24 hours since he'd left me a blubbering mess and now I was asking him to return to find me the same way.

Thirty-six
Arianna

My one phone call went to Joshua Berger.

The lawyer from Delaware I'd hired the last time I found myself in need of legal assistance.

With his help, I beat the bogus manslaughter charges the Los Angeles assistant district attorney managed to get a grand jury to indict me with in Chauncey's death.

This time was different, though.

Part of me wanted to pay for what I'd done to Nicole. Her baby would be alive if it weren't for my need for revenge. If I hadn't made the stupid decision to bring a loaded gun.

I fought with Kenny over the gun, even though deep down I knew if I let him have it, he wouldn't have used it against me.

He was only trying to protect himself.

He should have known I never would have used it on him, either. I was just frontin.' Letting my anger get the best of me. Once again, allowing a man to turn me into a fucking lunatic.

Though my guilty conscience wanted to atone for my sins against my best friend, the mother in me wanted to be free to finish raising my daughter.

I prayed Joshua Berger could help me do just that.

Though in the back of my mind, I wondered if Akilah would be better off without a mother like me.

Since they arrested me on a Sunday, I had to spend the night in the jail. I was processed, fingerprinted, mugged and locked behind bars.

They took my shoes, a pair of black heels, and replaced them with slippers made of the same kind of brown paper used for grocery bags. Something about shoes being possible as weapons and people using shoestrings to hang themselves.

The steel palette screwed to the wall they called a bed was as comfortable as concrete and cold as a meat locker.

There was a toilet but no toilet paper.

It was no wonder sleep never found me.

Joshua, short, white and Jewish, shook his balding head as he stepped into the interrogation room where the police let him meet with me.

"Can you please tell me how the hell you wound up in this situation again?" he asked. "It's not like you're a stupid woman or a career criminal, Arianna. Another accidental death? This one is not going to be easy."

"You got any good news?" I asked, sarcastically.

"Not really," he said. "It's not self-defense like last time. I read the police report. They got you dead to rights. Pennsylvania law says you are guilty of criminal homicide of an unborn child if you recklessly or negligently cause the death of one. And you did."

"I don't need you to cite Pennsylvania's penal code, Josh. I need you tell me what my chances are. Can we beat the charge?"

"It's gonna be difficult. How far along was your friend?"

"Five months."

"Good."

"Why?"

"Prosecutors are less likely to pursue charges unless a woman is further along. The whole when does a fetus become a living being argument."

"Five months isn't enough?"

"No. They usually need to be in their third trimester. There was a case last month where a man who was driving drunk killed an 18-year-old pregnant woman who was a passenger in his car. Turns out she was in her second trimester, like your friend, so the Perry County prosecutor decided not to charge him with the death of the fetus. Only the death of the mother. They wouldn't even issue a fetal death certificate because the child hadn't been born."

"Wow," I said, blown away by these fine legal details that determine when a person is a person. "So it's like her baby never existed?"

"According to the law. I'm sure the father of that child and the grandparents don't think that way," Joshua said matter-of-factly.

I thought about Nicole and Lorenzo.

Their baby was definitely a real human being to them. Not a fetus. Not a ball of splitting cells with their DNA as medical science would call it.

Guilt once again hit me in the gut.

"Like the parents of the baby I killed don't think that way," I whispered.

"I'm sure they don't," Joshua said.

"What if that girl was further along?" I asked.

"The prosecutor might have charged the guy."

"Might?"

"I can't tell you what he would've done, Arianna. I'm not him. I don't even know him."

"How do you know so much about Pennsylvania cases?"

"It's my job to know. That's what you expect from me, right? I'm licensed to practice here so I get regular information about cases, especially unusual cases like that one."

"So where do we go from here?"

"We get you out on bail and we prepare for trial."

"Trial? Do you think it's going to get that far?"

"Arianna, I just told you this is not going to be like the last time. There are going to be one of two outcomes. We go to trial or you take a plea. You need to start thinking long and hard about which one would be best for you."

"What kind of plea do you think they'll offer me?"

"At this point, I have no idea."

"If I get convicted at trial, what am I looking at?" I asked, not really wanting the answer.

"Well, because a gun was involved, there's a minimum mandatory of five years. The maximum sentence for third-degree murder, which is how this crime is classified, is 40 years. So you could be looking at anything in between."

"What! I shouted, as an earthquake begin to erupt inside me. "Five to 40 years? Are you kidding? I can't do that kind of time. In five years, Akilah will go from being a girl to a woman and I can't miss that."

"Like I said, Arianna, you've got some thinking to do. Right now let's see about getting you out of here."

Joshua sighed, shook his head again, and walked out the door.

Thirty-seven
Arianna

My empty house was eerily silent.

I'd almost forgotten what it was like to be home alone. I used to relish the peaceful Me Time.

This wasn't one of those days. I needed company. The company of somebody who cared about me and would tell me everything was going to be fine.

There was no one.

Amir had taken Akilah to my brother's house and went back to school. He didn't even bother coming to the arraignment.

Agnes didn't say anything, but I knew she was upset with me and I didn't dare burden her with the latest.

And the days of Kenny providing me with comfort were long over.

He and I had been arraigned in the same courtroom that morning. Janelle's arraignment was held later that day and she was bailed out.

Kenny's eyes looked as though they'd pop from their sockets when he saw the guards walk me in handcuffed and lead me to my seat.

It was beyond awkward.

The judge looked like he would release me on my own recognizance after Joshua explained the circumstances of the accident. Then the prosecutor told him that I'd brought the gun with me to Clay's house to kill Kenny.

Then he brought up Chauncey.

Joshua told him the gun was to scare Kenny, not kill him and Chauncey was irrelevant.

It didn't matter.

The judge determined I had anger management issues and was a danger to others. He set my bail at $150,000 dollars.

I only needed 10 percent of that. I dipped into my savings.

Too bad money couldn't solve all my problems.

Kenny's bail was only $10,000 dollars. He had no prior record, and wasn't accused of direct violence.

It was all I could do not to show how pissed I was.

His mother posted the grand he needed to get out.

I ran into them in the court clerk's office.

Unspoken words and anger lingered in the air, but neither was given voice. Mae just rolled her eyes. Kenny wouldn't look in my direction at all.

That was fine by me.

I was spent. Empty. I had nothing to say and didn't want to look at him, either.

I needed to rid myself of the foul odor of the jail cell and that horrid experience in the courtroom with my future ex-husband.

I soaked in the tub until my feet were shriveled and doused myself with raspberry scented body splash. Then I climbed under the covers and spent the day in bed.

The next day was even lonelier. I called Amir shortly after waking. He didn't answer.

When I called my brother's house to speak to Akilah, his wife told me he'd taken her to the school department to enroll her.

"What!" I shouted.

"Arianna, face reality," said my sister-in-law Gina, a stay-at-home mother who was born with a silver spoon in her mouth. "You are looking at jail time. You need to get your case together. You need to get yourself together. You're in no position to raise a child right now. Greg and I will take care of Akilah until you get your life right."

"That's not a decision for you and Greg to make without consulting me," I snapped.

"He was planning to call you about it today," Gina said. "Let us do this for you. Be grateful you have a brother who is willing to help you out instead of getting mad at him for doing it."

I lay still in bed, feeling defeated, unable to speak.

"Arianna? You still there?" Gina asked.

"Yeah, I'm here. Are you telling me that you guys want custody of my daughter?"

"Yes. Not permanently, of course. Just until you are better able to provide Akilah with a more stable home. You have to admit that with both you and your husband being arrested, your home is not stable right now."

"Let me call you back."

I hung up and lay back down, trying to wrap my mind around my new reality. Gina, as much as I hated to admit it, was right. My house, at the moment was not a good home for Akilah.

Plus, jail was a distinct possibility.

I couldn't believe it. Janelle had gotten what she wanted after all. I was losing everything, my husband, my business, my freedom, and my children.

I waited a few hours – the time it took me to swallow my pride – before calling Gina again.

"All right, Gina. You and Greg should keep Akilah. For now. But she is *not* going to public school in D.C. Can you and Greg please find a good private school? I'll pay for it."

"Are you sure…"

"I'm sure, Gina. This is my daughter's education we're talking about. Think what you want about me, I've always been a good mother and you know it."

"No need to get defensive, Arianna. I just didn't know if money was a problem with legal fees and everything. I'll talk to Greg about it when he gets back."

"Thanks, Gina."

"Take care, Arianna. Keep us informed. I know Greg wants to drive up there to see you and attend some of your court hearings for moral support."

"Yeah. I'll let you know," I said, pressing the end button on my cell.

I had no more tears. I'd used them all the night before and my eyes were so swollen I'd barely been able to open them wide enough to see the numbers on the cell phone keypad.

I stumbled to the bathroom and peed. As I washed my hands and stared at the tired face in the mirror, I knew I couldn't spend another day in bed.

Or another day alone.

I grabbed a bottle of douche from underneath the sink and stepped in the shower.

After toweling off and throwing on a pair of sweats and sneakers, I went outside and snatched the newspaper from my driveway.

I wanted to see if news of my arrest had made the papers, yet.

It hadn't. There were no reporters in the courtroom when Kenny and I were arraigned because our cases hadn't made it on the docket.

The *Press-Herald* only had a small item about Nicole, saying an unidentified woman had been shot in an apparent domestic dispute and the victim was in critical condition.

I turned on the radio and watched TV with the volume down. I knew if they had a story about me, I'd see my face splattered across the screen.

Nothing.

It was only a matter of time, however, before the whole ugly truth came out. So I seized on the small window of opportunity I had and called Randy.

I decided to take advantage of his ignorance about my situation. I needed the company of someone who had the power to make me forget, even for just a few hours, that my life was crashing down around me and I was facing many years behind bars.

I called Randy and apologized for my performance at his front door. He accepted and invited me over for dinner.

I wasn't going to throw myself at him, but if he put the moves on me, I damn sure wasn't going to turn him down this time.

Thirty-eight
Arianna

Randy greeted me with a rose and smile.

"Why are you being so nice to me after everything that happened?" I asked as he took my coat.

"Should I be mean to you because you made an error in judgment and timing? What would be the point of that?"

I shrugged my shoulders.

"You look great by the way," he said, smiling mischievously.

My body was completely covered with an ankle-length chocolate brown and blue-checkered wool skirt, a tight fitting cashmere brown sweater and knee-high brown leather boots.

Randy's pecs were bulging through a snug powder blue sweater and his tight ass was hiding underneath a pair of loose-fitting designer jeans.

"Thanks. You look nice yourself."

"Although I was hoping you would wear that peach thing you had on," he said winking. "I didn't see the whole thing 'cause your coat was blocking it. But I saw enough to know it was something skimpy and sexy."

"Something sure smells good," I said, changing the subject.

He sniffed the air. "Yes it does, doesn't it?"

"You gonna tell me what it is?"

"Sweet and sour soy chicken."

"Sounds interesting."

"You'll love it. I had it at this vegetarian restaurant I went to in Atlanta. Their food is off the hook. I liked it so much I bought their cookbook so I could get the recipe. You want some wine?"

"Sure, thanks."

Randy smiled. "You like white right?"

I nodded my head.

We ate at the dining room table by candlelight.

The food was excellent, the conversation easy.

I let Randy do most of the talking. His voice, sexy, deep, and sweet, provided a shield from the brutal reality of my world, allowing me to temporarily forget.

Sprinkled between current events, Randy's children, and the funny things his students did that kept him entertained, were personal tidbits that exposed our vulnerabilities. Those little details that allow others access to our inner selves, to the place where our happiness resides.

With a table between us, Randy and I became more intimate that night than Kenny and I had been in a year.

After we finished eating, I helped him wash dishes.

"So you wanna talk about whatever's bothering you?" he asked, passing me a plate to rinse.

"How do you know something's…"

"I can count on two hands the number of words you've said tonight. You're not usually this quiet."

"Oh," I said, with a faint smile. "It's nothing, really. I appreciate the offer, though."

"That's what friends are for. You sure you don't want to talk about it?"

"Yeah. I'm tired of listening to myself complain so I know my friends could use a break. Tonight, I just want to relax and enjoy your company. That's the best medicine I could have right now. "

"Well, that's an easy request to accommodate."

Randy bent over and pressed his lips against mine. He glided his tongue over my lips, and then slid it inside my mouth.

At first, our tongues danced the tango. Then he grabbed my tongue with his lips and began to suck it as though he were sipping through a straw. He sucked so hard I thought he would swallow it.

It felt weird, yet erotic at the same time. I wrapped my hands around his neck and pressed his face against mine. My hands were wet and sudsy, but he didn't seem to mind.

His wet hands found my breasts. He fondled them through my sweater, gently pulling at my nipples, making them hard. I reached down and grabbed the bulge between his legs.

Our breathing escalated and suddenly our movements were trying to keep time with our breaths. We were touching and licking, kissing and squeezing and trying to keep our balance at the same time.

Randy pulled my sweater from inside my skirt and snatched it over my head. Then he reached behind me and unsnapped my bra, dropping it to the floor on top of the sweater.

He bent down and put one breast in his mouth and caressed the other with his hand. I leaned my head back in pleasure as nectar flowed to my center.

Randy let go of my breasts and hiked up my skirt, pulling down my panties and inserting his fingers. He put a finger to his mouth and licked my essence.

"Thanks for bringing dessert."

He then proceeded to feast on the pink parts of me as I stood with my back to the sink, calling on God.

After extracting the fluid of two orgasms from my loins, he pulled a condom from his pocket and began to unwrap it. I stood there awkwardly waiting while he handled his business.

Once he was properly covered, he picked me up, sat me on the counter and entered me.

Both pairs of lips were screaming Randy's name.

"Ahhh. Ahhh. Oh, God," I moaned. "Shit, that feels good."

The more I talked, the faster came his thrusts.

He scooted me to the opposite side of the counter and placed each of my feet on a stool, giving himself a wider opening. I arched my back and tried to meet his thrusts, but my timing was off.

"Don't move, baby. I got this," he whispered.

I closed my eyes and allowed him to take over, sending my body into ecstasy.

His penis still snuggled tightly in my vagina; he picked me up and carried me to the living room. He laid me on the thick carpet, placed my legs behind his head and prodded himself deeper and deeper inside me.

Randy needed no help reading the road signs to my promised land. He handled me like a puppet in his personal theater. One minute I was on all fours and he was taking me from behind, the next I was on the couch with one leg on the floor and the other in the air.

My face contorted in all manners of ugliness as I invoked the Creator over and over again. The sweat pouring from our bodies was deep enough to bathe in. Randy was fucking me furiously and all I could do was beg him not to stop.

By the time he finally reached orgasm, I'd been there three more times.

He rolled off me and collapsed on the carpet in a puddle of liquid salt.

I laid my head on his chest and wrapped my arms around his six-pack. "That was amazing."

Randy coughed.

"Are you OK?" I asked.

"Yeah," he laughed. I got carpet in my mouth, that's all."

"It beats rug burn."

"You got rug burn?"

"Yeah."

"Why didn't you say something?"

"You were in your own world. I don't think you would have heard me. Besides, it was feeling too good for me to tell you to stop."

He reached over and kissed my forehead.

"How long can you stay?"

"Why? You planning an encore?"

"Well, the thought had crossed my mind. Can you handle it?"

"I can handle you all night long. The question is can you handle me?"

Randy laughed. "All night? What about your family?"

"They're taking a vacation from me right now."

"Huh?"

"Don't worry. They're fine. They won't miss me tonight."

"Arianna, what's going on with you, tonight?"

"You are Randy. You are what's going on with me. Can't we just leave it that?"

"If that's how you want it."

"That's how I want it. How about we take this conversation into your bedroom where we don't have to worry about rug burn."

He got on his knees and helped me up. Then he stood and we walked naked into his room where we made love again before I fell asleep in his arms.

※※※

My body was pleased, but my soul still in turmoil when I awoke beside Randy just before the sun rose.

I lie next to him lost in dreary thoughts of the future. Randy's alarm clock began screaming at six. He popped straight up like bread in a toaster, his erect nipples staring straight ahead. After taking a moment to adjust to his newfound state of consciousness, rubbing his eyes and running his fingers through his sexy dreadlocks, he noticed me.

"Forgot I was here, huh?" I said, smiling.

He returned the smile. "Actually, I dreamed about you."

"Really? What was I doing?"

"You really want to know?"

"Yeah."

"Giving me head and rocking my world."

I cracked up. "Is that a request?"

"Would you say 'yes?'"

"Maybe."

"Then *maybe* I'll ask next time."

"What makes you so sure there will be a next time?"

"All that screaming you were doing last night? There will definitely be a next time," he said, leaning over and planting a kiss on my lips. "But right now, I gotta get dressed and get to school. What about you? What's on your schedule today?"

He pulled off the covers and got out of bed.

A meeting with my lawyer, but I couldn't tell him that.

"I have a meeting and some editing to do," I said, staring at his perfect body and wanting him to come back to bed and wrap it around me.

"That's right, your friend's novel. How's that coming?"

"Great, she's a good writer."

"Cool. I'm gonna hit the shower."

"Can I join you?"

"I'd love for you to, but another time. If you come in there with me now, washing up is going to be the last thing on my mind."

After Randy left the room, I decided to get dressed and shower at home. I turned on the radio so the Tom Joyner show could keep me company as I put on my clothes. Those fools could always make me laugh.

I was caught up in their silly soap opera, "It's Your World," when Randy came storming back in the room waving the newspaper.

He threw it on the bed.

"It never occurred to you to tell me about this?" he said, scowling.

There in black and white was my shame.

Twist of Fate, Husband Charged in Cyber Sleuth's Shooting
Wife accidentally kills unborn child exacting revenge

The story began:

Author and entrepreneur Arianna Singleton is no stranger to payback. Two years ago, her desire to get back at a lover who wronged her landed her in a California court charged with manslaughter.

She got off scot-free.

Yesterday, the creator and owner of the popular and controversial Web site ExposeHim.com was charged with criminal homicide for allegedly killing an unborn child, an innocent victim in her effort to exact revenge on her husband, Kenneth Washington, for paying a man to shoot her.

After weeks of investigation, authorities arrested her husband and his alleged mistress, Janelle Bailey, for plotting to destroy ExposeHim.com and inadvertently causing Singleton's shooting.

When Singleton learned the pair was responsible, she went after them, beating up Bailey and attempting to shoot Washington, police said.

Instead, she shot her pregnant best friend and business partner, Nicole Tate, killing the fetus, police said.

So far she has not been charged with assaulting Bailey. Detective Lester Howard said there were no witnesses to the fight.

Experts say Singleton is not likely to be as lucky in court this time around.

"I...I'm sorry, Randy. I just wasn't ready to talk about it last night."

"No, but you were ready for me to fuck it off your mind, right?"

Silence.

"Right?!!" he yelled. "That's why you came over here isn't it? You used me to make your problems go away."

"That's not true, and it's not fair. You know I care about you. You and I were working toward something long before this shit happened."

"Fair? Who the hell are you to talk about fair? You know what, fuck it. Just leave, Arianna and take your drama with you."

"The drama you wanted me to tell you about last night? 'Cause you wanted to be my friend?" I yelled. "You wanna be my friend as long as it doesn't get too messy for you!"

"Messy? Messy is a husband. A crazy ex-boyfriend. Problems with your kids. You got murder charges. Not once but twice. That's more than drama, lady. That's insanity. And, yes, you can keep that shit."

I didn't bother responding.

He was right. I put on my boots, grabbed my coat and purse and stormed out, slamming the door on our friendship.

Thirty-nine
Nicole

Waking up without tubes down my throat was an answer to one of the many prayers I'd sent up since arriving at the hospital.

The doctors said I would make a full recovery. That was the answer to another.

The one prayer I knew wouldn't be answered was the one I wanted most of all. For God to give me back my baby.

The pain on Lorenzo's face when I opened my eyes in intensive care told me my baby was dead.

I'd never felt so alone, so empty in my life.

Nothing Lorenzo could say or do would make my pain go away. And boy, did he try.

He promised we would try again right away to get pregnant.

Promised we would have a service to mourn the baby we lost.

She was a girl. A daughter I'd never get to see. Never get to hold. Never get to buy pretty dresses for. Never get to do her hair.

It was the first time in my life I wanted to curse God like Job's wife had asked him to do.

My first love, my father, had been taken from me.

Jamal's father wasn't the man I thought he was, forcing me to end the first relationship I thought would last a lifetime.

Then there was Chauncey.

Then Lorenzo's betrayal.

And now this?

How much did God expect me to endure in one lifetime?

How much was I supposed to forgive?

As if on cue, Arianna walked into my hospital room as I pondered these thoughts.

She must've gotten one of the nurses to sneak her in while Lorenzo was gone.

At first, I pretended to be asleep, not wanting to deal with her. I didn't have the energy for drama. But after 20 minutes of playing possum, I realized she wasn't going to leave, so I opened my eyes.

Arianna looked like she was the one who belonged in a hospital bed. She was staring at me, her vacant eyes tired and lifeless.

From somewhere deep inside me, sympathy bubbled to the surface. How is it I could manage to feel sorry for the woman who killed my baby and put me in the hospital, I'll never know.

But I was determined not to let it show.

Arianna had seen that side of me often enough. It was time for her to meet the strong Nicole.

"Hello, Arianna, what are you doing here?" I asked coolly.

She could only manage, "How are you?"

"I'm blessed," I said. "And you?"

"That's not important. Do you honestly feel blessed right now?"

"Yes, I do," I said, careful to enunciate each of those small words, my voice scratchy and hoarse.

"I'm alive. I have a husband and son who love me. And pretty soon, I'm going home to be with them."

"And what about..."

"The baby I lost? The daughter I always wanted?"

The words fell from my mouth like arrows, striking a bull's eye in Arianna's heart. I knew she probably already felt lower than gum stuck to the bottom of a shoe, but it wasn't my job to make her feel better.

Not over this.

Tears welled in the corners of her eyes as she bowed her head and nervously began to speak. I'd never seen her so humble.

"Nicole, I don't know what to say. I know sorry isn't good enough..."

"I forgive you, Arianna," I interrupted. I'd made up mind to forgive her a few days before. Holding on to my anger for her would only keep me bound and give her power over me.

She looked up. "What?" she whispered, the shock stuck in her throat.

"I forgive you. I lost my little girl because of your anger and need for revenge. My being angry at you won't bring her back. I need to forgive you to move on. It's that simple."

"It can't be that simple, Nicole. You have to be angry with me. Hurt. Upset. Something. Not enough time has passed for you to be able to just forgive me like that. Yell at me. Hit me. I don't care. I deserve it. Whatever you want to do to me, I'll take it."

"Then take my forgiveness. Who are you to decide how much time I need? I'm not you, Arianna. Yes, when I woke up and Lorenzo told me our baby was dead, I screamed and I cried for days. I was all those things -- hurt, angry, upset. And I wanted to strangle you. For bringing that damn gun in the first place. For not listening to us when we asked you to put it away. I told you someone was going to get hurt. And someone did."

"Nicole..."

"Let me finish. You and I have been through some heavy stuff together and it doesn't get any heavier than this. You have a lot of good qualities. You have been a good friend. But at the same time, you can be like poison. And I don't want you in my life anymore."

"You just said..."

"That I forgive you. And I do. But forgiving someone doesn't mean you have to keep them in your life, or that you'll forget what they did to you. I'll never be able to look at you without thinking of the daughter I lost. Even if I could, Lorenzo would never accept us still being friends. And if it's a choice between the two of you, I'd choose my husband."

"But..."

"But what?" I asked, struggling to pull myself into a sitting position. "Did you honestly think we could still be friends after this?"

"So that's it? I'm forgiven and dismissed. Now go away?"

"Arianna, I'm not forgiving you for you. I'm doing it for me. 'Cause if I don't, and I hold on to all the anger, pain and bitterness, I'll end up like you."

I wasn't trying to be harsh, but I could tell my words crashed against her like hurricane force winds.

"Like me?"

"Yes, like you. You're a great mother, you have a big heart and you can be so generous. But there's another side to you. The angry, bitchy, spiteful side."

"I'm sorry about your baby, Nicole. But because I'm a strong woman who doesn't want people to get away with hurting me, doesn't make me bitchy and spiteful."

"Call it what you want, Arianna. I can't stand that side of you. That was the person in the room with the gun pointed at Kenny. The person who killed my daughter..."

"It was an..."

"An accident, I know. Just like Chauncey was an accident. How many more accidents do there have to be before you get it, Arianna? I don't want to be around for the next one. Lorenzo told me they arrested you and charged you with my baby's death?"

"Yes," she said, no longer able to fight back the tears.

I averted my eyes. I was fighting back tears of my own and looking at hers would make mine come cascading down.

"What does that mean?" I asked, looking past her at the picture of a unicorn on the wall.

"I could go to prison."

"I know that. Will there be a trial?"

"I don't know. It depends on how I decide to handle it, I guess. Take a plea or take it to trial. What do you want me to do?"

"It really doesn't matter, Arianna. Whatever happens, my baby will still be dead."

With that, she stood up and headed for the door.

"I really am sorry, Nicole," she said, the words trailing behind her. Once she was out of sight, I let my tears flow.

Forty
Arianna

Emotions held me hostage in my car for more than an hour after I left the hospital.

Paralyzed by the truth revealed in Nicole's room, I needed the one thing that could help me through anything: a hug from my daughter.

Once I pulled myself together, I got on the interstate. I called Gina from my cell and told her to expect me but to keep my impending visit secret from Akilah.

I wanted to surprise her. We'd spoken several times since my arrest, but our chats were short, punctuated by silence because neither of us wanted to talk about the very subject we needed to discuss.

The future.

Akilah was the one person who would forgive me for anything. She hadn't matured to the point where she felt like she had a choice in the matter. And above all else, I was and would always be her mother.

Amir was old enough to judge me. Or so he thought. I knew he needed his space and I was willing to let him have it. So though I was tempted, I didn't stop by his dorm on my way south.

I went straight to Greg's.

Even the smooth grooves of Dave Koz emanating from my CD player couldn't pull my mind from all that had happened in my life during the past few months.

The only silver lining was that when news broke about Nicole's shooting and the role Janelle and Kenny had played in mine, the mystery woman who'd been playing mattress tag with Eugene Rodgers came forward. Said she had no idea the chick was that damn crazy. She was scared of Rodgers, until I told her if he tried anything, she could sue him for sexual harassment. She decided to sue him anyway.

And with her sworn statement, the court dismissed Rodgers' suit against me.

I arrived at Greg and Gina's a couple hours before Akilah got home from her new school. The private school they'd found had longer hours than public middle schools.

Gina and I made an effort at conversation. We had little in common and had never forged a relationship. I hated the fact I was now in her debt.

I tried focusing my attention on my beautiful little nieces, but my back was killing me from the steep walk up to their row house. It seemed like a hundred stairs long.

Gina and Greg lived in the Northeast section of D.C. in a middle-class neighborhood only blocks from the ghetto.

Their house was beautiful. Four bedrooms, hardwood floors, marble counters in a kitchen filled with stainless steel appliances.

Greg worked his ass off as an engineer to provide for his family and to make sure Gina was able to stay home with their two daughters.

They had turned the fourth bedroom, which served as Greg's home office, into a bedroom for Akilah. I politely excused myself to that room, telling Gina I was tired from the drive. I slept until Akilah arrived.

I awoke to the touch of her lips pressed against mine.

"Hi, Mommy!" she said, excitement ringing from her voice. "How come you didn't tell me you were coming?" she asked smiling.

I returned the smile. "Hey, baby," I said, sitting up in her temporary full-size bed. "I wanted to surprise you. How you doin'?"

She poked out her lips and dropped her eyes to the floor.

"I miss my friends and my old school. When can I come back home?"

I exhaled enough air to a balloon.

"Sit down, baby."

"I don't want to sit down, Ma. Just tell me. I know it's bad."

"Why do you say that?"

"'Cause of the sound you just made. Plus you never ask me to sit down to tell me something good."

"It'll make *me* feel better if you sit down, OK?"

She reluctantly took a seat next to me on the bed.

"Akilah, I'm probably going to have to go to jail for what happened to Miss Nicole's baby."

"But you didn't mean to kill her baby," she wailed. "It was an accident. How can they make you go to jail for an accident?"

"They just can, sweetie. It's the law. It's like if somebody gets drunk and has a car accident and kills someone. They didn't mean to kill the person, but it's still their fault because they shouldn't have been driving drunk. So the courts make them spend some time in jail to learn their lesson about drinking and driving."

"So what lesson does the court want you to learn?"

"That having a gun is not a good thing, especially when you're angry. And not to take the law into my own hands."

Akilah angrily crossed her arms in front of her adult-sized breasts. "What does that mean?"

"What does what mean?"

"Takin' the law into your hands?"

"It means I should've just called the police when I found out what Kenny did instead of getting mad and going after him. He broke the law and it was up to the police and the courts to deal with him, not me."

"Oh."

"Do you understand?"

"Not really. If somebody did that to me, I would want to kick their butt, too."

"That's how I felt, but look where it got me. Promise me you'll learn from my mistakes, 'Kilah, and don't do the stupid things I do."

"I guess."

"That's not a promise."

"I promise," she sighed. "But how long will you have to go to jail for?"

By then, tears covered her sunflower colored cheeks. I wrapped my arms around her. She didn't return my affection, keeping her arms locked around herself in anger.

"I know it's hard, baby. Both your parents going to jail. I'm so sorry for doing this to you."

She yanked herself from my embrace.

"Kenny is not my parent! He's nothin' to me!" she screamed, her pain punctuating each word.

"OK... OK...I'm sorry. Come here, baby. It's gonna be all right."

I hugged her again. This time, she hugged me back, her warm tears moistening my blouse.

"I don't know if I'm gonna be locked up or for how long. But if I do go to jail, I'm going to ask your Uncle Greg and your brother to take turns bringing you to visit me. And I'll write you every day. And before you know it, I'll be out and you can move back in with me."

She pouted. "Amir won't bring me."

"How do you know that?"

"He told me. He said if you go to jail, he's never gonna go see you. He said he doesn't want anybody to know you're his mother."

My insides burned with guilt, hurt and anger, giving me nausea and indigestion. I stood up, holding my stomach, as if my grip could keep its toxic contents from overflowing.

It didn't.

Seemed like my stomach was a lot weaker since I'd left the hospital.

Seconds later, I found myself hovering over a toilet bowl with Akilah by my side crying, and Gina standing in the doorway, offering useless advice. "Put your head between your legs, Arianna," she said.

I didn't have the energy to tell her to leave me the hell alone. I just ignored her until she walked away.

When I felt like I was done, Akilah handed me a wet washcloth to wipe my face.

"How you doin', mommy?"

"I'm fine, honey. I'm just stressed out and stress is not good for you."

"I'm stressed out, too," she said.

I grabbed her hand and held it tight. "I know baby, I know. But somehow, we are gonna get through this."

Forty-one
Arianna

The courthouse was packed, filled with newspaper and television reporters, and lots of lawyers interested in my case only for its legal merits.

The majority of people there, however, didn't give a damn about the law. They simply wanted something to gossip about.

A sexy headline.

A salacious sound bite.

As Joshua and I made our way through the hallway, crowded with the photographers, TV crews and spectators who weren't allowed inside, I noticed Randy fighting his way through the throng, trying to get my attention. My body smiled at the sight of him in a navy designer suit, striped baby blue shirt and coordinating navy tie.

I'd never seen him so well dressed.

Damn, that man was fine!

Joshua, who was shielding me from the media pariahs, many of whom used to be my colleagues, thought Randy was one of them and tried to keep him away.

"He's a friend, Joshua," I said. "At least I think he is."

"I am," Randy said, taking my hand. "Can I have a minute with her before the hearing starts?" he asked Joshua.

"We have some time," Joshua said. "I still have a couple details to work out with the prosecutor. You can talk in his waiting room while we meet."

We followed Joshua down the hall, dismissing reporters, shooing photographers and swatting away microphones randomly shoved in my face.

"I'm sorry about the way we left things the last time we saw each other," Randy said after we found refuge in the district attorney's office.

"Why are you apologizing? I'm the one who wasn't honest with you. I should've told you what was going on with me," I said.

"True. But, you were right about what you said about me and friendship. A true friend doesn't disappear when things get rough."

"We've been dancing on this thin line between lovers and friends every since that first lunch date. We finally cross that line and then shit hits the fan at the same time. Too much, too soon, I guess."

Randy nodded his head in agreement.

"We should have fought our attraction for each other and worked longer and harder at being friends, Arianna. Sex changes things, and not always for the better."

"I know. I made that mistake once before and now Kenny and I are both headed to jail because of it. The difference is I was never really attracted to him the way I am to you."

"What do you mean you're going to jail? I thought this was just one of those pre-trial conferences."

"It is, but I'm gonna take a plea."

"What kind of plea?"

"Six months behind bars and two years probation."

"Damn!"

"I keep telling myself it'll go by quickly. And while I'm on probation, I have to go to anger management classes. Joshua persuaded me to agree to that bullshit. He claims the D.A. said it was non-negotiable."

"I take it you have a problem with it?"

"I do," I said, rolling my eyes. "My anger was justified. Most people would've responded the same way if they found out they were sleeping with the enemy and that enemy was responsible, intentionally or not, for two bullets shattering their life. It's not like I'm a danger to society who goes around waving a gun at innocent people."

"Most people would've been pissed, you're right about that. They would've confronted the person, yes. But bring a gun? I don't think *most* people would've done that, Arianna. Most people don't even own a gun. Why did you have one, anyway?"

"For protection?" I said sarcastically. "Somebody shot me and his accomplice was still out there. Or so I thought, before I found out I was sitting across the dinner table from him."

"All right I got it," he said. "So what's the deal with your husband anyway?"

"He was sentenced last week. Five years. He took a plea, too. Pleaded guilty to recklessly endangering another person and criminal conspiracy."

"Five years isn't a lot of time for putting two bullets in someone."

"I know, but he didn't actually pull the trigger. Crump got 10 and Janelle got five like Kenny."

"Ten is OK, I guess. He should've gotten 20. So are you cool with Kenny's sentence?"

"It doesn't matter what I think. I just want all this to be over with. And, the fact is I do feel sorry for Kenny. His pride was hurt and he let a manipulative bitch take advantage of that weak spot. I'm sure he didn't mean for me to get hurt. At least not in the way I did. Still, I can't believe he would slash my tires, send me hateful notes and try to have my place trashed. This shit is so damn complicated. Nobody meant for anybody else to get hurt, yet a baby is dead and two people are headed to jail."

"Are you kidding me? You're excusing him for what he did?"

"No, of course not. But whether he serves five years or 50, Nicole's baby is always gonna be dead. Kenny's punishment won't change that."

"What about your punishment? Do they have a strong case against you? Is that why you agreed to the jail time?"

"I took the plea to spare Nicole and her family the drama of a trial. I think there's a good chance I could beat the charges since she hadn't reached her third trimester. But six months is nothing compared to what I've taken from her. I owe her at least this much."

"I can't believe you're actually going to do time. I mean I know your friend's baby is dead, but I've seen drunken drivers get off without spending a day in jail for killing living, breathing people."

"I know, but a trial and the media circus that comes with it would make life miserable for my family, too. I can't do that to my kids. Did you see that shit outside? I used to be a reporter. I know how relentless they can be. This shit would only get worse with a trial. My kids have been through enough shit because of me.

"I know I'm robbing my daughter of time with her mother, but I'm praying she can forgive me."

"She will. Like you said the time will go by fast," Randy said, taking my hand in his. "Some kids spend half the year with one parent and half with the other. Six months is nothing. And I'll visit whenever I can."

"You don't have to do that, Randy."

"I want to. You know you're like a lot of my students, trying to cover your pain by acting tough. You don't have to pretend you're not scared, Arianna. You're a lot more vulnerable than you let people see. And going to jail is something to be scared about."

"I'm a little scared," I said. "So you sure about being the friend of jailbird?"

"I think so. Look, I enjoyed making love to you the other night, but that doesn't mean we can't take a step backward and reassess our relationship. We were moving way too fast. Maybe we should've put the brakes on. But like you said, lust gets the better of people sometimes. Now we don't have a choice but to take things slow. It means we can give this friendship thing a real try. You need a friend a helluva lot more than you need a bed partner."

"With all the drama in my life, Randy, why the hell do you want any part in it at all?"

"I've been asking myself the same thing. I just know I want to be there for you. Hey, we can even be pen pals," he laughed.

"So you'll write me about all the dates you'll be going on while I'm locked up?" I said, unable to hide my jealousy.

"Well, I won't lie to you. I'm not going to stop dating. It's not like you were the only woman I've been seeing anyway."

"I never thought I was. It's not like you were my man or anything. And I was a married woman. But that doesn't stop me from having feelings for you or getting a little jealous thinking about you with another woman."

"I'll tell you what. I'll spare you the details of my love life, if I have a love life. I'll tell you about the antics of my students. That always gets a laugh out of you."

I smiled. "Cool. I'd like that."

"And who knows what might happen when you get out. If somebody hasn't snatched me up, of course."

"Ha, Ha, Ha," I said with sarcasm.

But Randy was right. His friendship was exactly what I needed.

+++

Randy and Joshua accompanied me into the courtroom, each holding an arm as I inched my way through the scandal hungry mob. They were the only people at the courthouse who were there for me.

Amir wouldn't have come if I wanted him to. He was still treating me as if I had a deadly, contagious disease.

I didn't want him there anyway. He and Akilah didn't need the drama. I'd told Greg not to bother making the drive. The hearing wasn't going to last long.

Blanche, our mother, had called to say she was too sick to make it. I expected nothing less since I couldn't remember the last time she'd supported me with anything more than a roof and meal.

And my sperm donor hadn't checked on me since he walked out on her holier-than-thou ass. Hell, I wouldn't recognize him if he did decide to make a surprise appearance.

Agnes offered to come. I declined, though I was glad she was willing. It helped to know she still cared.

In the first row of the mahogany, pew-like seats were my unofficial jury, Nicole, Lorenzo, Pam and Mark, Nicole's brother.

When my eyes met Nicole's, my feet locked in place as if I'd stepped in a puddle of glue. Caught in the gaze of her sad eyes, I searched for the words to once again express my sorrow for her suffering.

Not one of the 26 letters of the alphabet could find their way to my lips.

It didn't matter. Nicole could see clear through to my heart. She nodded in my direction, letting me know she understood what I couldn't say.

I took my place at the table in the front of the courtroom, while Randy sat behind me in one of the few available seats for spectators Joshua had asked to be reserved.

He'd expected me to have more supporters. I didn't bother telling him I was trying to be noble by sparing my loved ones.

Several minutes went by before the bailiff, a short, pudgy middle-age brotha, called for us to stand for the judge's arrival. I spent most of that time avoiding Lorenzo's condemning eyes. The heat from his stare was making me sweat.

We took our seats after the judge took hers. She was a stern-looking, gray-haired woman whose milk-colored face was blanketed by wrinkles.

The bailiff called my case and Joshua and the prosecutor, an attractive, young blonde, stood. Nicole tugged at the prosecutor's arm and whispered something in her ear. The woman then asked the judge for a short delay.

Then she, Nicole, Lorenzo, Pam and Mark got into a heated discussion.

"Mrs. Evans is there a problem?" the judge asked the prosecutor.

"No, your honor. The victim needs clarification on a few points. I'll be right with you, Judge Chandler," she said, clearly agitated. She then turned back to Nicole and Lorenzo.

Minutes later, Lorenzo plopped back in his seat, looking defeated and Pam angrily folded her arms across her chest and shook her head. Mark threw his hands up in disgust. Then, Nicole headed toward me.

She took a seat next to Randy and asked Joshua and me for our attention.

"Don't take the plea, Arianna."

"What?" I said, shocked.

"I appreciate that you're willing to go to jail, but it's not necessary."

"The D.A. said..."

"Forget what they said. I just told her I don't want you to go to jail. I told her to void the plea agreement. If you don't take it, they'll have no choice but to take this to trial or drop the case."

"Then I risk being convicted and serving more time," I said, shaking at the thought.

"No. They won't take it to trial. The D.A. told me that when I first got out of the hospital. Crimes against unborn babies are hard cases to win. That's why they offered the plea in the first place. They figured if you took it, it's an easy win for them."

"Why are you telling me all this, Nicole?"

"I just told you. I don't want you to go to jail. That's not going to bring my baby back. Besides, you have a daughter to raise and you know I love Akilah. Why should she have to suffer? I know I couldn't bear to be separated from Jamal for six months."

"I don't know what to say."

"Say you'll throw away that gun. That you'll practice patience and learn how to forgive. Maybe even take your butt to somebody's church and find your way back to the Lord?"

"I threw away the gun. And I'll work on all those things, even going to church."

Joshua looked dazed. "You've got one hell of a friend here, Arianna," he said.

I smiled. "I know."

"I'll go talk to Evans and tell her we're backsliding on the plea agreement and see what she has to say."

Nicole returned to her angry family.

"Attorney Berger. Mrs. Evans. Do we or do we not have an agreement in this case? You are trying this court's patience," Judge Chandler shouted from her seat on high.

"Your honor may we approach?" Joshua asked.

"Please do," the judge insisted.

Next thing I knew, I'd gone from six months in jail to 1,000 hours of community service and court costs. And of course the anger management classes.

The buzz in the courtroom was loud enough that Judge Chandler was banging her gavel demanding order.

"This is bullshit!" shouted an angry voice. "I can't believe this shit!"

I turned around to see Eugene Rodgers ranting and raving.

"How many times is she gonna get away with killing people and ruining their lives? Huh, your honor? Huh?"

It was then that I recognized his voice as the one that taunted me in the hospital while I was in the coma.

When the bailiff couldn't get him to shut up, he removed him from the courtroom. Of course, reporters and photographers followed, taking notes and snapping pictures of his tirade.

When the bailiff returned, he was nice enough to escort all of us through the judge's chambers to avoid the madness. As Randy, Joshua, Nicole, Lorenzo, Pam, Mark and I were shuffled through the door behind the judge's bench, I felt a pull on my arm.

When I turned around, Lorenzo was glaring down at me.

"Can I talk to you for a minute?"

"Sure," I said, anxiously anticipating his wrath. I told Randy and Joshua to give me a minute and Lorenzo did the same with Nicole and his in-laws.

They waited with the bailiff in the quiet hall outside the judge's chambers. She was still inside the courtroom, hearing another case.

I spoke first once they all had left the room.

"Thanks for agreeing..."

"Don't thank me. That was all Nicole's idea. I was against it 100 percent," Lorenzo interrupted. "I wanted to talk to you about Amir."

"Oh," I said a little taken aback. "Don't worry, Lorenzo. I'm not going to tell Nicole about you and my son if that's what you're worried about."

"I don't want to keep any more secrets from her, but..."

"But telling her the truth serves no purpose, especially after everything else she's been through."

"So you agree she doesn't need to know?"

"Yes, you and I are on the same page. But, you have to promise that you won't hurt Nicole any more than *you* already have. I'm not the only one in this room guilty of causing her pain."

"You're right."

"By the way are you gay or straight? Do you even know?"

"I'm both. There are people who are one or the other and they don't have a choice. Like your son. I do have a choice. I like men and women. But I'm choosing to live straight. I lot of people don't understand bisexuality, but the only person I want to understand is Nicole. And she's trying."

"Are you choosing the straight life 'cause it's easier?"

"That's only part of it. The most important reason is because I love my wife."

"You know what, Lorenzo. I believe you do love her. I love her, too. Make sure you take care of her."

With that, we left the judge's office, joined our respective groups and went home.

Forty-two
Arianna

Summer found me in a new home, a beige Colonial split level on a quiet peaceful road in Blue Bell, a small town about 15 miles from Philly.

My four-bedroom sanctuary backed up to a watershed and nature preserve. It had two fireplaces and beautiful hardwood floors.

But I loved it as much for what it didn't have: Memories.

No memories of Kenny. No memories of Chauncey.

In the mornings when I descended the stairs from my master bedroom, where I slept peacefully alone, I swear I could hear Patti LaBelle's "New Attitude" ringing from my hips.

I edited books under one of the many trees that shaded the house. When I wasn't reading, I fussed with the perennials and impatiens in the garden that hugged the edge of my winding driveway.

I sold ExposeHim.com and EbonyLadiesofPassion. The businesses carried too much baggage. There was a still a need for the Web sites and I wanted them to continue and prosper. The new owner promised me they would.

Occasionally, I'd write a column under a pseudonym. And I couldn't help but still read the posts. It never ceased to amaze me how gullible some women are and how downright scandalous some men could be.

It didn't stop me from believing, though, that the right man was out there for me.

Giving up the dot-com businesses gave me more time to focus on my first love: Writing.

Agnes' agent was so impressed with my work, she recommended me to other authors and publishing houses.

I had more freelance work than I could stand and the best part was I could do it from home. That meant I could spend as much time with my daughter as I needed.

Amir still hadn't come around. I hadn't seen him since the day he took Akilah to D.C. He chose to spend the summer working a job on campus rather than come home. I didn't pressure him. He knew my love didn't have an expiration date and when he was ready, I would be there.

I was sitting under one of the big trees in my front yard fanning myself with the pages of a manuscript when I got a call.

"Arianna, I'm pregnant," said the jubilant voice on the other end of the phone.

"Who is this?" I said knowing full well the identity of my caller.

"You know who this is."

"Nicole? Oh, my god. I can't believe it!"

"I know you never expected to hear from me again, but I just had to call you and let you know. Lorenzo and I are expecting another baby."

"Nicole, I am so happy for you. Both of you. How is everything between you? How's Jamal?"

"Jamal's fine and Lorenzo and I are doing a lot better. We've been in counseling the past few months. He's working on his issues, I'm working on mine and we're working on ours. We pray together, we laugh together. He's not perfect, but he's perfect for me."

"And that's all that matters," I said, smiling from ear to ear. I didn't realize how much I missed talking to Nicole until I heard her voice.

"What about you?" she asked.

"I'm good. Akilah's doing great in school and I'm doing some freelance editing. It pays the bills and keeps me out of the spotlight. I'm living a quiet life and it's working for me."

"What about your love life?"

"What about it? It's nonexistent. But even that's cool. I figure love will find me when I'm ready for it. And until then, I've got plenty to keep me busy."

"That's good," Nicole said. "Well, I won't keep you. I just wanted to share my good news with you. I thought you might like to hear it."

"I loved hearing it, Nicole. I really am happy for you. I'm going to pray for you and your baby. And Lorenzo."

"Pray? You?"

"Yes. Me. I found a church I like. One that teaches the principles I believe in and I'm finding my way to the Lord just like you asked me to."

"That's wonderful, Arianna. I hope everything works out for you."

"Nicole... I love you."

"I know."

Just as I was about to hit the end button, I saw Randy's number pop up on my screen. I clicked the talk button.

"Hey lady, how you doin'?"

"Great actually. I just got off the phone with Nicole. She's pregnant."

"That's great news and it's great that she called to tell you."

"Yeah, so what's up with you? You wanna do something tonight? Dinner? A movie? Or do you already have a date?"

"No. That's cool. And maybe we can go back to my place afterward."

"For what? So you can kick my butt in Scrabble again?"

"No, I had something a little more intimate in mind."

"Meaning?"

"Meaning, I think we've got this friendship thing down pat, and maybe we can put the pedal back to metal so to speak?"

I was aroused immediately.

"How 'bout I come over now and we can skip the appetizers and get right to dessert."

Randy laughed.

"Wear that sexy peach number."

Forty-three
Arianna

Bouyed by Nicole's good news and my night of passion with Randy, I drove the next day to SCI Coal Township, the medium security prison where Kenny was being held.

"I didn't expect to see you here," Kenny said when he took his seat across from me at the table in the dark, ugly room where inmates met with their visitors.

The room was loud with conversation. Most of the women were black, wore cheap wigs in various shades of red and blonde and scant clothing.

They looked as though they'd spent the night working on their backs.

I looked and felt completely out of place.

Kenny looked like a big-ass tangerine in his bright orange prison uniform.

"I never expected to be here," I said.

"How are you, Arianna?"

"I'm good."

"You're not going to ask how I'm doing?"

"You're in prison, Kenny. I think it's obvious how you're doing."

"Good point. But I'm fine, too."

"Really?"

"Yeah. I mean this is no country club, but I hear it's way better than the maximum security place where the murderers and rapists go."

"Where Darryl Crump is?"

"Yeah. Why? Do you think I should be in the same place as him?"

"It doesn't matter what I think, Kenny."

"It matters to me."

"Why?"

"'Cause I care about you. I know you find that hard to believe, but I do. How's Akilah?"

"She's fine. She's adjusting to our new house, her new school, life without you."

"I don't suppose I could talk you into bringing her to see me? Give me a chance to try and explain to her what happened?"

"I don't know, Kenny. She's still so angry with you. She's hurt. But then again it might actually do her some good to talk to you about all this, hear your side. It might give her some closure. But, I'm just not sure."

"Well, at least it sounds like you're open to it. That's all I can ask for."

"I'll think about it."

"So what brings you here?"

"Well, I came...I came here to tell you that I forgive you."

"What?"

"I forgive you. I realized I can't move on with my life until I put all this stuff behind me. And that means forgiving you."

"Wow. I didn't think I'd ever hear you say those words."

"They're not for you, they're for me. I learned that from Nicole. I think if I'd forgiven a few more people in my life, you and I wouldn't be where we are. But I can't change the past. I can change my future though."

"How can you change the future when you don't know what's in it?"

"By making sure I don't carry any excess baggage on my trip there."

Kenny smiled.

"That's what I am? Excess baggage?"

"It's not what you are, but it is what you represent. Anyway, I need your forgiveness, too. Do you think you can do that?"

Kenny's eyes opened as wide as the space between us. "My forgiveness? What the heck do you need me to forgive you for?"

"For marrying you when I shouldn't have. For not listening to you when you tried to tell me how much what I was doing was hurting you."

"Well, if you think you need me to forgive you, then, yes, Arianna. I forgive you."

"Thanks, Kenny."

"No, thank you, Arianna. I really appreciate you coming here today."

"I'll let you know what I decide about Akilah. By the way, Nicole called. She and Lorenzo are pregnant again."

Kenny smiled wide. "That's great. I'm happy for her, really. You have no idea how guilty I feel for everything, but especially for her losing that baby."

"Actually, I do have an idea, Kenny. Take care of yourself."

"You, too."

After leaving the prison, I headed for New York.

Chauncey's grave was my next stop. I brought flowers, impatiens from my garden.

I laid them on the grave and said a prayer for his soul. I also asked him for forgiveness even though he couldn't give it.

I stood there waiting for an answer, a taunt, his evil laugh. Any sign that his spirit was still alive.

Nothing.

There were no ghosts. Trees and silence were my only companions. Fear had finally left me alone and sent peace to fill its place.

When I arrived home that night, Amir was sitting on the porch waiting.

Happiness overwhelmed me. I hugged him so tight I almost knocked him down.

"I'm so glad to see you," I said when I finally let him go.

"I can tell," he smiled.

"Come inside so I can give you the tour," I said.

Amir entered the house cautiously, as if he'd lost his place in my home.

"Boy, come on in here," I said. "Sit down. Can I get you something to eat or drink?"

"Nah, I'm good. This is a nice place."

"Thanks. You sure I can't get you anything?"

"Yeah. Look, Ma. I came over to apologize. I...I...I should've been there for you...at your hearing...to help you move in here. To help you when Kenny left. I just should've been here, period."

"Amir, you're here now. That's all that matters. Come upstairs. I'll show you your room."

"I still have a room?"

"Of course, you do. I still expect you to come home for Thanksgiving and Christmas. Next summer. Wherever I live will always be your home."

Amir hugged me like he did when he was a little boy. He wrapped himself around me so tight I couldn't breathe.

But I didn't complain.

I gave him a tour of the house, then made dinner. It had been a long time since I cooked for my son.

Amir sat on the living room couch watching TV as I made his favorites -- salmon croquets, rice and gravy and string beans."

Amir, honey?"

"Yeah, Ma."

"I love you."

He came in the kitchen and gave me a peck on the cheek.

"I love you, too, Ma."

ABOUT THE AUTHOR

Rhonda Swan is a syndicated columnist and an award winning journalist and poet who works as an opinion writer for *The Palm Beach Post* in Florida. Her columns have appeared in newspapers across the United States, Canada and abroad.

She is the author of two novels, *Busted: Never Underestimate a Sista's Revenge*, and the sequel, *Exposed: The Consequences of Truth.* She also has penned a volume of poetry titled, *Speaking My Mind in Poetic Verse.*

She also is the author of a self-help book titled, Dancing to the Rhythm of My Soul: A Sister's Guide for Transforming Madness into Gladness.

Rhonda is the mother of three adult children and has one grandchild. Find out more at www.rhondaswan.com. Email Rhonda at: thewordzlady@hotmail.com.

www.ingramcontent.com/pod-product-compliance
Lightning Source LLC
Chambersburg PA
CBHW072214170626
46813CB00003B/930